WAR'S PEACE

CLUB APOCALYPSE
BOOK ONE

RAISA GREYWOOD

Cover art by Wicked Smart Designs
Editing provided by Amy Briggs

Ebook ISBN: 978-1-952596-17-9
Print ISBN: 978-1-952596-18-6

Playlist

PROLOGUE

"So, this is what the Horsemen have come to. Why do I have a feeling we're living out an old Eagles song?"

"Don't be like that, War. You aren't seeing the possibilities." Scowling, Ryan grabbed a pair of gloves from the first-aid kit he always carried and retrieved a used needle from the broken concrete leading to the main entrance.

Mark Luciano grimaced at Ryan but didn't respond. It had been hilarious at the time, but the nicknames they'd given each other during BUD/S training didn't seem to fit anymore. He wasn't sure he liked the reminder.

Ryan Wood, their field medic, just cried out to be called Pestilence. Mark could still catch a whiff of Betadine from him when the wind was right. Jake McBride's nickname, Famine, was easy. He could turn an MRE into haute cuisine with little more than ketchup packets and Tabasco sauce. Sean Franklin's nickname didn't take much thought either. Silent unless he wanted you to hear him coming, he was Death.

That left Mark with War, yet he chafed under its weight.

Jake laughed sourly. "Possibilities for what? Scorpions and armadillos in the kitchen?"

Ryan disposed of the needle in a sharps container then shook his head. "Nah, the old place just needs a little paint and—"

"A wrecking ball, maybe a backhoe," Mark finished. "What the hell are we supposed to do with a condemned motel on a two-lane stretch of decommissioned highway?"

"It's close enough to civilization to open the BDSM club we always wanted," Sean said. As always, he was the ultimate peacekeeper. "We can build an addition for the dungeon and Jake can take over the diner. We'll even clean up a few of the rooms for anyone needing a bed for the night."

"Yeah," Jake replied, pointing at the spray-painted graffiti. "Like the nice, upstanding folks who left that art on the building."

Mark privately agreed with Jake. According to the sign hanging drunkenly from the twenty-foot post in the parking lot, it was the finest motel on Route 66 with daily blue-plate specials. No matter how much he squinted and cocked his head, the sun-bleached skeleton of The Majestic didn't improve.

The only thing missing was the—aw hell, there it was—a cow skull mounted over the open space where the lobby door should have been. The accompanying wagon wheel had probably been stolen.

It had the right mix of kitsch and Wild West glamour that would have made it a popular stop on the Mother Road back in the day, but it was a moldering eyesore now. Paint chipped and peeled from the cinderblock walls, leaving scabrous trails of ochre that fought with virulently colored gang tags. Most of the windows were gone; either scavenged or broken as the desert reclaimed the building.

He left his friends and walked around back, trying to get a sense of his surroundings as the burning cerulean sky beat down on his head. The landscaping was overgrown with invasive plants. Dirt bike and ATV trails crisscrossed the property, and a trash heap slash junkyard stretched around the west wing.

Despite the mess, life flourished without the threat of bombs, blood, and battle. Kneeling, he touched the budding blossom on a succulent, then caught sight of faint prints left by a bobcat.

Centered between the right-angle wings of the motel, he found the pitted remains of a swimming pool. Empty for years, the concrete was cracked, allowing woody brush to sprout in the sloped bottom. A mermaid was picked out in faded blues and greens, and a sapling grew from the cavern of her smiling mouth.

Twenty miles east of Winslow, Arizona was as good a place as any to settle down and try to make some sense of what they'd become. No longer boys with crisply pressed uniforms, but men with bowed shoulders and the heavy tread of people carrying too many demons.

Mark's footsteps on the hard-packed earth were silent as he returned to his friends. No trucks rumbled in the distance. There were no people shouting outside boundary fence. No sense of humanity at all, save the Four Horsemen.

For the first time in years, he almost felt like he could... breathe. His lungs could fill with air untainted by cordite or gun oil. There was no sense of too many people pressing too close. No desire to lash out just to get a single fucking moment when nobody was touching him.

"Are we still planning on calling this dump Apocalypse?" Jake asked, unwittingly dragging Mark from his dark thoughts.

Ryan grinned, rubbing his hands together in glee. "Yeah. It'll be awesome." Pointing to the broken glass door, he added, "Let's go see what's in the kitchen. Maybe you can fix us one of your mama's pies."

Laughing, the Horsemen followed him into the decrepit structure they now called home.

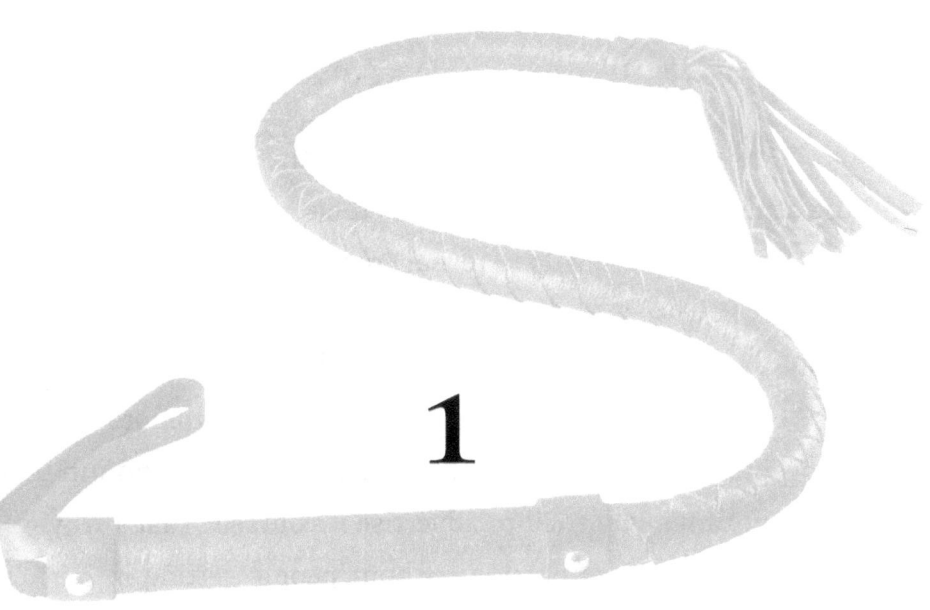

1

MARK

"No." Mark calmly folded a paper airplane and sent it sailing over Ryan's head. It crashed against the far wall of his office behind the bar, then spiraled to the floor. He hated morning meetings.

"War—"

"The name is Mark...*Ryan*," he snapped, emphasizing his friend's given name. "We're not in the Navy anymore."

Of all of them, Mark thought Ryan had changed the most in the five years following their discharge. He used to be easygoing and just a little on the sloppy side. Now, he looked like a stockbroker in tailored three-piece suits that he never, ever unbuttoned. Who the fuck wore suits in a bondage club?

"Come off it." Ryan flopped down in the leather chair on the other side of his desk and rubbed his face, the sleeves of his suit jacket pulling up to reveal French cuffs with gold and onyx cufflinks. "We have to do something, man. Those protesters are eating our business alive."

"I told you years ago I didn't want to promote the dungeon. You promised you'd let me keep it small and intimate, but then you tried to advertise it yourself. That's why none of us can step outside without people getting in our faces demanding we shut down."

"I made a mistake, okay?" Ryan took a breath and exhaled through pursed lips. "I thought we were big enough to handle it, and now we need help."

"Close down for six months and wait until they find someone else to bother?"

"What about our employees? Are you suggesting we lay off over fifty people?" Sean asked, quiet as his nickname suggested until he had something to say. No, death wasn't nearly as silent as Sean could be.

Fuming inwardly, Mark sent another paper airplane over Ryan's head. "Can we do it without this fancy marketing specialist?"

"I've tried," Ryan said, sounding tired. "Publicity obviously isn't in my skillset, but I had to do something. We've been losing money hand over fist for months, and it's draining us dry. The events are still selling well, but reservations are down across the board."

"The restaurant isn't doing any better," Jake added. "I've lost four of my best servers already because they're afraid to cross the protester lines, but it's just as well since I get no walk-in traffic anymore. If the restaurant closes before we pay off our upgrades, we'll all be Famine, not just me."

"Fine." Mark got up and reached for the darts standing in the board behind his chair, then let them fly one after the other in an attempt to control his irritation. "Who are we hiring?"

He didn't want strangers coming into his space, much less someone who would turn Apocalypse into a carbon copy of every other club in the world. Part of him wanted to shut Club Apocalypse down until the bad publicity blew over, but that would put too many people out of work. Aside from that, it wasn't in him to let himself be bullied by a bunch of redneck fuckers with nothing better to do with their time.

Then again, they could use the marketing guru for long enough to get rid of the protesters, then go back to business as usual. It wouldn't be a permanent situation, and with luck, Mark could keep them out of the dungeon entirely.

"Her name is Kendra Hall. I headhunted her from one of the luxury hotel chains, and she has an excellent reputation. It's going to cost a fortune, but my contacts say she's the best in the business."

"I thought you preferred women who stayed home to play housewife."

Ryan shrugged, then smiled crookedly. "I'm well aware

women are just as capable and intelligent as men, and I have no intention of dating her. She can do whatever the hell she wants in her personal life."

"Fair enough."

"Good, because she's scheduled to arrive this coming Monday afternoon. That leads me to another item on our agenda."

"Shoot," Mark replied, aiming a dart at the elusive triple twenty on the top of the board. It was Friday, giving him the weekend to figure out how to keep Ms. Hall out of his business.

"I hired someone to upgrade and reinforce our computer security."

"I can take care of it," Sean replied. "We'll just—"

"There have been two hack attempts in the last week," Ryan interrupted. "I'm not willing to give them a chance to get in."

Sean grunted sourly but nodded. "Who is it?"

"Dr. Gabrielle Knox from MIT. She's agreed to a short-term contract."

"No idea who that is."

"Unsurprising," Ryan said. "She designs kid's computer games for profit but does corporate security for fun. She got her PhD at nineteen, specializing in counterespionage and trackable viruses."

"Dr. Knox has a strange idea of fun," Sean replied. "She's over twenty-one, right?"

Ryan arched a brow. "Ask me if I care. All I want is for her to do what we're paying her for. She'll be here tonight, but she's driving from Massachusetts, so we didn't set a firm arrival time."

Mark was more concerned about Kendra Hall. Would a fancy hotel exec have any idea how to market an adults-only resort?

There was only one reason Club Apocalypse existed. They'd all wanted a play space everyone could enjoy without the outrageous membership fees of other clubs. Kinksters weren't just beautiful millionaires; they came from all social classes and were all ages and body types. The one thing they had in common with the rich fuckers in those expensive clubs was a desire to be with others like them.

Hell, one of his regulars was an elderly Gorean master from Holbrook whose *kajira* was seventy-five and grand-mother to twelve. Could he make the place grow and keep that intimate atmosphere welcoming to everyone? Grumbling under his breath, he paced, wondering how he was going to keep Kendra from changing everything that made Club Apocalypse special.

"All right," Mark finally said. "Ms. Hall will be here Monday. I'll deal with her. Sean, you'll handle Dr. Knox since you know about the security we already have in place."

"Poker tonight?" Jake asked, getting up from his chair.

"Yeah."

His friends wandered out, leaving him alone with his thoughts in an empty dungeon. He hated seeing it like that.

———

KENDRA

Surrounded by desert on all sides, Kendra Hall's new workplace was like a mirage. The setting sun bathed Apocalypse in reddish light, making the stark white of the vintage motel look like it had been covered in blood. A sign on a tall post stood at the entrance to the parking lot. It looked like it might have been original, but it had been painted black. The Apocalypse logo was picked out in red and purple neon lighting, paying homage to the old motel's roots.

Parked cars lined both sides of the road and dozens of protesters marched across the parking lot entrance. Her new boss, Ryan Wood, had warned her about them so it wasn't a surprise. Slowing down, she weaved her way through the gauntlet of vehicles and read a few of the signs.

We don't need a brothel in Winslow.

Repent and send the Horsemen back to Hell.

God is watching you!

Making sure her doors were locked, she kept her speed steady, but didn't stop. Unsurprisingly, the protesters moved out of her way when it became clear she'd run them down if they didn't. Although she didn't want to hurt anyone, there was no way she was stopping her car or getting out.

Despite the protesters, there was a line of cars waiting at the valet station. Kendra allowed herself a small smile. It was always easier to promote a popular business. Getting rid of the demonstrators wouldn't be a great challenge, and after that, she could get to work.

Judging by the parking lot, the joint was hopping—just as she'd hoped to see. This was why she'd shown up early. Her actual start date wasn't until Monday, but she'd wanted to see the property on a weekend—and without the owners expecting her.

Leaving her vehicle running, she stepped out and accepted a claim ticket from the valet, then walked through the frosted glass doors into the lobby.

Freshly divorced at the ripe old age of thirty-six, Kendra Hall was ready for her new gig as the vice president of operations for what was supposed to have been one of the hottest adult resorts in the western United States. Well, that's what the brochures said anyway.

Maybe it had been hot once upon a time, but the financials she'd been sent by Ryan Wood, one of the owners, proclaimed the property to be lukewarm at best and it was hemorrhaging money.

Their concept was on point. The name, Club Apocalypse, was gold—especially since it was owned by military veterans who called themselves The Four Horsemen, complete with War, Famine, Pestilence, and Death. There was even a picture of them in one of the brochures. Unfortunately, it hadn't been labeled, so she had no idea which of them was which.

At least she knew their names: Ryan Wood, Mark Luciano, Jake McBride, and Sean Franklin. Not that it really mattered. She'd been too desperate to get out of Houston and away from her ex. The offer had been too good to pass up, and it had come at exactly the right time—namely, the minute she had her divorce decree clenched in her hands.

She pulled the glossy trifold brochure from her pocket, tracing her fingers over the dark-haired man with sinful whiskey brown eyes and a jawline sharp enough to cut glass. He was off limits though. Aside from being one of her employers, she'd sworn off pretty men. They were more trouble than they were worth.

Case in point, Daniel, her ex. His ginger hair and soulful brown eyes had caught her in a web of lies and mental abuse that trapped her for a decade.

However, this was exactly the challenge she most relished. Her career and the salary she could command relied on understanding the nuances of what made people spend money and how to bring ailing properties back to profitability. She thought she had a decent grasp of how the world worked, but when she walked in, she realized there were levels of adult entertainment she hadn't been aware of. Namely, a naked man on all fours wearing a puppy mask and a collar, with a glittery chain leash and a furry tail hanging from a butt plug.

Towering over him in black boots, a corset, and a teensy black miniskirt, his gorgeous blonde partner leaned down and stroked his head between the leather ears of his mask.

A lovely brunette wearing an apron and a collar offered her an appetizer from a tray. A similarly attired blond man followed with champagne flutes. Although she wouldn't have minded sampling the food, they were violating at least a half dozen health codes.

In her soft cotton maxi dress, Kendra couldn't decide if she was overdressed or underdressed. Even if she had any, fetish wear wasn't the best idea for road tripping across three states from Texas.

Head held high, she wended her way through the somewhat shabbily retro lobby to the front desk. Kendra wasn't here to play or ogle the scenery; she had a job to do and couldn't do it in a leather corset.

Her biggest challenge wouldn't be getting rid of the protesters camped just over the property line. It would be convincing the owners to update. Club Apocalypse had to look like it was worth the five hundred dollar a night rack rate. It needed to be decadent and opulent, with fixtures and furnishings designed to tease the senses into believing the fantasy the owners wanted to present. Instead, it looked like a chain motel. Maybe the suites were better, but the lobby needed a renovation.

"Welcome to Club Apocalypse," the woman behind the desk said. "How can I help you?"

Wearing what Kendra decided was sexy professional, the desk clerk was impeccably groomed, with silvery blonde hair tied in a wavy ponytail. Her black suit was cut low to reveal generous décolletage and was very short. Her name tag read Sierra.

"Hi, I'm Kendra Hall. I'd like a room for the weekend if you have one available."

Obviously recognizing the name, Sierra's smile faded, then returned as she typed furiously on her computer. "We weren't expecting you until Monday, but your suite is ready. Did you have a pleasant trip from Houston?"

"Yes, thank you."

"I'm glad." Sierra looked down at her computer terminal and swiped a keycard. "Would you care for valet service for your luggage?"

"Please." Kendra laid the valet ticket on the desk. "There are two suitcases in the trunk."

"I'll have them delivered to your suite shortly." Sierra handed her the card. "You'll be staying at the end of the east wing closest to the pool. If you're ready for supper, the restaurant is just past the atrium in the west wing. I can have someone give you a tour if you prefer."

The décor might be dated and shabby, but what she'd seen of the staff had been beyond reproach aside from their attire. That was a very definite plus in Kendra's book and would become part of her marketing plan.

"A tour would be wonderful. I had a late lunch, but I'll try to visit the restaurant later."

Lifting her hand, Sierra snapped her fingers and an adorable young man with dark hair appeared, wearing a pair of tight leather shorts and a collar.

"Ezekiel, Ms. Hall is our new vice president of operations. You'll be giving her a tour of the facility. Make sure to include her new office down the hall from Master Ryan's, and the staff conference room adjacent to the restaurant, please."

"Yes, ma'am." Ezekiel inclined his head, peeking at Sierra from under thick eyelashes.

"Thank you, Ezekiel. Ms. Hall, it was a pleasure to meet you. Please let us know if we can assist you further."

Clearing his throat, Ezekiel looked at Kendra's collarbones, then said, "The Majestic was built in 1935 and had sixty rooms, plus a diner that served breakfast and lunch. The rooms were converted into forty suites, four of which are handicap accessible. It was purchased by Masters Ryan, Mark, Sean, and Jake five years ago, and has undergone—"

"It's okay," she said, laying a hand on his arm. "I read the brochure. I'd love it if you'd show me around though."

"Yes, ma'am."

"And you can call me Kendra."

"Yes, ma'am... I mean, Kendra."

She tried for a smile to show her approval, but he made her feel old. Had she ever been that innocent and shy? Then again, Ezekiel was working at an adult resort, meaning he couldn't have been as young as he appeared.

As he pointed out features, she typed notes on her phone, cataloguing changes she'd suggest during her meeting with the owners. Although she might have gone faster had there not been a crowd, it allowed her to see two significant problems.

The traffic flow was a potential fire hazard, and nobody was spending money.

"Ezekiel, is there an event scheduled for tonight? I'm curious about why so many people are milling around the lobby."

"No, ma'am... I mean, Kendra. They're all just visiting."

"Do they have rooms?"

"No, well, maybe some of them. Mistress Sierra would know."

"I see. And how often do these guests visit?"

Brightening, he grinned. "Every Friday. The Horsemen call it *Get Your Freak on Friday.*"

Kendra had a problem with that. Not because of the dumb name, or because people were running around mostly naked, but because the resort was spending money feeding hors d'oeuvres and champagne to freeloaders. There was no incentive for them to pay membership fees, buy food, or reserve rooms when they had free run of the lobby.

Parties could be a beneficial marketing tool but having them every week was a serious financial drain, and they should have been located somewhere that wasn't the freaking lobby.

Forgetting all about the protesters, she typed furiously, barely looking up as he led her through an open plan atrium toward the restaurant. Even the empty space was an offense. It should have been filled with vendors and shops for an additional source of revenue. There wasn't so much as a traveler's store where one could buy a forgotten toothbrush.

Without warning, she slammed into something hard and unyielding, the impact making her drop her phone. Swearing softly, she crouched to pick it up.

"I'll take over Ms. Hall's tour," a gravelly voice said. "It's clear she needs to pay more attention to where she's going."

She rose slowly, and her breath caught. It was one of the Horsemen. Not just any of them, but Whiskey Eyes himself. She looked up into those compelling eyes and forgot every last thought in her head. He was imposing, but not because of his size. Although only a few inches taller than her, he exuded presence as if his skin was too small to contain him.

Thankfully, he was fully clothed in a pair of dark jeans, boots, and a black polo with Club Apocalypse's logo stitched on the breast. Kendra wasn't sure she could have maintained her composure if she'd seen him dressed as the servers were. Muscular arms bulged, stretching his sleeves to bursting, and there were prominent ridges of a defined abdomen under his tight shirt.

Ezekiel muttered an apology and disappeared, leaving them alone.

"Excuse me," she replied, trying to shake off the spell he'd cast over her. "I was taking notes and I should have found a place to stop. Are you Mr. Wood?"

"No." He tugged the phone from her hand and pocketed it. "Ms. Hall, you are not above the rules. We don't allow electronic devices in public areas."

Taking her arm, he walked quickly down the corridor, forcing her to trot to keep up. "Sir," she said, trying to make him slow down. "You need to return my phone. That rule isn't visibly posted, nor was it communicated in any way."

"Don't worry. You'll get your phone back."

Instead of slowing to allow her to keep up, he walked faster, leading her back through the lobby and into the east wing past several numbered doors. At the end of the corridor, he swiped a master keycard through the slot, then opened it to reveal a comfortable suite. The décor was tasteful, yet bland. Although it was spotlessly clean and inoffensive, it could have been better.

Giving her a smile that didn't reach his eyes, he returned her phone and inclined his head. "Enjoy your evening, Ms. Hall."

The door shut behind him, leaving her speechless.

Kendra had spent over a decade dealing with prima

donna managers, overly dramatic chefs, and needy guests, but had never once been treated like a naughty child sent to her room without supper. For a moment, she considered chasing him down to explain the facts of life to him, then decided against it.

She wasn't at all upset about the rule prohibiting electronic devices. It made perfect sense, and she should have thought of it herself. However, it needed to be clearly posted throughout the property. She also wasn't about to let someone walk all over her like that—especially when he hadn't even bothered to introduce himself.

At least her luggage had already been delivered and rested on the floor next to the closet. The owners—at least one of them—left her cold, but the staff was definitely five-star.

"More flies with honey," she muttered, opening a suitcase. She pulled out a black cocktail dress, then hung it in the bathroom to steam while she showered. This engagement called for proper armor.

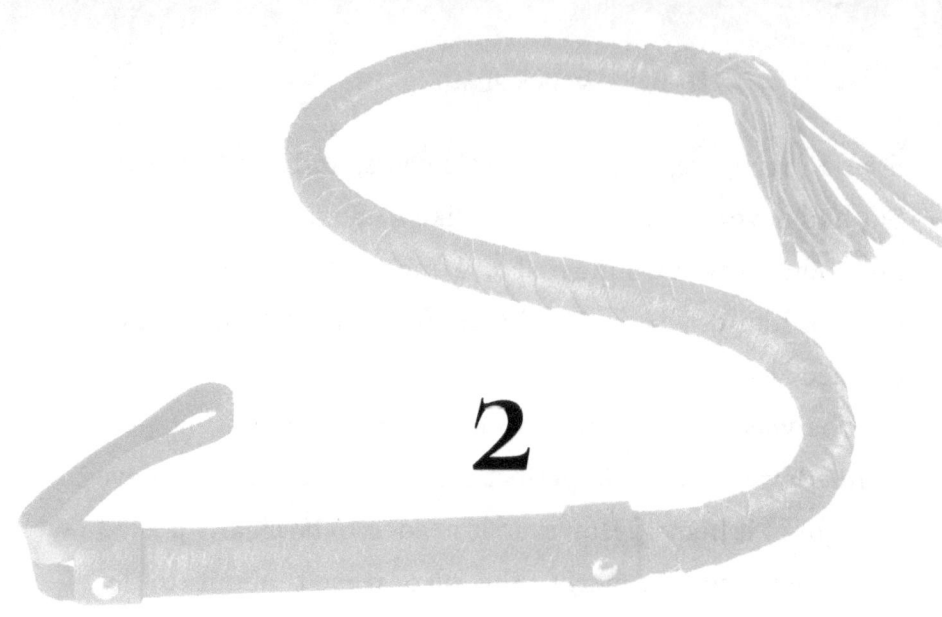

2

MARK

Chuckling to himself, Mark returned to his office. He had no idea what Ryan had been thinking to hire a woman like Kendra Hall. With disheveled blonde hair clipped in a messy bun and that long dress, she looked like she should have been serving cookies at a PTA fundraiser—not traipsing around a BDSM club three days before she was supposed to show up.

That wasn't entirely fair of him though. Wincing, he vaguely remembered Ryan had said she'd be driving from Houston, meaning she'd just arrived after a two-day road trip. He wouldn't be looking like he'd just stepped away from a photo shoot either.

And he certainly wouldn't have smelled like citrus and

vanilla, scents that made his mouth water for Jake's limon-cello pound cake. Or looked all soft and sweet, like she'd just tumbled from someone's bed wearing a floaty cotton dress sheer enough he could almost see through it.

Mark shook the thought away. He didn't do soft or sweet, and Kendra would be safe in her room until he had time to deal with her. He'd have to scrounge up a few hours after their morning meeting to take her around when the place wasn't full of guests.

Leaving his office door open, he sat behind his desk to double check the schedule before the dungeon monitors started arriving. As he was finishing, he heard the unwelcome voice of one of his least favorite people.

"Master Mark, I've been a very bad girl."

Mark pinched the skin between his eyes and bit back a groan. Shelby Baldwin, one of the club submissives and the bane of his existence, sauntered into his office wearing a schoolgirl outfit with a skirt so short he could see her panties, and a sleeveless white blouse with most of the buttons undone. Her blonde hair was tied into pigtails with red ribbon, and thick makeup outlined her hazel eyes until she looked like a doll.

Not for the first time, he wondered if he ought to cut her loose. Instead of working the floor, she followed him like a puppy. It irritated the hell out of him and her coworkers.

Maybe this was a blessing in disguise. As bad as business was, they didn't have space for dead weight. He needed employees who would work toward making the resort a success.

Careful to keep the smile off his face, Mark gestured to invite her in. Teetering on six-inch heels, she flounced to his desk and bent, putting her elbows on the polished wood. Looking over her shoulder, she batted her lashes at him.

"Have a seat. I was going to talk to you after your shift tomorrow, but we might as well do it now."

Giving him a pout, she sat on the edge of the chair, leaning forward to reveal her cleavage. "I know I'm not scheduled tonight, but I just had to tell you how bad I've been. I—"

"Shelby," he said, trying to keep his tone gentle, "I'm not your dom. I'm not anyone's dom, but especially not yours. I'm a sadist, and you're most definitely not a masochist, or even someone who can take more than a few whacks with a strap before melting down."

Shaking her head, she said, "No, you're not a sadist. If you were a sadist, you'd be mean all the time, and you're nice. I think all you need to do is cut your hair and shave, and maybe get some nice clothes like Master Ryan, and—"

He gave her the smile that usually sent submissives to their knees in terrified anticipation. "You say you need to be punished, right?"

Her eyes drifted shut and a pleased little smirk played about her lips. "Yes, sir, and you're the one I want."

"Uh huh. Well, why don't we get started with that?"

Mark opened his lower desk drawer and pulled out a bag of rice, a short candle, and a blindfold, tucking the items to his chest so she didn't see them. Detouring to the umbrella stand next to the door, he got a lightweight cane.

Shelby blinked at the sight of the cane, her breath coming faster between parted lips as he lit the candle. Ignoring her giggles and squirming, he covered her eyes with the blindfold, then quietly spread dry rice on the hardwood floor behind her.

He helped her from her chair, leading her forward to position her over the rice. "I think this is the perfect punishment for bad little subs," he whispered, letting his breath tickle the shell of her ear. "I want you on your elbows and knees, ass in the air."

"Should I undress first?" she asked, her hands flying to the few buttons holding her shirt closed.

"No. You're perfect just like you are." She wasn't perfect for him, but he was sure there was someone out there who would think she was. "Elbows and knees, please."

"Yes, sir." The bratty little smirk still on her lips, she crouched, then eased herself to the floor, hissing out a breath as her knees met the sharp grains of rice.

"Elbows, Shelby. Now," he barked, swishing the cane through the air.

She whimpered as her forearms settled into the rice. The smirk was finally gone, and she sniffed as she tried to hold back tears.

"Master, it hurts! I don't think I can do this!"

"You're the one who asked for a punishment, sweetheart. I'm not one to deny a lady's requests."

Maybe this would teach her not to play with sadists. Picking up the candle, he pinched the wick between his fingers, extinguishing the flame. The wax was hot enough for her to feel warmth but wouldn't hurt her if she moved and spilled it.

He set it gently at the base of her spine, just above the curve of her ass. "I suggest you hold very still, Shelby."

"Oh, my God, you're going to burn me!"

He snapped the cane against his hand, making her jump. "No, if you get burned, it will be because you moved. I think five minutes is sufficient for your crimes, don't you?"

With a piercing scream, Shelby leaped to her feet and tore off the blindfold. She stared down at the rice and unlit candle, then looked at him, her eyes wide.

"You asshole! You were fucking with me? Why?"

"I'll never let the opportunity for a mind fuck go to waste when it's so freely offered." He bared his teeth and slapped the cane against his palm. "I told you I was a sadist, and you chose not to believe me."

Her face purple with anger, she screamed, "How dare you! I should have you arrested! I should—"

"For what?" He leaned back against his desk and gestured at the red lights of the security cameras mounted on either side of the room. "You and I are both dressed.

We've never kissed, much less had intimate relations. You let me blindfold you and knelt on that pile of rice of your own free will."

"How can you be such a dick?" she asked, folding her arms across her chest. "All I wanted was a chance to date you and make you see I'm the woman you need."

Sighing, he rubbed his face. "Sit down, Shelby."

"No! I want you to admit you were mean to me."

"Sit down!" he barked, suddenly out of patience.

Letting out a squeak of fear, Shelby obeyed and sat, cowering under his angry glare.

"First off, being mean to people is what a sadist does. Making pretty girls cry is my favorite thing in the world to do."

"But I know I can make you different!" Tears filled her eyes as she gazed at him. "I just want to make you into the sweet guy I know you have inside."

"You don't know shit, honey. I like being a sadist, and I'm happy with my choices. There are people out there who enjoy it, but you are not one of them." He pushed a box of tissues toward her, then leaned back in his chair, steepling his fingers as he waited for her to stop crying.

Normally, a woman's tears made his dick hard, but Shelby's were just annoying. Even if he had interest in finding a woman, it wouldn't have been her. She was too young, for one thing, and he didn't tolerate brats. With some irritation, he glanced at his watch, hoping she'd hurry it up.

When she sniffed and dabbed at her eyes, he said, "Now that you've calmed down, we need to discuss your job."

"What about it?" she asked, her eyes focused on the wadded tissue in her hands.

"We're going to talk about why you're not doing it. You aren't required to accept a scene with anyone, and you know that. You're also aware you're not permitted to accept financial compensation even if it's offered."

"Yes, I know. What's the problem?"

"The problem is you don't do anything else. You follow me around all night, and I've had several complaints from your coworkers saying you're not carrying your weight."

She muttered something under her breath and scowled. Mark didn't bother to waste time arguing over it and let it slide.

"So, here's the deal. I can't afford to pay you to stand around. If that's all you intend to do, put your name on the waiting list and pay your membership fee. I'll give your job to someone who wants to work."

Shelby lifted her chin and her eyes narrowed. "Are you firing me?"

"No. Not yet anyway. I'm giving you a week to decide whether you want to work here or not. If it isn't what you want, you're welcome to leave at any time."

She bit her lip, and he wondered what she would decide. He hoped she'd quit and get out of his hair, but the small, hidden part of him he didn't like to show hoped she'd learn from this experience and do her job. Maybe there was someone out there for her, but if she didn't stop looking at people as pets she could train for obedience, she was destined to be disappointed.

Standing up, she dropped the tissue on his desk. "Fine. You want me gone so bad, asshole? I quit."

"All right. Stop by Ryan's office on your way out to arrange for your last paycheck and the return of your keycard. I wish you the best of luck in your future endeavors."

"That's it? That's all you have to say?"

Mark had maybe another minute of patience remaining before he had security throw her ass out. Gritting his teeth, he got up and walked to the door, then opened it. "I can't think of anything else that needs to be said, aside from reminding you of the nondisclosure agreement you signed. If you need assistance, I can have security escort you."

"I'll make sure Ms. Baldwin gets to Ryan's office." Sean stood behind her, his hands tucked into the pockets of his slacks as he leaned against the wall. Two members of his security team stood behind him.

Sean must have been watching from his command center in Security. Mark had protested the cameras in their offices at first but was grateful for them now. He had a feeling if they hadn't been there, Shelby would have tried to have him arrested as she'd threatened.

Shelby gave him one last poisonous glare and stomped

out, following the security guards down the corridor.

"You found yourself a crazy one, that's for sure," Sean murmured.

"Yeah, I should have fired her months ago during her probationary period."

"Well, it's done now. I'll let you get back to work and make sure she's escorted off the property. Do you want to ban her?"

"I'd like to say it won't be necessary, but..." He shrugged, then swept Shelby's used tissue into the wastebasket. "Thank God I didn't scene with her."

"Shelby was more than clear about what she was trying to do, but maybe you should have just fired her instead of giving her a mind fuck. Save those for someone who might appreciate it." Sean studied him for a moment, his dark brown eyes calmly assessing. "Speaking of which, when was the last time you had a scene with a submissive?"

"Last week. I did a demo with that couple from Ohio. You remember, Siobhan and Jackson McKenna?"

"Not a demo. You need a partner who isn't someone else's submissive."

Grunting in acknowledgement, Mark turned back to his paperwork. "I'll take it under advisement."

"Do that. Don't be the only dominant in Club Apocalypse who hasn't had a real scene since we opened."

"Sure. Whatever."

"And stop scratching your forehead with your middle

finger, asshole. We're not in middle school." Sean's phone chimed and he frowned as he glanced at the device. "I have to go. I just got the background check on Dr. Knox."

The door shut behind him before Mark had a chance to tell him Kendra had arrived.

At least he'd be left alone until the dungeon opened. So what if he hadn't had a sub? Was that a crime? It wasn't as if he didn't want to. He just...

Sighing, he scrubbed his hands over his face. He still couldn't stand to be touched. He was okay touching other people—mostly—but what was the point of sharing a scene if he couldn't also share the aftercare? Aside from that, he'd never consider asking a sub to put up with that shit.

He got back to work, pushing the thought from his mind. Yet he couldn't get rid of the image of Kendra Hall quite as easily.

———

KENDRA

"Table for one?" the hostess asked, giving Kendra a wide smile. She wore a white shirt with a black bow tie, and black trousers. Behind her, hung a professionally printed and framed sign, large enough to read from the corridor.

Nude dining in outdoor areas only. Please ask your server for special accommodations.

"Please," Kendra replied. Considering the decided lack of attire on the servers in the lobby, she'd been worried about even more health code violations, but the sign and the hostess's uniform put those worries to rest.

"Right this way, ma'am. We have a table with a wonderful view of the gardens. In fact, the solar lights should be coming on shortly, so you'll be able to see our resident porcupines come along for a snack. Later, we might even see a mountain lion or two."

The hostess pulled out Kendra's chair. Dressed simply in white linen, the table bore a pink rose in a bud vase, along with a single place setting of plain, but obviously expensive tableware.

"Sounds wonderful, and the gardens are lovely."

"We don't see the mountain lions often, but we're not busy tonight, so we might get lucky. The lights are only good for an hour or two because we don't want to interfere with nocturnal wildlife too much. The website hosting our trail cams is on a printed card in your room if you'd like to take a peek."

"Thank you. I'll do that."

"Great! Master Jake will be with you in a moment to tell you about the menu. We have standard a la carte options, as well as a tasting menu which includes wine service. May I bring you a cocktail? We also have a selection of virgin cocktails if you plan to play in the dungeon."

"Just water for now, please." The dungeon could wait.

She wanted to see that in the light of day. Ryan had already assured her there were no liability or safety issues, and it wasn't her area of expertise, so it was probably better if she didn't see it full of guests.

Then again, she wouldn't mind seeing Whiskey Eyes in a pair of leather pants and nothing else. He might be a jerk, but he was a pretty one.

"My pleasure. I'll be right back."

The staff—aside from Whiskey Eyes—was perfect. Even when they weren't wearing much, they were knowledgeable, polite, and charismatic. She'd place them in any of the properties she'd managed without question.

Elegant and tasteful with well-spaced tables and impeccable décor, the restaurant would be a perfect showpiece for Apocalypse's new marketing. Although there were only two couples in the dining room, the outdoor seating area was full of people in various stages of undress, all very clearly enjoying their meals.

The bar was an antique mahogany edifice with mirrored shelves and intricately carved finials. Leather upholstered stools with chrome footrests stood in regimented precision along its length, mixing vintage with modern, and she blinked at a few of the exposed labels.

There were easily six figures in alcohol resting on those shelves. It didn't make sense. Why would the restaurant look so amazing while the rest of the resort was threadbare and dated?

Carrying a manila folder under one arm, Sierra exited the door leading to the kitchen. Smiling, she veered toward Kendra's table. "Hi, Ms. Hall. I'm glad you decided to try our restaurant. May I also say you clean up very well."

Kendra caught the interested gleam in Sierra's eye and her face heated with embarrassed pleasure at the compliment. "Thank you."

"Was Ezekiel helpful?"

"Very much so," Kendra replied, deciding not to tell Sierra what an ass her boss had been. "It was very educational, but if you have a few minutes, I'd like to pick your brain."

"Of course." Sierra sat across from her and folded her hands on the table. "Pick away."

"When I passed through the lobby on my way here, it was empty. What happened to all the people?"

"About a third of them will be heading to the dungeon now. The rest went home."

The answer tied with what Kendra suspected and she nodded. "And how many reservations do you have for tonight, not including me?"

"Six, plus another new employee."

Meaning, they were at fifteen percent occupancy on a Friday night. "Is that standard for weekends?"

Grimacing, Sierra nodded. "We used to run at capacity every night, but..." She gestured toward the road and shrugged. "We're lucky to get fifty percent these days."

"Do you think the al fresco diners will reserve rooms?"

"We might get another five. Maybe."

Leaning back in her chair, Kendra tapped her lower lip with a fingernail, then nodded. "Thank you. You've been very helpful."

"Any time." Rising to her feet, she grabbed her folder. "I need to get back to work but stop by the front desk if you have more questions."

"I appreciate your time. Oh, one more thing. Just out of curiosity, is the rule about cell phone use in public areas posted anywhere?"

"No, I don't think so. It used to be, but most people know better."

Maybe most people except Kendra, because it hadn't occurred to her, nor had it been mentioned in any of the employment documents Mr. Wood had sent. The NDA simply said she wasn't allowed to take pictures, which she understood completely.

"Ah, yes, I suppose that's true. Thanks again."

"Enjoy your supper. Master Jake will be out in a moment to tell you about tonight's tasting menu."

Instead of using her phone, Kendra pulled out a legal pad and started writing notes the minute Sierra walked away. The atrium, the impromptu parties in the lobby of all places, the lack of appropriate signage. Dwindling occupancy. The dismal financials...

And really, there was an awful lot of booze in the restaurant for a place where people would be picking up whips and things but weren't allowed to drink and participate in those activities.

She tapped her pen on the page a few times, wondering if Club Apocalypse would be the one property she couldn't bring back. No, there was that boutique hotel in Paris with rats in the basement, a broken elevator, and a kitchen she still had nightmares about. If she could make that one profitable, this one should be a snap.

"Welcome to Club Apocalypse, Ms. Hall," a man in chef's whites said, striding toward her. Thankfully, he wasn't Whiskey Eyes. They were about the same height and build, but the chef was clean-shaven with cropped blond hair, vivid blue eyes, and had a friendly smile for her.

"Thank you." She accepted the offered handshake, pleased when he didn't try to squeeze her fingers.

"I'm Jake McBride. I hope everything is to your satisfaction."

"It's gorgeous. I'd love to get a photographer in here for some marketing shots."

"We have a photographer for private events. She's already signed our nondisclosure agreement, so I'd prefer to use her." He sat across from her, then rested his elbows on the table. "I'm sure Ryan told you it's mandatory for all employees and vendors."

"Yes. I've already signed mine and sent it back." Leaning forward, she met his blue eyes. "I'd really like to talk about the restaurant though. It's very impressive, but it almost seems as if it doesn't fit with the rest of the property."

"That's because it doesn't. We just finished renovating about six months ago. Before that, it was the original diner with an open grill and a counter."

"A little at a time then?"

"As we can afford it, yes. We don't want to bring in outside investors unless we absolutely have to, so we did the rest of it ourselves as best we could."

"Thanks for the information," she replied. "I'm trying to get a sense of what I think the place needs versus your budget, and this is very helpful."

"My pleasure. Would you like to hear tonight's menu?"

"Please."

His eyes brightened and he grinned. "I have a tasting menu with wine pairings for you. We'll start with seared weathervane scallops wrapped in applewood smoked bacon and served with a California chardonnay. After that, we're serving—"

Whiskey Eyes appeared in the entryway, looking just as sour and unpleasant as he had before. She considered leaving but wasn't about to give him the satisfaction of chasing her off. Straightening her spine, she met his gaze and flushed when he looked her up and down like a dog sizing up a bone.

It seemed her black cocktail dress had worked a little too well. She absolutely hated herself for the low thrum of arousal blossoming in her core. He might be a jerk, but he was an incredibly handsome jerk.

It was almost a relief to meet a man who, for whatever reason, didn't like her. She'd rather know where she stood at the beginning than spend another decade of her life being gaslit by someone like her narcissistic ex-husband.

He crossed the dining room and grabbed a chair from another table, then sat next to her, much too close for comfort. "You don't have to introduce every course, Jake. Just bring out the food."

"We're supposed to be nice to Kendra, asshole. I'm not seeing nice."

"I haven't thrown her out for having a phone in the lobby yet, have I?"

Then again, Whiskey Eyes was going to be one of her new bosses.

She did a quick mental tally of how long she could live off her savings, then laid her napkin on the table and stood. "Gentlemen, if you'll excuse me, I have somewhere to be."

"Where are you going?" Jake asked, sending Whiskey Eyes an angry glare. "If it's because of this guy, ignore him like the rest of us do."

"I just remembered I had a better offer. Please tell Mr. Wood I'll be exercising the three-day grace period of our contract, and that he'll receive formal written notice tomorrow morning."

Unsurprisingly, neither man followed her as she strode

to the front desk. This had been an utter waste of time. She should have kept going to her second offer in Reno but hadn't wanted to deal with the weather. She'd take a dozen feet of snow over having to see Whiskey Eyes again though.

With a practiced smile, Sierra greeted her. "What can I help you with, Ms. Hall?"

"I'll be checking out tomorrow morning, so—"

"I will not allow a convicted thief anywhere near my security system!" a man shouted behind her.

Turning, she blinked as one of the men from the brochure photo towered over a young woman with multicolored hair and tattooed sleeves on both arms. A tasteful gold ring pierced the septum of her button nose, and she had another in one eyebrow. She was absolutely adorable in a purple pinafore dress with a pony on the front, and knee length black engineer boots.

"I haven't stolen anything in almost fifteen years, you git! Do you honestly think I'd risk my bloody security clearance over a failing business I could buy with cash?"

She had a thick Scottish accent, and the most charming vocabulary of swears. Kendra was almost immediately entranced by her—especially since it seemed they had the same trouble with Horsemen.

"Language!"

The woman tossed her hair and flipped him off. "Bugger it, and you, Mr. Franklin. I'm going to get a suite for the night, and—"

"We're full." He gave her a nasty smile and pointed at the door.

"No, they're not," Kendra said. "They've only managed to fill six rooms out of forty."

At least now she had all their names. This jerk was Sean Franklin, and she'd already met Jake. Aside from their voices being dissimilar, Ryan wouldn't have been antagonistic. That left Whiskey Eyes as Mark Luciano.

She probably should have kept her mouth shut and loaded up her car. It would have been the easy way out, but she wasn't about to let another woman get bullied without fighting back. Aside from that, she was exhausted, and the other woman looked like she could use a good night's sleep as well.

Sierra let out a tiny snort, then nodded, trying to hide a smile. "We already have Dr. Knox's luggage in her suite. It's right across from Ms. Hall's."

"Dr. Knox," Kendra said, "will you join me for supper? I was chased off mine by a different asshole, and I think we could both use a drink and better company before we leave in the morning."

"You too, eh?"

To Kendra's surprise, Dr. Knox's eyes were damp, and she blinked furiously to hold tears at bay. It made her realize how very hurt the woman was, and she wanted to squeeze her into a tight hug.

And then she wanted to punch the man who had

insulted her. Instead of doing either of those things, Kendra pointed toward the restaurant. "You might be interested to know there's a lovely bottle of Glenfiddich in the bar with our names on it."

Dr. Knox sniffed, then ducked her head to surreptitiously wipe her eyes. "With our names, you say?"

"Yes. It says Property of Kendra and—"

"Gabby." She linked her arm through Kendra's and tugged her toward the restaurant. "If it has our names on it, we must introduce ourselves before it gets lonely."

"And the chef is nice. His name is Jake, and I understand his food is very good. I imagine he'll let us eat at the bar while we talk to our new friend."

Two hours later, Kendra's sides hurt from laughing, and most of a five-hundred-dollar bottle of scotch was gone. Gabby was the single most interesting person she'd ever met, and she didn't understand why Sean had taken such an immediate dislike to her. Then again, Mark had done the same thing to her.

Jake kept bringing them small tidbits of food and had a smile for them no matter how loud they got. The scallops were every bit as good as they'd sounded and were followed by succulently spicy bang bang shrimp paired with appetizer-sized spring rolls. The decadent artichoke dip accompanied by crusty bread almost made her cry.

"You are my new best friend, Jake McBride," she said, drunkenly waving a skewer loaded with rare bits of prime rib and grilled lobster. "If only Whiskey Eyes could be like you."

"Whiskey Eyes? Who's that?" Gabby asked.

"Mark. He has eyes like whiskey, but he stole my phone, then sent me to my room like a child. We should just call them assholes, but different assholes so we don't get our assholes confused."

Lord have mercy, she was drunk. Kendra tried to repeat her words to see if they made sense the second time around, but it didn't help.

Snorting, Gabby sprayed criminally expensive scotch down the front of her pinafore, then burst into laughter. "Oh, I like that. Asshole One and Two, then?"

"But which is which?" Kendra grabbed a piece of bread and swiped up the last of the artichoke dip.

"Problem is, Sean was right, so it doesn't really matter." Sighing, Gabby took another shot, then looked out the window. "Anyway, I'm going to bed. Thanks for supper and the conversation."

Before Kendra could ask what she'd meant, Gabby hopped off her barstool and walked away, her steps wavering only slightly. Jake caught up and gently took her arm, escorting her out.

When he returned a few minutes later, he cleaned up their empty plates and wiped the bar. "I had a security guard escort Gabby back to her suite. I fed you both enough to soak up all the booze, so I think she'll be okay."

He started to say something else but pressed his lips together and scrubbed at a spot on the bar.

Kendra drained the last of her scotch, then stood, not curious enough to press him. "I hope so. Thank you for feeding us, and for being the one Horsemen who isn't a jerk. What do I owe you?"

"It's on the house as a gift for having to put up with Sean and Mark. Anyway, you haven't met Ryan yet, but considering the odds, I'm pretty sure he'll do something to piss someone off." He sobered and sighed heavily. "For what it's worth, I hope you change your mind and decide to stay."

"Thank you, but it's best I move on." She handed him a business card with her private number. "When Club Apocalypse fails, please call me. I'd be delighted to help you find another restaurant. What you've done here is nothing short of outstanding."

Jake flushed and grinned. "You think so?"

"The whole property should look like this, but that's all the free advice I'm giving you."

"Not even for a slice of death by chocolate cake?"

Shaking her head, she chuckled. "No, I'm too full. Besides, I hate to say it, but unless you make some changes, you have two years at best. After that...well, you'll all be looking for new jobs."

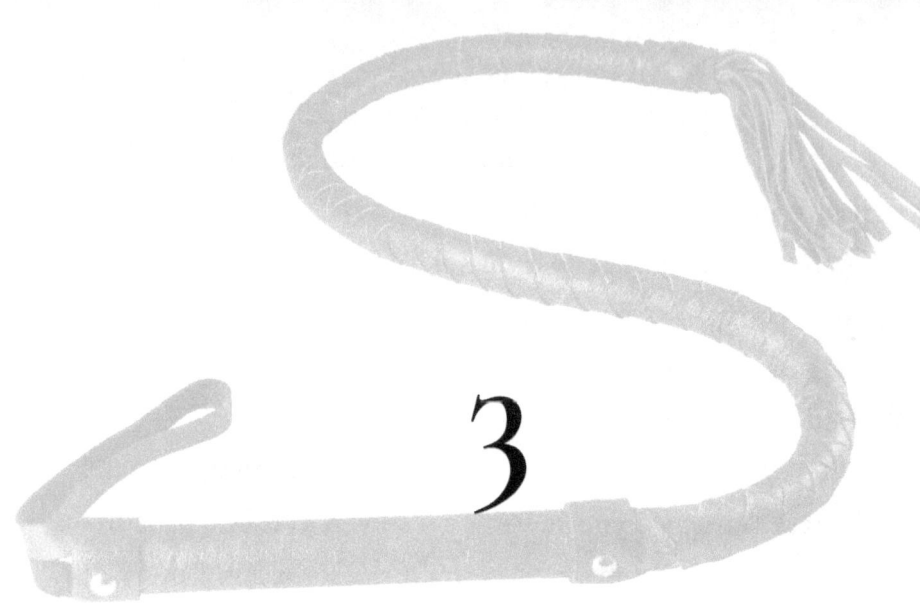

3

MARK

Leaning against the entrance to the restaurant, he scowled as Kendra laughed uproariously at something her companion said. He didn't know the other woman but assumed her to be Dr. Knox. It seemed as though he hadn't been the only asshole in Apocalypse, yet he couldn't imagine what would make Sean be anything but polite to a woman.

He might not have wanted Kendra Hall messing in their business, but he hadn't needed to be such a dick to her. Unfortunately, seeing Jake look at her in that slinky black cocktail dress and those sexy heels made jealous rage replace every logical thought in Mark's head. Both women were smiling at him, and even included the bastard in their conversation as he fed them the supper Mark should have been eating with Kendra.

Her companion finished her drink, then walked out, passing by him without a word. Mark didn't think she saw him though. Between the alcohol and her obvious exhaustion, she seemed too focused on putting one foot in front of the other to pay attention.

Jake caught up to her, giving Mark an ugly glance as he passed, then escorted her down the corridor toward the front desk.

After waiting until Jake was out of sight, Mark took a step into the restaurant, meaning to apologize to Kendra now that she was alone. Before he could reach her, Jake caught his arm and spun him around.

"Don't even think about it, asshole. In fact, get out of my restaurant."

"What? I'm just going to—"

"Turn your ass around and leave her alone. You and Sean have done enough damage for one night."

"I was going to apologize." He gritted the words past tight lips, trying to resist the urge to punch one of his best friends in the face.

"Do it tomorrow. If you want to be helpful for a change, find Sean and kick his ass for making Dr. Knox cry." Giving Mark a shove, he added, "Now, get lost before Kendra sees you."

It was one thing to make a submissive cry during a

consensual scene or a negotiated punishment. Verbally abusing a woman until she cried was anathema. Mark would have cut off his left nut first. Although he had made Shelby cry, her tears were because she hadn't gotten her way —not because he'd physically hurt her or said anything that wasn't the truth.

He refused to believe Sean had struck Dr. Knox. Then again, he wouldn't have thought Sean capable of verbal abuse either.

"Why was she crying?"

"I have no idea. She was trying to hide it and I didn't get a chance to ask." He shoved Mark again, then glanced over his shoulder. "I swear to God, I'm going to beat you with your own tawse if you don't get out of here before Kendra sees you."

Giving Jake a curt nod, Mark walked out, but didn't go far. Positioning himself behind a large ficus, he waited until Kendra left, then followed, his steps silent on the industrial carpet. He hadn't needed to go to so much trouble though. She was lost in her own little world and barely acknowledged Sierra's greeting.

When she reached her suite, she held the card above the slot, then turned, frowning at the door across from hers. Instead of swiping her card, she crossed the corridor and knocked softly.

"Gabby, are you okay?"

The door opened suddenly, making him duck into the alcove containing the ice machine before they saw him.

Wearing a short nightgown with a unicorn on the front, Dr. Knox appeared, clutching a large teddy bear. Tears streaked her face, and she wiped her nose with the back of her hand, then smiled wanly. "I could use a hug if you're offering."

It took Kendra a bare second to take in the scene and make a decision. "Let me get changed and we'll have a cuddle, okay?"

Mark waited to make sure both women were safe in Dr. Knox's room, then left them alone. He might have been a dick but couldn't understand what had possessed Sean to abuse a woman like that. Not that it mattered. This wasn't a contest to see who could be the biggest asshole.

Retracing his steps, he trudged to his private suite adjacent to the dungeon, torn on what he really wanted. They didn't need Kendra to make Apocalypse successful. It was fine the way it was. Yet he wanted her to stay. Maybe it was the haunted look in her eyes when she thought nobody was watching.

It might have had something to do with that hot little body all wrapped up like a present in black silk. The dress had been a power move on her part. He'd recognized it the minute he saw her in it, yet it didn't make it less effective.

Most likely, it was her self-contained attitude. She didn't need him, Apocalypse, or anything else. She was mature—

mid to late thirties if he had to guess—meaning she knew what she wanted and could probably get it for herself. Mark wanted her to need something too badly to walk away, and he wanted it to be him.

Unfortunately, he'd fucked it all up by being a jerk to her. Knowing he wouldn't be able to sleep, he went into the dungeon and got some work done overnight, including the inventory he'd been putting off. With luck, she'd accept his apology and maybe stick around long enough to share a scene or two with him. For her, he might even resist the urge to fuck with her head while he fucked with her body.

He finished up the last of his supply orders in plenty of time to grab a shower and get to the conference room fifteen minutes early. Jake was already there with the usual cart full of pastries, a coffee urn, and pitchers of juice and water. This time, there were mini quiches too.

When he reached for one, Jake slapped the back of his hand with a metal spoon, making him bite back a curse. "What was that for?"

"They're for Gabby and Kendra, jackass. Hands off until after they eat."

"What's for Gabby and Kendra?" Ryan walked in, then grabbed a coffee cup and filled it. For once, he wasn't in a suit. Instead, he wore his usual weekend attire of jeans and a polo shirt.

Jake covered the tray with a linen napkin. "The quiches.

And don't you touch them either. I'm still holding judgment on whether you're going to be a dick too."

"Oh, you can bet I'm going to be a dick." Ryan took his coffee and sat at the head of the table. "I happened to have a charming conversation with Sierra this morning before her shift ended, in which I learned she's scheduling two of my three best friends as demo dollies for her next single-tail class. We'll wait until asshole number two gets here."

"I'm going to apologize." Mark got his own coffee and doctored it with cream. "I don't think we need Ms. Hall, but I was out of line."

"You won't be getting an apology from me." Sean strode in, then sat across from Ryan, glaring at him. "What possessed you to hire a fucking car thief? Are you just asking for her to open our client list and bank accounts to every hacker in the world?"

"You weren't complaining yesterday," Ryan replied. "Why now?"

"I did a background check. Her juvenile record is sealed, but—"

"Let me get this straight." Ryan stood, resting his hands on the table. "You're judging a woman for crimes she committed as a juvenile when she was living in the Scottish version of the projects?"

Sean scowled, then stood as well. "You mean to tell me you knew and didn't tell us?"

"Why would I? Show me a kid with that upbringing who didn't do stupid shit to survive."

Ryan might not have come from an inner-city tenement, but he'd been raised in poverty. He glared at Sean, as if daring him to say something.

Sean swore under his breath. "Sorry."

"Whatever." Ryan pushed his coffee aside. "Frankly, it's none of our business, especially since multiple governments have already decided she's trustworthy. You know how deep they crawl up people's asses for security clearances."

The door opened, revealing Kendra, with Dr. Knox close behind. Kendra looked sleek and professional in a black pantsuit and another pair of wicked sexy stiletto heels. Her hair was pinned up in a neat chignon, and she carried a manila folder in one manicured hand. Incongruously, she was sucking on a lollipop.

Dr. Knox wore a yellow pinafore dress with pink Doc Martens and had her rainbow-hued hair tied in pigtails. Large sunglasses covered her eyes. Waving a hand at them, she went to the cart and filled a plate with mini quiches and a small bunch of grapes.

"Inside voices, gentlemen." She sat as far from Sean as she could, then tossed a balled-up piece of paper at Ryan. "Miss Gabby is slightly hung, so I'll eat my breakfast while Mr. Wood accepts the dissolution of our contract."

"Here, try this." Kendra handed her a wrapped sucker.

"What is it?"

"Ginger candy. It will settle your stomach. I get them from an amazing lady named Rhonda in Oklahoma."

Gabby unwrapped it and giggled as she held up a molded candy phallus. "Is this your way of telling me to suck a dick?" Her laughter cut off abruptly. She replaced the wrapper and tossed it across the table at Sean, then ate a quiche.

"Savage." Smirking, Jake poured her a glass of water. "I love it."

Mark shared a look with Ryan, but before he could give Kendra his apology, she laid her folder next to Ryan's coffee cup.

"This is mine. You'll also find a check reimbursing your signing bonus. If you'll recall, it wasn't refundable, but as I didn't perform any work on your behalf, I thought it best to return it."

"Good on you to get a bonus," Dr. Knox said, her mouth full. "I took the job at a tenth of my normal rate."

"Why on earth did you do that?"

Shrugging, Dr. Knox ate another quiche. "They couldn't afford me otherwise. Something Ryan said about the hack attempts sounded familiar and I decided to make a vacation of it so I could track it down."

Mark stood and walked around the table, blocking Kendra's departure. Sean might have been a bigger dick, but that didn't lessen his own culpability. "Ms. Hall, I owe you an apology. I'm sorry I was a jerk to you last night. I was out of line, and I'd like to start over."

She blinked in surprise, then gave him a tentative smile. "Thank you. I wish you and your friends the best with your business."

———

KENDRA

"Wait." Ryan pushed Mark out of the way to block her path. "What would it take to get you to stay?"

She considered him for a moment, gazing up into pale gray eyes the color of smoke. They were almost chilling, yet she didn't feel threatened. Ryan was almost unnaturally gorgeous with chiseled features and a lean, muscular build, yet she felt nothing aside from momentary appreciation of his appearance.

Although Mark had apologized, she got the distinct impression he didn't want her at Club Apocalypse. Truly, they seemed divided. Jake and Ryan were both willing to consider hiring outside talent, yet Mark and Sean were not.

"Let me ask you something, Mr. Wood. What are your goals for Apocalypse?"

"I want it to grow and continue making a profit so we can expand."

"And yours, Jake?"

"The same as Ryan."

"How about you?" She looked at Mark.

"I don't want to grow, but I do want to continue making a profit."

"And you." She faced Sean, then waited for his answer.

He didn't take his gaze off Gabby. "Profit, and also keep Apocalypse secure for our guests and members. I don't care whether we grow or not."

Gabby snorted and sipped her water. "Least they agree on something. Sounds like you'd be herding cats."

"Dr. Knox makes a fair assessment." Kendra poured coffee for herself and studied them. "You all want profit, which goes without saying. There's no point in operating a business at a loss. Data security is also a concern with any hotel or resort. Those two items are going to be important regardless of your growth path."

"What do you suggest?" Mark leaned forward intently, his dark brown eyes seeming to bore into her.

"Unfortunately, I don't think it will matter. Last night, I took a harder look at your financials. If you can't control your expenses, bring in additional revenue streams, and increase your overall marketability, you'd be better off cutting your losses and selling Apocalypse to a developer. I estimate you have less than two years before it goes under."

"I might be willing to invest," Gabby said. "I have a few million dollars that isn't doing anything important."

"We are not taking outside investors," Sean muttered between clenched teeth. "Especially not you."

"You shouldn't anyway," Kendra said, cutting off their exchange. "You'd be throwing good money after bad."

Ryan winced, making her feel a bit sorry for how she'd worded her comment, but she wouldn't take it back. It was the truth as she saw it. The four men stared at each other for several seconds, then turned to face her.

"We don't have to grow," Ryan said. "I think that was the only true disagreement we had, so I will go with Mark on the current size of the resort. Will you consider staying, please?"

Sighing, she looked at them. Restoring Club Apocalypse had sounded like such a good time, but she wasn't interested in what could potentially be a toxic environment. "I'll stay on one condition."

"It's yours if it's ours to give."

"Dr. Knox has to agree to stay too."

Gabby laughed, then put her empty plate in the bus pan on the lower shelf of the cart. "I'm afraid not. As curious as I am about your cyber intruder, I have better things to do with my time than be abused by a perfect stranger."

"Can you tell us about the hacker?" Mark asked. "What makes you so curious?"

Frowning, she stood, then paced across the room. "I'm not sure, actually. It's just something familiar about the pattern and I keep thinking if I can just find a few more clues..." She stopped, then turned and smiled. "I was ever one for a puzzle, but I think you're more curious about why your friend thinks I'm a thief."

"According to Ryan, it happened when you were a child. You don't owe us an explanation," Mark said, his gaze softening into something almost kind.

"Yes, she does."

"Shut up, Sean."

Mark, Ryan, and Jake spoke in unison. There was apparently something else the Horsemen agreed upon. Gabby had told her the story once she'd calmed down, but Kendra wanted to see their reactions before she made a final decision.

"I was twelve, actually, and yes, I was a car thief. Quite a good one too, until I stole the wrong vintage Jaguar and got caught by an elderly barrister who had no business running as fast as he did. I'm not sorry, in fact, I'm very grateful to him, especially since it wasn't good for his heart to chase me down."

"Why were you grateful?" Ryan asked.

Gabby's eyes went distant, and she looked over his head. "People will do almost anything when they're desperate, even when they don't want to." She smiled brightly, then added, "In any case, he taught me to read, then mathematics, and the next thing I knew I was fourteen and MIT snapped me up like a biscuit. I make more now than I could have ever hoped to in a dozen lifetimes of stealing."

"You're still a thief," Sean snapped. "How do you explain

the Jag sitting in our parking lot? It's the same damned car you stole!"

Gabby stared at him long enough that Kendra thought she might not answer. Finally, she appeared to shake herself, then moved to the door. "The barrister's name was Nigel Barryson, and he left it to me when he died. I'm sure you can find the paper trail if you look. Now, if you'll excuse me, I'll be on my way."

The men were silent for several seconds, watching as she walked out. Eventually, Sean wiped his face, then stood. "I... um... I owe her an apology."

Jake let out a low curse, pinning Sean with an angry glower. "Fix it, asshole. If you don't convince her to come back, you will never eat in my restaurant again."

"And then we'll drown you in the pool," Mark added.

"After we stake you out in the desert for a few days." Ryan jerked his head toward the door. "What are you waiting for?"

Once Sean was gone, she took control of the meeting. "All right, gentleman. I'm going to lay out exactly what you need to do to have any hope of surviving."

"That sounds ominous." Jake pulled a bottle of champagne free from the lower shelf of the cart. "I think we'll need proper sustenance."

"Put it away and have a seat. We have a lot of work to do."

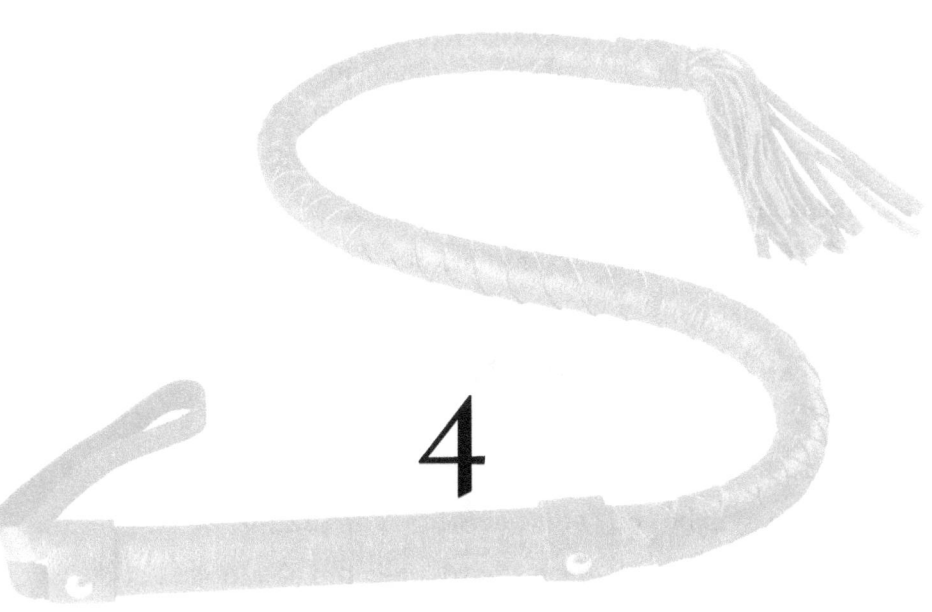

4

MARK

There was something very sexy about a woman who knew enough about her business to make Ryan shut up and listen to her. Mark studied her intently, trying to follow the conversation, but got lost when she started throwing around words like ROI and income streams.

As she spoke, Sean slunk into the conference room, Dr. Knox in tow. Judging by his expression, he wasn't happy, but Mark didn't miss the matching smirks of satisfaction on both Dr. Knox's and Kendra's faces.

Kendra's entire demeanor changed. Instead of pacing the room like she was a second away from leaving, she sat at the head of the table, crossing her legs to reveal a slim ankle and the pointed toe of an incredibly sexy stiletto pump.

"What do you recommend about data security?" Ryan asked.

"I'm afraid that isn't my area of expertise. Aside from making sure it's there, I don't know the first thing about how to implement it." She inclined her head toward Dr. Knox. "Gabby will be your point of contact on that."

Her warm brown eyes hardened, and she looked at Sean when she spoke. "Dr. Knox will bring any problems to me, and I'll make sure they're dealt with. For now, we're going offline for reservations and financial transactions until she can put countermeasures in place. I realize it's an inconvenience, but until the systems are secure, it will be the safest option for everyone."

Mark didn't miss the change in her phrasing. Before Dr. Knox's return, she worded everything as suggestions. Now, they were orders, and he didn't like it. Who was she to be ordering them around?

Oh, yeah. She was the fixer Ryan thought they needed.

"What about advertising?" Jake asked. "You mentioned wanting to use the restaurant."

"Yes. Until you can do something about that eyesore of a lobby, I recommend your focus remain on food service and your incredible staff. You should also consider promoting the landscaping. Your artist was truly gifted, and the live streaming trail cams are brilliant. That, plus your proximity to Homolovi is perfect for getting outdoorsy types into the resort."

"What's wrong with the lobby?" Mark asked, trying to control his fury. He'd done the lobby himself, despite not knowing the first thing about construction or design, and thought it came out well.

"Nothing, if you're running a hundred-dollar a night chain motel, but Club Apocalypse is a destination resort. The lobby is the first thing a guest will see, and it needs to show them what to expect."

Pulling out her phone, she tapped the screen and laid it on the table. "This is a BDSM resort near Toledo, Ohio, and it—"

"We know the place," Mark interrupted. "It's a freaking castle."

"I realize that. It's simply an example of how everything fits together into a seamless product. When people go there, it's an immersive experience from the moment they reach the property until they leave. That's what you need to achieve here."

Ryan nodded, his gaze fixed on the image on her phone. "I thought the Friday parties would do that."

"Well, they do, but they don't."

"Explain," Mark ordered.

Kendra arched a brow. "Let me ask you something first. Do you see any conversion from those parties?"

Ryan pinched the skin between his brows and held up a

hand. "Small words, please. It's more than clear we don't know shit about marketing. I have a nursing degree, Mark got his in history, Jake was chemistry, and Sean was criminal justice."

She shook her head. "No, you're all clearly intelligent. You just need some new vocabulary. How many new members do you get each week from those parties? Do people stay the night?"

"Sometimes," he admitted. "Maybe one or two new members a month, and we usually run fifty percent occupancy on the weekends."

"I see. And do those one or two a month pay for the parties? That's what I mean by conversion. You want to convert the expense into revenue. I'm guessing they were successful at first, but people are using them for a source of free entertainment now."

"So, cancel the parties."

"No. I'd say have them twice a year and move them from the lobby into a larger area that showcases what you want potential members to see. Right now, that many people crowded into such a small space is against fire code and it inconveniences guests trying to check in. These events should be highly anticipated, rather than something to do on a Friday night."

"The atrium? It's close to the restaurant," Jake said.

"No. I have plans for the atrium. I was thinking the dungeon, but I need to see the space first."

"No," Mark said. "The dungeon is off limits, and I refuse to allow you to change it."

"We could do them outside. The restaurant pavilion has enough room," Jake said.

She held up a hand, cutting Jake off. "May I ask why, Mr. Luciano?"

He wanted to wrap a hand around her throat—not to strangle her, but to force her to feel helpless. He wanted to feel her nails digging into the back of his hand as she struggled for air. Anything to destroy that rigid, sharp-edged perfection. Letting out a breath, he tried to center himself as the shrink from the VA said, but it didn't help.

"Mr. Luciano?"

Without conscious thought, he bared his teeth into a rictus grin. "I'll take you into the dungeon on one condition, Ms. Hall."

"And what might that be?"

"The dungeon is mine. You go in there, you obey."

"Fine." She turned her attention to Ryan, seemingly dismissing Mark without a single thought. "Let's get back to the lobby. At the very least, we need to stop using it as a party space. It simply isn't safe or functional. We won't be changing fixtures right away, but we can add relatively inexpensive art, plants, and soft furnishings to achieve a more approachable look. I found an artist for permanent art, but she's very expensive, so it will have to wait until next year. Her name is Natalie Mercer. As I was saying—"

"We already have a whole series of her work in the dungeon," Mark interrupted. It was an offhand comment though. He was too busy thinking about what he'd do to Kendra once he had her in his lair to focus.

"Why on earth would you spend that much money on art no one sees? Arrange to have it moved, please."

Fuck no. Kendra hadn't even seen the dungeon and she was already making changes to *his* space. He'd known this wouldn't work out, but he'd already said his piece, and nobody was listening.

"I'd like to get started," Dr. Knox said, interrupting the uncomfortable silence. "I'm rubbish for all of this, and the sooner I can get the system locked down, the better."

"Unsurprising, considering you have the fashion sense of a colorblind toddler," Sean muttered.

Her eyes glittering with moisture, Dr. Knox lifted her chin. "I—"

Jake rose and walked around the table to offer Dr. Knox his arm. "I'll show you to your office. We can stop in the kitchen on the way for a slice of my world-famous limoncello pound cake and a glass of strawberry milk, okay?"

She blinked several times, then nodded and stood. "Thank you."

Jake escorted her from the room, shooting Sean a glare promising retribution.

Mark scowled. Sean's behavior was inexcusable. Before

he could speak, or better, punch him in the face, Kendra lifted her hand for silence.

"Is there a problem, Mr. Franklin?" she asked, her tone communicating her irritation. "If so, direct it to me. Otherwise, I'll ask you to kindly shut your damned mouth before I get testy."

Sean crossed his arms over his chest but didn't meet her steely gaze. "Fine. I'll behave myself."

"Do that, and stop being a jackass to the woman who will save your asses from a security breach." She rose to her feet, then gave them an abrupt nod. "I believe you all have your marching orders, gentlemen. Mr. Luciano, the dungeon, if you please."

She walked out, clearly expecting them to follow.

To Mark's disgust, Ryan sent her heart eyes and sighed. "Damn, that was hot. She'll be giving Sierra a run for her money in the dungeon."

Didn't it just figure? The one woman to catch his interest in years had to be a domme.

————

KENDRA

She paced off the atrium while she waited for Mark, calculating how best to use the space. It was large enough for maybe four small shops, or multiple kiosks, but the retail space would have to fit the Club Apocalypse brand. At the very least, they needed a gift shop with branded merchandise and sundries.

There had been a spa intended for the space in their original business plan, and while it was a good idea, the atrium wasn't the best place for it. She made a note on her legal pad to examine the blueprints for an alternative, but it could wait until the resort was in a stronger financial position.

"You never told us what you wanted for the atrium," Mark said, surprising her. She hadn't even heard him walk up.

Kendra turned to face him, getting caught in his hard brown eyes again. "Retail space. Shops and the like."

"This isn't a straw market, Ms. Hall."

She counted to ten in a desperate attempt to keep her temper. "Of course not. I want to bring in artisans who create bondage equipment, plus a small traveler's shop with personal necessities and branded merchandise."

"We don't need that. Everyone brings their own gear."

"Yes, but what if someone forgets their favorite cane?"

"The dungeon will—"

"Or their toothbrush, or wants a coffee mug with the Club Apocalypse logo?" When he didn't answer, she continued, "You'll also be charging the vendors rent, and they'll pay it for an opportunity to sell their wares to a captive audience."

"That sounds too good to be true. What's the catch?"

Despite Mark's surly attitude, this was one of Kendra's favorite things to do. She loved exposing property owners to new revenue opportunities.

"There really isn't one. You'll have to find appropriate vendors and hire an attorney to draw up lease agreements, but aside from that, it's passive income."

He rubbed his forehead and sighed. "Lay it out for me in layman's terms, please."

"Okay. Let's use the Disney properties as an example. You can't walk into a park without being bombarded by merch. With me so far?"

Mark shook his head, his nose wrinkling with a sneer. "That is not what I want for Club Apocalypse. This isn't a theme park."

"Think about it. The mouse excels at separating tourists from twenty-dollar bills, and a large percentage of their profit comes from souvenirs and food service. That isn't a model you want for Club Apocalypse, but you can do it on a smaller scale—especially since your food service game is on point."

"But you just said—"

"I'm not talking about mouse ears every ten feet. That would be inappropriate and cheapen what you're trying to do. Let me ask you something." When he nodded, she continued. "If you were a guest and passed by an artisan creating a beautiful flogger, would you stop to look? And maybe purchase something? Remember, you'd be on your way to a dungeon, so you'd have an almost immediate chance to try it out."

"I..." His surly expression cleared, and he gave her a panty-melting grin that transformed his face into sheer gorgeousness. "I get it. Fuck, why haven't we done this before?"

"I don't know." Actually, she did. The four men were very protective of their space and didn't want to share. It was a common failing with small businesses.

He rubbed his hands together and the glee on his face was palpable. "Best of all, we'd be supporting small vendors who might not have a real store."

"Yes, but they'd have to be vetted and produce a safe, quality product to fit with your brand."

"We could even get Natalie Mercer to install a few pieces and sell them on consignment. It would be free decorating!"

"By George, I think he's got it," she murmured, smiling at him.

"Smart ass." He sobered and touched her arm, then pulled his hand away as if she'd burned him. "I'm sorry I was such a dick last night."

"It's okay. Change can be difficult, and Club Apocalypse is your baby. It's never easy to see a business failing."

"Will retail sales help?"

"Yes, but it won't be enough by itself." Her cold black heart softened at his crestfallen expression. She tried to lay a hand on his shoulder, but he flinched and stepped away, somehow making the gesture look as if he was examining one of the skylights.

She frowned but dismissed his odd reaction. "Come on, let's see the dungeon. We're going to get Club Apocalypse back, I promise."

"Don't make promises you can't keep."

"Oh, I can keep this one," she replied, letting him lead her from the atrium. "You just have to do as you're told."

He chuckled softly as they reached a black-painted door. "Except here. You already agreed to obey me in the dungeon."

Kendra's voice caught and she had to swallow before she could speak. "I did, but I'm not—"

Turning to face her, he tipped up her chin with a gentle forefinger. "I won't ask you to do anything you don't want to, but I do ask you to keep an open mind—exactly as you asked of me."

He swiped his keycard through the lock and opened the door. "After you, Alice. Welcome to wonderland."

"Nice," she murmured, taking in the elegant hostess podium and intimate illumination focused on tasteful art and bronze statuary. A red velvet curtain divided the vestibule from the rest of the club, but it was pulled aside to allow her to see into the darkened play area. "Can you bring up the house lighting?"

"Of course." Mark went to a bank of switches and turned them on, flooding the dungeon with bright light. "During business hours, these are dimmed. We use this setting for demos, classes, and cleaning."

"Perfect." She scribbled more notes on her legal pad. "I want a schedule for your classes and demos. There should be at least two a month because everyone who takes a class is another potential member."

Laughing softly, he turned down the lights. "Give me fifteen minutes before you start thinking up changes."

This was a mistake. Kendra knew she'd be better off focusing on business, but when Mark held out his hand, she took it. He tightened his fingers, trapping her, and a surge of need surprised the air from her lungs.

"What can you show me in fifteen minutes?" she asked once she regained the ability to speak.

"Possibilities. I'm just returning the favor."

The click of her heels on polished concrete echoed. The space looked almost industrial with exposed beams and conduit, yet still gave the impression of sumptuous luxury.

Cushions were strewn across the bare floor, positioned near comfortable armchairs and couches. What could only be described as stations with equipment she'd only seen in porn movies were surrounded by cocktail tables and chairs. A bar, more utilitarian than the one that graced the restaurant, occupied one corner. To her relief, the booze selection was sparse and limited, but she saw mixers and a fountain for soft drinks.

Natalie Mercer's art took up one whole wall opposite the

bar, the pieces illuminated with indirect can lights mounted in the ceiling. Her breath caught at one painting of a man with a neatly trimmed gray beard holding a knotted flogger in one clenched fist. His chest was bare, and he wore unzipped black trousers that revealed a prodigious erection. The naughty smirk curving his lips was both cruel and loving, and she nearly reached out to touch the large silvery ring piercing the crown of his cock.

"It's called *The Heart of a Masochist*," Mark murmured. "That's Natalie's husband, Henry. What do you think about it?"

"It's..." Kendra let out a breath and tried to formulate a response that wouldn't make her sound like an idiot. "It's compelling."

No, it was visceral, heartbreaking, joyful, sexy... She ran out of descriptive adjectives, but knew this particular series was too...intimate to be in the lobby.

Mark moved behind her, almost too close. His warm breath brushed the back of her neck, stirring the short hairs left free from her updo. "And what does it compel you to do?"

Beg you to fuck me until I lose consciousness.

"Nothing," she finally said. "Shall we continue the tour?"

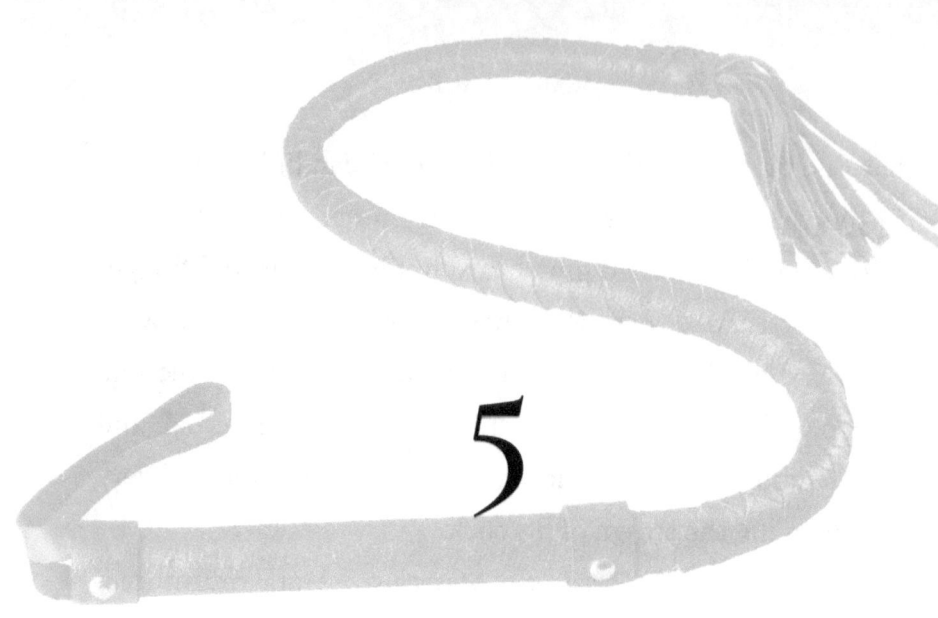

5

MARK

Kendra had a decent poker face, but Mark was experienced enough to know when someone was aroused. Her breath was short, and she blushed a perfect shade of pink.

"Tell me about the St. Andrew's cross," she said, walking to the fixture.

"That's from Chelsea Barber in Vermont."

"Looks like you already have two potential vendors." She laid her palm against the knotted rope carved into one of the beams. "She's brilliant."

"Don't look at it for too long," Mark warned. "People get lost in her carvings. They're like hidden object games."

"I..." Her voice trailed off as she moved closer and

narrowed her eyes. Obviously, he'd been too late with his warning. "Holy moly, this is amazing."

"Come on. There's more to see." Mark had to forcibly turn Kendra away from the cross, but to her credit, she didn't protest.

"You can stop now. This isn't my area of expertise, but I wouldn't change a thing except for getting more people in to see it. I think you'll find your parties will be much more successful if they happen here."

"Nope. You promised me fifteen minutes." He led her to the aftercare and triage rooms. "This is for post-scene cooldown. We also have a first-aid room complete with defibrillator and medical supplies in case of emergency. We're all CPR certified, and Ryan is a registered nurse."

He opened a sliding pocket door, revealing an aftercare room. The small cubicle had a double bed and refrigerator for snacks and water, plus condoms, blankets, and everything a dominant might need to care for a submissive.

"I assume you have liability waivers for your guests." She walked into the triage room and swiped a finger over a light fixture, obviously checking for dust.

"Yes. Everyone has to sign one whether they're playing or not, plus the standard NDA."

"Good. I saw quite a bit of alcohol in the restaurant. How are you making sure everyone stays sober for play?"

"You're not as innocent as you like to pretend." Mark twisted a loose piece of her blonde hair around his finger and tugged gently, then took a step back. He wanted to see how she'd react to a blatant tease.

Although she arched an eyebrow, she made no other reaction. "Mr. Luciano, I'm closer to forty than thirty. I might not spend time naked and on my knees, but I'm not blind."

"It's interesting you place yourself as a submissive." He circled her, forcing her to move to hold his gaze.

"Are you going to answer my question regarding the alcohol?"

"Everyone gets two dated and personalized drink coupons, and guests have to show ID, so they don't get passed around. We also have a Breathalyzer if one of the dungeon monitors feels it's necessary."

"That's a good plan." She moved toward one of his favorite spanking benches and stroked the leather bolster. "What are you doing about recreational marijuana? If I recall, that's legal in Arizona."

"Kendra, eyes on me."

Her flush deepened as she faced him, and he resisted the urge to pump his fist. Maybe she wasn't as dominant as she wanted everyone to think. Many powerful people were sexually submissive though. It wouldn't be unusual.

"What?"

"I still have ten minutes. Let me show you what makes this place special."

"Mr. Luciano, I—"

"Call me Mark."

"Thank you, but as we'll be working together, I don't think this is appropriate."

"I won't be touching you unless you ask for it, and we will both stay dressed." He winked, then added, "Or are you scared?"

"Hardly." She straightened her shoulders and tried to peer down her nose at him. If she'd worn glasses, she'd have looked like a disgruntled librarian.

A very sexy librarian. And for some strange reason, he hoped she'd agree to let him touch her.

He held out a hand, silently willing her to take it. "What do you have to lose?"

"Professionalism," she retorted. "I believe your biggest objection to me was the possibility I might change your dungeon."

"How do you figure that?" He leaned against the spanking bench and crossed his ankles. She was right, but he hadn't said as much to her.

"Your facial expression when I mentioned moving the art." She turned to study the paintings again, tapping her lip with a forefinger. "You want to protect your domain from the interloper."

"Well, to be fair, that's how it was presented to me." Mark straightened and shrugged. "What other changes do you suggest?"

"Get rid of the booze in the dungeon completely and cut back the stock in the restaurant." She sighed and touched his shoulder. "As much as I love a good martini, mixing BDSM and alcohol isn't safe or sane, and a drunk person can't give consent."

He nodded grudgingly. She had a very good point. "Most of the dungeon patrons don't imbibe before play, but we do allow observers to drink."

"And then you have to watch them like hawks to make sure they don't get drunk and stupid, right?"

"Sometimes, yes. Anything else?"

"I'd like to move the parties into the dungeon."

"No. This is a members-only space."

"Letting them in doesn't mean they'd get to play. Set up demos and let them watch. Show them what they're missing out on if they don't join. This is a well-equipped play space. It's clean and safe. I truly believe you should show it off."

He blinked, unable to hide his surprise. "I was expecting you to want to hide the dungeon."

"No, that would be counterintuitive. I'm asking you to make better use of your assets. Are you inviting non-members to your classes and workshops?"

"Why on earth would we do that? They're a member benefit."

"Because you can charge non-members and they'll make up the guest lists for the parties. Aside from being another source of revenue, you'd also have the opportunity to get to know new members before you accept them."

"I—"

"Tell you what," she interrupted. "Make a list of all your objections and have it on my desk by the end of next week. This back and forth isn't productive, so we'll meet on Friday to go through them."

"And I assume you'll give me your list of changes then too?"

Sighing, Kendra rubbed the bridge of her nose and squeezed her eyes shut. "I just did. Get rid of the booze and host new member parties in the dungeon instead of the lobby. That was it, but I also want signage mentioning the rules against electronic devices, and house safe words if you have them."

"All our members already know them."

"Probably so, but you'll be getting lots of new people in soon, if I have anything to say about it. Signage is cheap, and nobody will be able to claim they didn't see them."

Mark didn't believe a word of it. She had an end game, and it wasn't leaving the dungeon more or less untouched. "All right. I'll make a deal with you."

"What do you have in mind?"

"I'm in need of a demo partner for a workshop tonight. Agree to do that for me, and you can make all the changes you want."

She glanced at her watch, then at her legal pad. "Fair enough. What time?"

"Six. Wear a tank top and shorts."

After scribbling a note on her pad, she nodded. "I have a

full schedule today, so I might be a few minutes late. If you'll excuse me, I have a meeting in Winslow, then an angry mob to disperse."

As she walked out, she added, "And have that workshop schedule on my desk by Monday morning, please."

Mark touched his fingers to his forehead and smirked. "Yes, ma'am."

———

KENDRA

She was almost to Gabby's office before she could convince her knees to stop shaking. What the hell had she been thinking to agree to a demo with Mark? She'd been in too big a hurry to get away from him to even ask what sort of debauchery he was plotting. Worse, it would be in front of strangers.

The thought of being exposed—letting someone perform intimate acts on her in public—made her swallow hard against nausea crawling up her throat. Hell, even the equipment made her tremble with a mix of arousal and outright terror.

Mostly, it was arousal, which was absolutely inappropriate.

"Pull yourself together," she muttered to herself. "He'll stop if you use a safe word."

She didn't know any of the Horsemen well, but she was certain of that, at least. After patting her hot cheeks, she knocked softly, then entered when Gabby invited her in.

It looked like Gabby had made herself at home. The desk had been pushed into a corner and held nothing but a pair of massive computer monitors mounted on adjustable stands and tilted down. Gabby sat cross legged in a poufy pink bean bag chair. She still wore her pinafore dress, but had taken off her boots, revealing toes painted with sparkly purple polish.

"How's it going?"

"I'm currently plotting the demise of whomever designed this infrastructure. It's like these idiots wanted to get hacked." Gabby muttered, her fingers moving rapidly over the keyboard perched on her knees. "Will you let everyone know it's down for at least another few hours? I'm moving the whole thing to a secure server, and then I'll start over."

"Okay. Do you need a purchase order for the new server?"

"No, it's going on my personal system. It can stay there until I build the new site. It's faster and more secure than anything commercial anyway."

"Okay." Kendra tore a piece of paper off her legal pad and wrote her phone number on it, then laid it on the desk. "Here's my cell number. I have to go to Winslow for a meeting. I won't be back until about lunchtime but call or text if you need anything."

"Can you bring back chicken nuggets and French fries?" She waved a hand at a Kate Spade purse embossed with a cat spilled carelessly on the floor. "I think there's money in my handbag. If not, there's an Amex in there somewhere. Don't forget to get something for yourself and ask Jake and Ryan if they'd like something too."

As she spoke, Kendra heard a noise from the hall and looked up to meet Sean's eyes as he took a step inside. Before Gabby could see him, Kendra gave him her patented death stare, promising untold hell would rain upon his head if he bothered them.

Still watching him, she knelt and righted the purse, then put everything away. "Eight hundred in cash, plus a black Amex on the floor. I put it all back in your wallet."

"It should be enough for lunch then. Take whatever you need, but no lunch for Sean or Mark. I'm not sure about Mark yet, but Sean can bloody well starve."

"I'm sure Jake would make you nuggets and fries if you don't want to wait."

Gabby looked up from her work, blinking behind cat's eye glasses covered in rhinestones. "I completely forgot about the restaurant here. Can you ask him on your way out?"

"Okay. Anything else?"

Instead of answering, Gabby turned back to the monitors and grinned. "Oh, you naughty little wanker to build such a clever back door. I'll have to send you a pressie."

Sean scowled and took a step inside, but Kendra held up a finger, stopping him in his tracks.

"What kind of present would you send a hacker?" she asked.

"Oh, just a little something that will make them sorry they ever touched a computer. If I'm very lucky and they're careless, it will get them a prison sentence." She giggled and kept typing. "I love my job."

Sean scowled thunderously, then strode away.

Chuckling softly, Kendra left her to her work, only stopping to talk to Jake about Gabby's lunch and tell Ryan about the computer systems. She would have told Sean too, but he'd vanished.

Two hours later, she completed her business with a local towing company and with a very pleasant young woman at the police department. The protesters would soon find themselves ticketed and towed for illegal parking.

She couldn't help but wonder why the Horsemen hadn't tried a legal solution. Perhaps they simply hadn't thought of it, or like many people faced with public scrutiny, had hoped ignoring the problem would make it go away. It was more likely to be the latter. Albeit stubborn, they were all intelligent and she didn't believe it hadn't occurred to them.

By the time she reached the resort, a pair of officers were already passing out tickets, and she was just in time for her conference call with the first of three potential graphic designers for promotional materials.

As she slipped her wireless headset on, Jake tapped on the doorframe and carried in a tray. "Lunch is served," he said, laying the tray in front of her.

"Oh, thank you, but I'm afraid I—"

"Have plenty of time for a delicious lunch," he interrupted. "BLT with bourbon-infused bacon, heirloom tomato, organic romaine, and fresh mayo on toasted multigrain bread baked this morning."

"Your food porn should be outlawed," she muttered as she picked up the sandwich. "Has Dr. Knox had lunch yet?"

"Don't forget the hand-cut potato chips. And yes, she got tempura battered chicken nuggets with spicy peanut dipping sauce, fries, fruit salad, and ice cream with sprinkles."

"Thank you. I'm sure she loved it."

"No problem." He looked away for a moment, then touched her shoulder. "And thank you for looking out for her. She's—"

"I know, but keep it to yourself, please." Kendra didn't share what she and Gabby talked about after their impromptu supper the previous night. It wasn't Jake's business, but she was glad to see he recognized Gabby's needs.

"I will if you eat your lunch. It's time for someone to take care of you now."

She took a bite and moaned, chewing slowly. The lettuce and tomato tasted like summer, crisp and brilliantly fresh with a touch of cracked pepper, while the bacon was sublime with rich bourbon and smoke. Kendra didn't have words for the toasted country bread, and the mayonnaise was creamy and delicious—so much better than premade from a grocery store.

After swallowing, she said, "Get thee from me, demon."

Chuckling, Jake pushed a white ramekin toward her. "You can't abjure me until you eat the chocolate pot de crème."

"Hello treadmill, my old friend." She finished half her sandwich and glared up at him. "You are evil."

His blue eyes seemed to glitter, and his lips quirked into a half-smile. Some trick of the light made him look almost demonic and she shivered.

"You have no idea, little girl," he murmured. He lifted his chin and grinned, erasing the predatory gleam in his eyes. "Enjoy your lunch."

Kendra wasn't Catholic, but she resisted the urge to cross herself and ate the rest of her meal. She'd say one thing about Jake's food—it kept her mind off what would come during Mark's demo.

Unfortunately, by the time she finished her last task of the day, she could barely focus, and the delicious sandwich had turned into a lead ball in the pit of her stomach. She closed her eyes and did a few deep-breathing exercises, trying to calm her racing heartbeat.

Mark wasn't going to hurt her. This was his business, and he had to know better than to introduce a newbie to heavy kink. At least, that's what she told herself when she picked up the small bag containing the shorts and tank top he'd asked her to wear.

There wasn't time to go back to her suite to change, but she wished for a few more minutes before she had to face the lion in his den. Actually, she wanted to hide under the covers and pretend to be sick, but she was a grown-ass woman who had made a promise.

And she wasn't about to give Mark the satisfaction of seeing her run.

6

MARK

Kendra was late, but he couldn't exactly punish her for it—especially when she'd already warned him she might be.

In one afternoon, she'd gotten rid of the protesters, sourced several quotes for new marketing graphics, set up an interest form for retail vendors to fill the atrium, gotten the lawyer started on rental contracts, and had managed to keep Sean from bugging Dr. Knox long enough for her to get the computer systems back online.

The woman was a damned machine in red-soled stiletto pumps.

As he made the rounds through the crowd, he kept an eye on the curtain dividing the vestibule from the dungeon, waiting for her to show up. Apparently, word had gotten around about the protesters being run off, and tonight's demo had a capacity crowd of almost a hundred participants.

It made Mark think hard about what she'd said. If half the attendees weren't members and paid to attend... Even with a nominal fee for non-members, the dollar signs started adding up and that didn't count any new memberships.

Best of all, she wasn't changing anything that mattered. Truth be told, it would be easier not to do weekly parties. Housekeeping would certainly be happier not to have to clean up after them.

Despite his vigilant attention, he nearly missed her as she slipped into the restroom, heels in hand. At exactly ten after six, she emerged wearing black yoga shorts and a green tank top over a sports bra. Her feet were bare.

Her crimson lipstick was gone, but her hair was still twisted into a professional updo. He'd fix that first. She had gorgeous hair and he wanted to see it tumbled into sexy curls.

"Excuse me," he murmured to the couple he'd been talking to. "My demo partner is here, so we'll get started soon."

"She's late," the dom, Randy Simpson, said. "Do we get to watch her punishment?"

Randy was a retired Marine Corps pilot with enough

commendations to make his uniform hang wrong. Although his silvery hair was still cut military short, his full beard made him resemble a kinky version of Santa in a leather vest and tight black jeans.

"Ms. Hall is our new vice president of operations. She's had a very busy day, and graciously worked us into her schedule."

"If she was the one who got rid of those fucking protesters, I'd say she gets a pass, sir," Joshua, his sub, murmured, his eyes downcast.

"Language, boy," Randy said, tugging on Joshua's collar. "But agreed. She's a pretty little thing too. Submissive?"

"Not during business hours," Mark muttered. He wasn't sure he appreciated Kendra being objectified like that. He might have had his doubts about bringing her to Club Apocalypse, but he wasn't about to denigrate her accomplishments.

"Lucky man." Randy clapped a hand on his shoulder and Mark hid a grimace at the touch. "A partner who can hold their own during the workday is always the best kind of sub to have. Just like my Joshua here."

He tousled his sub's hair, then hugged him close as Mark left them to collect Kendra.

When he reached her, she said, "Sorry I'm late. My last conference call ran long."

"Don't be." Surprising himself more than her, he inclined his head to kiss her cheek. "You're moderately amazing."

"Only moderately?" A blush traveled from her upper chest to her cheeks, and she gave him a tentative smile. "I'll have to up my game."

"Just getting rid of the protesters deserves a reward."

"It might not be permanent," she warned. "With luck, I've made it inconvenient enough that they'll bother someone else, but there's no telling what religious nutjobs will do."

He offered her his arm to lead her to the freestanding massage table set on the demo platform. "I'm sure you'll have a solution if that happens."

Arching a brow, she laid a warm hand in the crook of his elbow. "Who are you and what did you do with War?"

He almost shivered at her touch. Offering his arm had been an unconscious gesture left over from his mother's etiquette lessons—one he thought he'd gotten rid of. Yet it wasn't unpleasant, and he didn't want to jerk away.

"How did you know? We don't advertise who those names belong to."

Holding his shoulder for balance, she hopped up on the stage. "I guessed. You confirmed it. Jake is Famine, of course. Ryan is Death, and Sean is Pestilence, right?"

"No, that's Ryan. Sean is Death."

"He's going to be if he doesn't leave Gabby alone," she muttered under her breath.

Mark choked out a surprised laugh, then adjusted the microphone attached to his wireless headset and turned her to face the crowd. Usually, he hated demos, but this one seemed different somehow. Maybe it was the air of excitement and anticipation, but it was most likely his partner.

"Welcome to Club Apocalypse," he said after turning the microphone on. "It's wonderful to see you all here tonight. I'd like to introduce you to the woman responsible for us being able to get together again without being bothered."

Grinning, he waited for the cheers to die down. "This is Kendra Hall, our new vice president of operations, and she's graciously agreed to be my demo dolly for tonight's presentation. We have a live feed on the overhead monitors to make sure everyone can see, but as usual, the demonstration will not be recorded."

As people jockeyed for position and found their seats, he helped Kendra up on the sheet-covered massage table and turned off his microphone. "Do you mind the cameras?"

"No, but that gives me an idea I'd like to discuss next week. What are you teaching tonight?"

"It's a surprise. Also, if you don't mind, I may ask you to take off your top, depending on how messy things get."

She arched one of those expressive brows and pursed her lips. "Messy?"

"You'll see. And you don't have to take anything off if you prefer."

She gazed at the crowd for a moment. As always, there was an eclectic mix of attire, ranging from suits to old-guard leather and cocktail dresses, to jeans and T-shirts. Several submissives wore nothing but their collars. Body types, ethnicities, and ages were just as widely represented.

"Just my tank top," Kendra finally said, pulling the green shirt over her head to reveal a black sports bra and a sweetly rounded abdomen.

"Okay." Resisting the urge to play with the small piercing in her navel, he folded her top and set it aside, then turned to face the crowd. "As you all know, ninety-nine percent of sexual pleasure and arousal is in the mind, but sometimes it's hard to get the brain and body on the same page."

Laughter rose from the crowd and Mark smiled at the knowing nods. "Tonight, I'm going to teach you how to bridge that gap with sensation play."

"And it's going to hurt, right?" someone shouted.

Mark gazed at the middle-aged man who had spoken. He was one of the new members they'd gotten in the last few months, and had ignored a sub when she called yellow, forcing the dungeon monitors to get involved. He'd claimed he hadn't heard her, and without evidence to the contrary, he'd been allowed to stay. Everyone was keeping an eye on him though.

Kendra probably hadn't considered the scenario when she recommended using parties and demos to evaluate potential members, but it was a good idea. Instead of getting on with the demo, he decided to remind everyone of BDSM 101.

"I was actually just about to mention that. Before

starting any play, consider your partner's level of experience and their hard limits. Since I just met Ms. Hall last night, I don't know any of that. It would be beyond irresponsible for me to touch her before learning that information. Let's get into safety first. For dominants only, what do we do when a sub says green?"

"Keep going."

"Don't stop."

"Good!" Mark replied, nodding at the two people who had spoken. "How about yellow?"

"Pause what you're doing and fix what's wrong," Sierra said, crossing one long leg over the other. "If your sub calls red after you've ignored a yellow, you'll be the next contestant on *The Bullwhip is Right.*"

Mark laughed, then wagged a finger at her. "And anyone who ignores red will be banned from this property without a refund. Any evidence of assault will be turned over to law enforcement as well."

"Submissives," Sierra said, pitching her voice to carry, "vet potential partners. Ask for references, ask the dungeon monitors for recommendations, and above all, listen to your gut."

"Would you like to do the demo, Sierra?" Mark asked, grinning at her. She was a known Mama Bear for submissives.

"Not unless there are whips involved!"

When the laughter died down, Mark said, "Now, since

Ms. Hall has been working very hard to make Club Apocalypse an even greater place to be, we haven't had a chance to negotiate our scene. We'll do that now."

―――――――

KENDRA

She'd been so nervous at the size of the crowd, she'd almost bailed. She felt exposed in her bra and shorts. Academically, she'd been able to accept that Club Apocalypse was safe. There was even an ASL interpreter several feet away for hearing-impaired members.

She wasn't a complete novice and had seen the dungeon before. It was so different now that it was full of people—all of whom were enjoying themselves. Yet with every word, Mark made her feel more comfortable.

It almost seemed as if his persona had changed too. Instead of the surly grump he'd been the previous night, he was charming and engaging. The audience seemed to hang on his every word, even when he went over the basics regarding safe words and negotiation—a slight detour she suspected was for her benefit, rather than that of the attendees.

He'd also called out what she'd done over the course of the day, giving her full credit. It was sweet, but she'd been doing what they hired her to do. Still, it made something warm and happy unfurl in her stomach when she saw how much everyone appreciated the absence of the protesters.

Mark moved closer to her. "Do you understand the safe words, Kendra? They're known as traffic light signals. Green for go, yellow for slow down. Red stops the scene."

"I understand."

"Good." He tapped the mic button, then whispered, "I want you to say yellow for the vampire glove so we can demonstrate. It doesn't matter if it's real because I'm going to stop and make sure everything is all right. Just tap my hand if you mean it, okay?"

Vampire glove?

"Got it."

"Great. I'm going to sit next to you so the mic picks up your answers. First things first, do you have any experience with D/s?"

The heat of his thigh next to hers sent a twinge of longing into her core, but she tamped it down. Doing a demo was one thing. Lusting after one of her bosses wasn't going to happen.

"No, not really." She wasn't about to admit how many smutty books were on her e-reader. Reading wasn't doing.

"Okay. Do you know what a hard limit is?"

"Yes. It's something I won't do."

"Good. A soft limit is something you might consider doing with the right partner. Do you have either hard or soft limits?"

"I... I'm afraid of mice?" It was a dumb answer. She'd said the first thing that popped into her head. Gentle laughter filled the room, but it wasn't unkind.

"Trust me. There are no mice in Club Apocalypse," Mark replied. "Do you prefer not to kiss? How about needles, water sports, or diaper play?"

"Water..." She frowned, then suddenly understood his meaning. "Kissing is okay, but no water sports or diaper play. I'd need to see what was done with the needles before I answer."

"Perfect." He stood, then faced the crowd. "I'm sure you all know about the checklists available on the internet. If Kendra and I were doing an actual scene, we'd both fill one of those out and talk about our answers beforehand. And remember, sometimes limits change, so it's a good idea for even long-term couples or groups to revisit those lists."

"Master Mark," a woman said, "do you have a preferred checklist?"

"No, not really, but involved parties should use the same one."

"Thank you, sir."

"My pleasure. We'll get into sensation play now, but if we have inexperienced players in the audience, Mistress Sierra offers an intro course on the fourth Saturday of every month."

Kendra wished she had her legal pad for notes, but hopefully she'd remember to recommend that all new members take that intro class before being allowed to play.

He picked up a long piece of black cloth. "Blindfolds can enhance any sensation play because the sub can't see what's happening. Kendra is a novice though, so I won't be using one."

"I... I'm okay with the blindfold," Kendra said softly. Maybe it would be easier if she couldn't see what Mark was planning. If it wasn't, she'd take it off.

Mark turned to look at her, and a wicked, utterly naughty grin changed his professional mien into something sinfully sexy. He moved behind her and pulled the clip from her hair, then tied the fabric over her eyes.

The darkness was almost comforting, but it seemed as if her other senses woke up. The brush of his hand over her hair sent prickles of sensation down her spine, and a faint whiff of citrusy aftershave made her inhale deeply. Warm breath tickled her ear, and she nearly came on the spot when he said, "Good girl."

Kendra felt him step away and wanted to whimper. What the hell was wrong with her? She breathed out through pursed lips, trying to focus on keeping her cool. She was doing Mark a favor—nothing more or less—and it wasn't meant to be titillating.

She wasn't even sure she liked him. He might have apologized, but he'd been an absolute ass to her.

Something soft touched her knee and she almost jumped

out of her skin as it traveled down the front of her shin to trace circles on the top of her foot.

"Feathers can be used all over a sub's body but be careful not to tickle. You just want to wake up nerve endings and prepare them for play."

Kendra bit her lip, trying to hold back a giggle, and jerked her foot away. "My feet are ticklish," she murmured.

"Good to know. Everyone, Kendra just gave me a nonverbal yellow when she pulled her foot out of reach. It let me know she wasn't enjoying what I was doing. Watch your subs carefully, especially when they're bound. The idea is to adjust your actions so they never have to use a safe word."

The feather moved up her body to her abdomen and she sucked in a gasp. The touch on her stomach moved to her hand, then up her left arm and across her collarbone, leaving gooseflesh in its wake. Her breath stalled as he dragged a gossamer line up her throat to just below her ear, and she imagined it was his lips caressing that sensitive patch of skin.

Cursing herself, she quit fantasizing and tried to focus on something else. Bereft of sight, nothing caught her attention. Aside from a few rustles and whispers, the audience was silent.

Without warning, Mark pulled the feather away. "Kendra has already said she's ticklish, so we'll try something else. Remember, the object of sensation play is to tease. You want to get your sub's focus on what you're doing, but not to the point you make them uncomfortable."

He moved behind her and she resisted the urge to turn and see what he was doing. The only thing that stopped her was knowing she wouldn't be able to see anything unless she took off the blindfold.

"Kendra, the mic is off. How are you doing?" he asked, his mouth close to her ear.

Her mouth dry, she swallowed hard. "I'm okay."

"Good. Can you stretch out on your back, please?"

She laid down and found a pillow under her head. "Like this?"

"Yes, thank you. Put your arms over your head, please."

"Okay." She folded her arms behind her head, trying to decide if she felt too vulnerable to maintain the position.

"Good girl." She felt the brush of his shirt against the inside of her arm before he added, "The vampire glove is next. The fingers and palm have short metal spikes, and it will feel like someone with long nails is scratching you. Unless you really hate it, wait about thirty seconds before you say yellow."

What was it about being called good girl that made her cream her panties? Kendra crossed her fingers and prayed she wasn't leaving a wet spot in the crotch of her shorts. Thankfully, her sports bra had some padding, so her painfully erect nipples weren't visible.

"Yes, Master Mark."

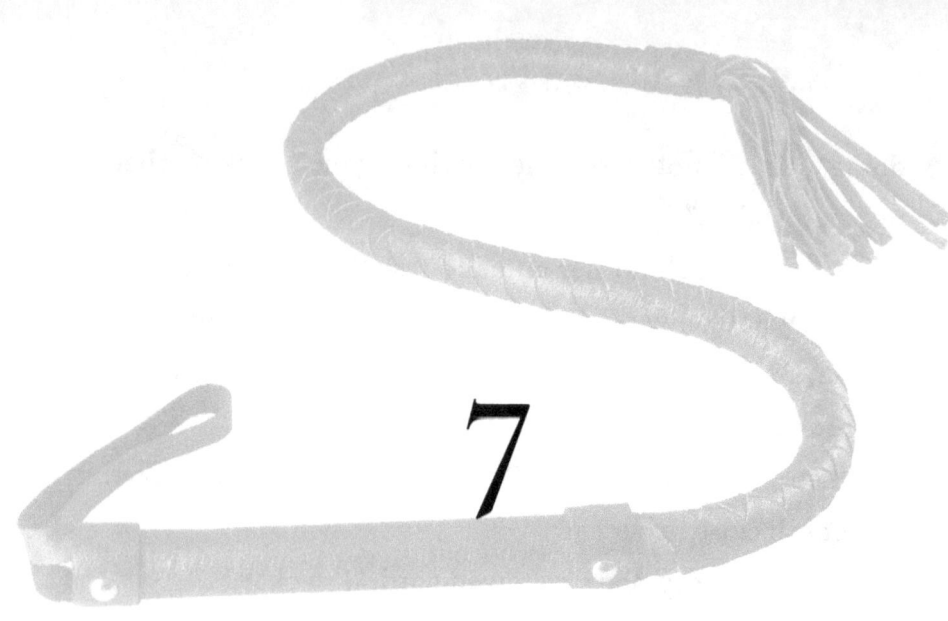

7

MARK

He stiffened and caught his breath at the formal address. Had Kendra said it to fuck with him? Or was it something else?

A public demo wasn't the time to ask about it. Instead, he grabbed the vampire glove and put it on, forcibly calming the tremor in his hand. Kendra was only repeating what one of the attendees had called him and probably didn't know what it meant to call someone master.

Focus, dumbass.

Before turning the mic back on, he put his lips close to Kendra's ear and inhaled the sweet scent of her floral perfume. "I'm going to touch you with the glove now. Just remember to give me about thirty seconds before you say yellow."

Her throat worked and she licked her lips. "Where?"

"Ah, ah." He stroked her thigh with the back of the glove, biting back a laugh when she flinched. "That would ruin the surprise."

Her breath stuttered on a nervous exhale and a rapid pulse fluttered under her jaw, signaling her trepidation. Kendra couldn't hide her body's reactions, and he didn't want her to. Instead of turning the glove over to let her feel the spikes, he kept stroking her with the back of his hand.

Goosebumps blossomed along the path he traced down her toned arm. A gentle glide over her belly made her suck in her stomach, and his cock thickened, straining at the zipper of his jeans when she whimpered softly. He was so entranced by her reaction, he nearly forgot about their audience.

This untutored, uninhibited reaction was his favorite part of sensation play, and Kendra was everything he'd ever wanted in a demo partner. Her heated scent rose, and he inhaled the perfume of arousal greedily, then turned his hand over to stroke the sensitive skin covering her ribs, just under the band of her sports bra.

"Ahhh!"

Mark chuckled at her squeak of surprise, then gently petted her side, leaving faint red lines scored into her skin. Without warning, she arched into the touch, muscles flexing as she panted. To his shock, a barely visible damp spot appeared in the gusset of her yoga shorts.

Making sure the mic was off, he moved the glove up her neck and carefully circled her throat, squeezing just hard enough to make her still without causing her discomfort.

Unable to help himself, he bent down and nipped her earlobe. "Did you forget something, Ms. Hall?"

"Oh, God." She tightened her hands, the tendons flexing as she let out a breath. "Shit, I'm sorry."

"Whenever you're ready."

He straightened and turned the mic back on. "As I was saying, make sure to watch—"

"Yellow."

He lifted his hand and stripped the glove off, then tossed it on the worktable. "Do you want the blindfold off?"

"No! I..." She turned in the direction of his voice and her lips parted, making him realize he hadn't told her what to say. "Um...can we do something else?"

"Master Mark," his middle-aged problem child said, "isn't that topping from the bottom?"

Mark massaged Kendra's shoulder with his bare hand, letting her know he was still present while he spoke. "When a sub gives clear preference with one of the traffic signal colors, especially if you haven't partnered with them before, then it wouldn't be considered topping from the bottom."

The older man looked thoughtful for a moment, then nodded. "Thank you."

Maybe he'd been wrong, and the man wouldn't be a problem. He hoped the issue was more a lack of education rather than malfeasance.

"My pleasure." He took his hand away from Kendra for long enough to light a few candles and open the small cooler full of ice. "Now, since Kendra let me know she wasn't enjoying the vampire glove, we'll move on to something else."

He almost wished he hadn't picked the vampire glove for Kendra's safe word demonstration. It had been more than obvious she was a fan, yet he wanted to make sure she knew her safe words would be obeyed without question.

"Temperature can also be used to wake up nerve endings," he murmured, picking up a piece of ice. Putting it in his mouth, he bent and brushed his lips over her abdomen.

She flinched at each drop of cold water, her stomach hollowing out as if to escape the frigid sensation. Instead of touching her, he moved the ice in his mouth and clamped it between his teeth, then traced circles around her navel.

Her hips bucked, nearly making him drop the ice, but he kept going until it melted. Mark grinned and straightened, then swirled a finger through the cold water, spreading it across her stomach.

After wiping his hands on a towel, he grabbed a candle and held it several inches above her bare skin. He tipped it slightly to allow a small stream of warm wax to land on her.

"Sweet baby Jesus!" Kendra bucked and nearly fell from the table before he could catch her.

Hurriedly, he set the candle aside and repositioned her, but didn't remove his hand from her chest. "Give me a color, honey. Green, yellow, or red?"

She arched against him, pressing her breast against his palm. "More, or I'm going to beat you with a stick."

The audience burst into laughter, and shaking his head, Mark joined them. "That, my friends, is topping from the bottom, but since Ms. Hall has expressed a clear preference, we'll continue."

She arched, her spine curving as her chin went up to expose her throat. Her vulnerability was unconsciously, effortlessly sexy and he bit back a groan, wishing she was naked so he could decorate her beautiful body the way he wanted.

He drew a spiral on her bare belly, watching her reactions carefully as she relaxed into the heat painting her skin. When the pooled wax was gone from the candle, he grabbed another piece of ice and chilled the cooling wax until it was hard and flaked off easily.

"Now for the fun part," he said softly, before picking up a slender rattan cane. A few members of the audience gasped, and he added, "Don't try this at home, children."

He took a step back and shook out his wrist. Watching her carefully, he let the cane fly to flick off a section of the dried wax. It would give just the faintest of stings, yet this wasn't the time to be careless—especially when she was wiggling around.

When all but the smallest bits of wax were gone, he set the cane aside and leaned down to kiss her softly. She whimpered and traced his lower lip with the tip of her tongue. Mark almost jerked away, but it was so...fucking...good. He cupped her head and deepened their kiss, letting her tongue tangle with his.

And still, she didn't touch him. Her hands were clenched together behind her head as if she kept them there by sheer force of will. Unable to help himself, he palmed her breast, feeling her erect nipple through the padding of her bra.

She arched into him, her body shaking. "Please, oh God, please."

"Such a good girl to ask so nicely." Slowly, he drew his hand down her stomach to her core, relishing her heated wetness. The crotch of her shorts was soaked with arousal, and he resisted the urge to strip her bare so he could feast.

This was Kendra's first time in a dungeon. Maybe she didn't care now, but she wouldn't be happy if he made her lose control and come in front of an audience. Aside from that, he was greedy. He wanted to keep her orgasm for himself.

That didn't mean he couldn't tease her. He circled her clit, finding the tiny bundle of nerves easily through the thin, clingy fabric.

She jerked and shuddered, her face flushing red, and she bucked against his hand. "Master, please!"

His cock hardened to bursting and he bit back a curse, then yanked the wireless headset off and tossed it aside. "Tell me your color, Kendra."

"G-green." She blinked, opening eyes glazed with need. "Please, don't stop."

He'd never seen anything so beautiful as Kendra in the throes of passion, but he wasn't about to allow her to get off so easily. Laughing softly, he tweaked her nipple, then pinched hard enough to make her squeak. "Patience is a virtue, Ms. Hall. You're going to beg first."

———

KENDRA

Holy... Damn.

Sting. Hot. Soft. Cold. The scent of his citrusy aftershave tickled her nose and she inhaled deeply, catching a faint hint of musk. The mixture of sensations Mark had given her swirled into a muddled, aroused mass careening through her body. Her skin twitched, missing his touch.

And his words. She imagined herself on her knees, begging as he'd suggested. Her swollen clit throbbed with need and the fabric of her shorts was almost enough to send her over the edge.

Aside from the vampire glove, he hadn't explained a single thing to her. Instead, he'd allowed her to experience everything as if she was in an actual scene with a dominant determined to fuck with her head.

Normal, not crazily aroused Kendra would have balked at letting someone have that much control over her, yet it was the most incredibly intimate thing she'd ever done.

And with a perfect stranger—who she was supposed to dislike. She was too drunk with pleasure to even care about the audience.

"I've got you," he whispered, tugging the blindfold away before cradling her in his arms. In a louder voice, he said, "Mistress Sierra will be available to answer any of your questions while I give Kendra the aftercare she needs. Thank you all for coming."

"Hottest demo I've ever seen," someone muttered.

"Set the whole place on fire," a woman said. "I might need to see if Kendra is up for a scene with me."

"I can do Kendra's aftercare," Sierra said, stepping in front of them. "And take care of the part you didn't finish, because that's just cruel."

Smiling fondly, she stroked Kendra's cheek and brushed a piece of hair off her face. The touch was sweet and tingled at her nerve endings, but it wasn't what Kendra wanted.

"No. Sadist, remember? Piss off and get to work."

Kendra peeked through her lashes, then hid her face, wondering at Sierra's look of astonishment. Although

Mark's reply had been terse to the point of rudeness, she didn't understand why Sierra would be so surprised when the tone seemed to be his usual speaking voice—at least toward Kendra.

She couldn't say she was surprised to learn he was a sadist either. Why wasn't she struggling? She should be halfway to her suite instead of cuddled in Mark's arms like she belonged there.

"Shh," he murmured, carrying her into one of the small cubicles. Turning, he slid the door shut behind him, then set her gently on her feet. "Are you still green?"

"Y-yes."

"Mmm. Good to know. Finish undressing for me, please."

Kendra shook her head in a desperate attempt to understand. "I thought we were done."

"Oh, no, sweetheart." He chuckled and traced a burning path over her collarbone with a gentle finger. "We're in an aftercare room because I didn't think you'd want an audience to see me make you beg to come."

Mark crossed his arms and leaned against the wall, simply watching her. He gave her every opportunity to leave. He didn't paw at her, restrain, or threaten her, or do anything else that would have made her run. He was an implacable presence she couldn't ignore. A caustic reply hovered on her lips but went unsaid.

Hands shaking, she unhooked the front closure of her bra, and her nipples tightened into achy points under Mark's avid gaze. It felt almost like he touched her, and she shivered.

"Are you cold?"

"I don't know."

He laughed softly but didn't move from his position. "Shorts too, unless you want to use a safe word."

"What happens if I do that?" She pushed her thumbs into the elastic waistband of her shorts.

Despite Kendra being almost naked, Mark kept his eyes on her face. "I give you a snack and let you rest, then take you back to your suite where I'm sure you'll finish what I started, then have a good night's sleep."

Was that what she wanted? Despite her growing need, the thought of crawling into her solitary bed with a toy didn't appeal. She needed more. Closing her eyes, she pushed her shorts down over her hips and let them drop to the floor.

"There's my very good girl," he murmured, still keeping his eyes on her face. "Fold your arms behind your back."

The position was inherently submissive, one that would put her at his mercy for as long as she held it. Yet he made her feel *seen*—like she was more than a body to admire. Another shiver worked its way down her spine to pool in her core. Mark hadn't even touched her, and she'd never been so aroused in her life.

Mark straightened and stalked toward her, moving as silently as a cat, then traced a gentle fingertip across her collarbone and down her arm. His body heat caressed her, warming her from the inside out.

"So pretty." He circled her nipple, making her gasp. "And so responsive."

"I—"

"What's your color?" he asked, moving to stand behind her. He pushed her hair over her shoulder and feathered a kiss over the back of her neck.

"Green."

"Good girl. Lie down on your side, please."

"Yes, Master Mark." The honorific came out without conscious choice, both surprising and horrifying her. Yet she obeyed and stretched out on the freshly laundered sheet.

His eyes sparkled and a faint smile crossed his lips. "I'll remember you called me that the next time you order me to do something."

She turned and looked up, giving him a halfhearted glare. "I'm probably not going to be great at submitting."

"Not true." He sat next to her and stroked her back, making her shiver again. "Just because you have a position of authority in your work life doesn't make you a bad submissive. You're being a very, very good girl."

"Thank you." It sounded stupid, but she couldn't think of anything else to say.

His boots thudded against the floor as he kicked them off, then he stretched out next to her. Without warning, he pulled her into his arms, spooning her against his broad chest. He bent her knee until she was open to him, his touch almost scalding as he petted her inner thigh. She felt bound, yet his touch was the only thing holding her still.

"What's your color, Kendra?"

"I'll tell you if it's not green."

His hand moved from her thigh to her breast almost too quickly for her to process, and he pinched her nipple hard enough to make her cry out.

"Ow! That hurts!" She wriggled, trying to get free, but he tightened his fingers on the abused bud until she stilled, and tears popped in her eyes. The pain surged and ebbed in time with her heartbeat, sending a shard of pleasure into her clit. She wanted something—anything—to touch her, yet Mark made no move to assuage the ache between her legs.

"Just a reminder to behave," he replied. Although he didn't let go, the pressure eased. "Would you like to answer the question again?"

Kendra let out a breath she hoped didn't sound like a whine. "Green, Master Mark."

"Mmm. I love hearing that."

He finally let go, but the ache didn't stop. Instead, it flared brightly as blood surged into her nipple. He stroked her stomach, the gentle touch of his palm confusing her nerve endings, then circled the piercing in her navel before slowly moving his hand to where she most needed his touch.

Circling her clit with a fingernail, he brushed kisses over

the sweet spot under her ear. Her hips bucked and he pulled his hand away. "Let's play a game."

Kendra swallowed hard and bit her lip against an order to get the hell on with it. "What kind of game."

"It's one of my favorites. I call it, *hold still or you won't get to come.*"

"Oh, fuck." There was no way. She was about to jump out of her skin as it was.

"Such language from a professional."

He waited until she managed to still her body, then brushed her clit. That single glancing touch made her bite her lip until she thought she'd taste blood, but she didn't dare move a muscle.

"There's my good girl, but the swear is going to cost you."

"Cost me what?" The words felt like they were edged with glass.

"In punishment for the f-bomb, you don't get to come until I say so." Without warning, he slid two fingers into her soaking channel and rubbed her clit with his thumb. She'd never been so close to climax after so little time. Desperate for more, she arched her back to deepen the penetration, but he yanked his hand away.

"Ahhh! God dammit, Mark!"

He laughed softly, making her want to bash his head in with a hammer. Maybe run him over a few times. "Naughty, naughty. Bad girls don't get to come."

8

MARK

"Please, Master Mark."

The sound of begging was music to his ears. Best of all, it was Kendra Hall doing it. It was almost as good as holding her in his arms—something he'd never thought possible with anyone.

He almost wished he was facing her. He'd have given anything to watch her face when she finally let go.

Well, not quite anything. He wasn't about to risk her touching him, and wished he'd tied her. Thankfully, her hands were clenched into fists in front of her and she wasn't thinking about anything except the orgasm he planned to give her.

"One more chance," he finally said. "But if you move again, you won't get to come."

"I...okay." She hauled in a breath and shuddered as she let it out. "I can do this."

Instead of going straight to her pussy, he petted her, allowing her to get used to his touch. Although her muscles tightened, she didn't move.

"Good girl." Mark kissed the tendon on the side of her neck then nipped her ear, relishing her pleasured whine as he eased two fingers into her tight channel.

He imagined sinking his cock into her and hardened uncomfortably. The zipper of his jeans felt like it was going to cut off his circulation, but he was too busy enjoying Kendra's uninhibited desire to bother with it.

"Feels so good." Her words were slurred, almost unintelligible, and hearing her lose control was everything he'd hoped it would be.

"You're holding so still for me." He brushed her clit with his thumb, making her jerk, but she settled quickly. "And good girls always get rewarded."

He curled his fingers inside her, seeking out the roughened area of her g-spot, then pressed hard. Her body seized and quivered, and the tendons in her hands stood out in sharp relief under her skin, telltale evidence of her struggle to obey.

"Ahhh! Mark! Please, please, please!"

"Soon," he crooned, rubbing circles around her clit with

his thumb.

"Master Mark, I...please!"

Tears thickened her voice, and he bit back a groan as his cock surged behind his zipper. If she had any idea how her desperate tears affected him...

"Come for me, baby."

With a tearing scream, she exploded, drenching his hand with slippery moisture. Resisting the urge to lick her clean, he gentled his touch and eased her down as he murmured soft nonsense into her ear.

"Such a good girl," he whispered.

"I...oh, God." She shivered, and he heard the faint click of her teeth chattering.

For the first time ever, he wanted to do aftercare. He reached to the foot of the bed and pulled up a blanket to cover her, then tucked her against his chest once more.

"Would you like a snack or some water, sweetheart?"

"No, I'm okay. I should probably get back to my—"

"Later." He pulled the blanket up to her chin and tightened his arms around her. "Rest, and we'll talk afterward."

"No, thank you. I'm fine." She wriggled free and tossed the blanket aside. "I'm just going to go back to my suite and get a good night's sleep."

"I guess we'll be doing this the hard way."

"Doing what the hard way?"

"Aftercare." Without another word, he caught her and wrapped her in his long arms, forcing her to lie back down.

Still keeping her trapped, he dragged the blanket over them and spooned her against his chest. "Now hush and rest."

She huffed irritably then squirmed again. Her perfect ass brushed against his cock, and he swallowed an ugly curse.

"Hold. Still."

She froze, then lurched from the bed, her eyes wide, but glazed with lingering passion. "Yellow!"

Who the hell used a safe word during aftercare? Instead of spanking her butt, he forced himself to stay where he was. "Thank you for using your safe word, Kendra. Would you like me to get Sierra for you?"

She grabbed her shorts and sports bra, then dressed hurriedly. "I... No. I'm sorry. I have to go."

Despite his aching cock, Mark choked out a laugh as she scampered from the room like she was racing from a burning building. He hadn't believed anything would make Kendra Hall run.

Not even a grumpy sadist with an aversion to physical contact.

Touching Kendra was different. He didn't recoil at the feel of her soft skin, nor did he want to jerk away from her. She'd been so deliciously responsive. Turning his back to the open door, he readjusted his pants, silently ordering his dick to behave so he could exit the aftercare room without embarrassing himself.

"I saw Kendra leave," Sierra murmured, stopping him

before he could join the guests for the question-and-answer session. "Do I need to sign you up for a bullwhip demo?"

"No, I don't think so. She called yellow when I tried to cuddle her, so I let her go."

Sierra blinked, then tugged at her ear. "I'm sorry. I understand all those words, but they don't make sense coming from you."

"Bite me." Mark scowled and stepped around her, then focused on what he was supposed to be doing. Her laughter chased him through the dungeon, but he ignored it.

The biggest question of the night was whether the demos would open for non-members. Apparently, everyone had friends they wanted to invite, but hadn't wanted to subject them to the protesters. With that problem solved— at least for the moment—the members were itching to celebrate.

Just as Kendra had predicted.

Maybe Ryan had a point about growing their membership. He couldn't ask the same dozen couples to show up every weekend. They needed fresh blood to keep things interesting.

"Are you going to open the dungeon for play?" Randy asked, his arm around Joshua's shoulders.

"Well—"

"Actually, sir, I thought we might have supper instead," Joshua said softly. "Neither of us had time to eat before coming here, and if Jake has the restaurant open..."

Randy chuckled and kissed Joshua's cheek. "Damn. I was going to call dibs on the cross, but you had me at Jake's food."

"He's still doing a *prix fixe* tasting menu," Mark said. "There's prime rib and weathervane scallops on it. The dungeon will be open until two as usual."

"We'll see you later!" Joshua called, dragging Randy from the dungeon.

The news about Jake's prime rib traveled fast, and the dungeon soon emptied as the rest of the attendees followed Randy and Joshua. He didn't blame them a bit. Jake had collaborated with Lauren Johansen from JoJo's in Connecticut for the recipe, and it was a crowd favorite.

Mark hoped at least a few of the attendees would decide to stay overnight. The dungeon wasn't the only empty space on the property.

Chuckling softly, he got to work helping his staff with cleanup. As he was wiping down tables and chairs in preparation for later, his phone vibrated with an incoming text from Jake.

Get your ass to the restaurant. I need help.

Frowning, Mark put away his cleaning supplies and hurried down the corridor to Jake's domain. To his shock, the place was standing room only, meaning that for the first time in ages, people had stopped to eat instead of going home.

"Thank God." Jake tossed an apron at him as he walked in. "Get to work cleaning the empty tables."

"Okay, but I need to get back to the dungeon soon, so I can't help for long."

"It can wait. The restaurant being full is more important."

"Jake, I have a present for you," Sierra called. She strode toward them, dragging a curvaceous woman with brown eyes and long dark hair behind her. "This is Olivia Rivera. Say hello to your new sous chef."

"Welcome to Club Apocalypse," Jake said, pumping her hand. "Where did you go to culinary school?"

Olivia's chocolate brown eyes widened, and she looked toward the door as if seeking an escape route. "Well, I—"

"Great. Grab a hair net and a set of whites from the laundry room on the way in and get to work on the side salads. Supplies are in the walk-in, and there are spare knives in the utility cupboard if you didn't bring your own. The ingredient list and proportions are posted above the salad station. Any questions?"

"I—"

"Fantastic. Glad to have you aboard." Jake gave her a pointed glance, then added, "Kitchen's that way and we have hungry diners."

Olivia jumped like she'd been goosed and hurried toward the kitchen. Before Jake could follow, Sierra stepped in front of him.

"There are two things you need to know," she murmured. "First is, if you decide to be an asshole like Mark and Sean, I will literally kick your ass."

"Hardly. I'm the one cleaning up after them, remember?"

"Second, Olivia just got out of prison. She's a bit gun shy, so give her a little time before you start barking orders at her."

"Did Sean approve her employment?"

"Yes, but she—"

"Then I don't care. If her parole officer has a problem with it, he can kiss my ass." Thrusting a bus pan into her hands, he added, "Now, unless you have something better to do, get to work."

Without waiting for her to answer, he turned and strode to his kitchen. Mark risked a glance at Sierra and wisely swallowed his laugh.

A former Marine drill sergeant and talented dominatrix, Sierra usually kept the staff under rigid control. Even the Horsemen stepped carefully around her. It was a measure of Jake's stress level for him to speak to her with anything but respect.

To his surprise, she smiled instead of chasing Jake down to chew on him. Setting the bus pan on her hip, she arched a brow at Mark.

"You say one word about this and—"

"I know," he replied. "I'll take the sections on the right and you take the left."

"Okay. We both have to get back to our own jobs soon though."

"Yeah, but it can wait until after we help Jake out. Nobody will be getting rooms or using the dungeon until after they finish eating anyway."

"True, but—" She glanced over his shoulder and blinked. "Well, will you look at that."

He turned to look where Sierra pointed, and his lips twisted into a grudging smile. "Seems our new vice president is a woman of many talents and has more endurance than a SEAL."

Wearing a huge grin, plus black pants and a white tuxedo shirt, Kendra carried a tray of entrees to one of the larger tables, along with a folding stand. She bent her knees and slid the tray to the stand, then started serving, making it clear this wasn't her first rodeo waiting tables.

Her movements precise, she pulled a pepper mill from the pocket of her apron and went around the table, adding the spice to the food according to each diner's preference. All the while, she kept up a steady stream of conversation.

"Luciano, these tables aren't going to clean themselves. Quit watching the hot chick," Sierra murmured, bumping him gently with her shoulder on her way to the kitchen with a full bus pan.

"Sorry." After tying the apron around his waist, he got started. As he worked, his attention wandered, but not to Kendra.

Ms. Rivera wasn't the first ex-con they'd hired, and she probably wouldn't be the last. Although the Horsemen drew the line at anyone convicted of a violent crime and those who had served time for a financial crime wouldn't have access to money, they believed in second chances.

The rules were more guidelines though. Their head of housekeeping had done five years for killing her abusive husband. The Horsemen figured she'd been taking out the trash and hired her on the spot.

All things considered, it seemed very odd that Sean would throw such a fit over Dr. Knox, then turn around and hire Ms. Rivera. Maybe it was simply a personality conflict, but it was still perplexing.

It was possible Sean was pissy because Dr. Knox had taken over their computer systems, which Sean had designed, yet she had a government security clearance and enough personal wealth to buy Club Apocalypse at least twice over. Mark didn't think it likely she'd risk her reputation over a small resort property.

After the last of the diners were seated, he pushed a full bus cart into the kitchen, nodding at Ryan and Sean as they loaded dishes into the industrial dishwashers.

"I need to get back to the dungeon soon," Mark said, catching Jake's attention. "Looks like everyone is seated and has ordered."

"Thanks." Jake rubbed his face, but grinned. "I'm wondering if I can convince my old staff to come back."

"You got a new sous chef though."

"Yeah, but..." His smile fading, Jake glanced at Olivia, who was putting several salads together. Although she faced away from them, Mark saw tension in her shoulders, and she hunched like she expected a blow.

"But?"

"She's not as experienced as I'd hoped." He shrugged and his smile returned. "Oh, well. It's nothing a little practice won't fix, and I'm sure I can't screw it up any worse than you and Sean did with Kendra and Gabby."

————

KENDRA

"I'll take this when you're ready, sir," she murmured to the older gentleman at table four. She recognized the couple from the demo and couldn't decide whether to be embarrassed or pretend like he and his partner hadn't seen her almost beg to come in front of a hundred people.

"It seems you're a Jill-of-all-trades." He slid a credit card into the folio and handed it to her. "Vice president of operations, a demo dolly, and a damned fine server."

Smiling, she nodded. "Thank you. I haven't waited tables since college, so I'm glad to hear I still have skills."

"We're headed to the dungeon after we finish our coffee." He studied her for a moment, his blue eyes intent.

"Will you be joining us? Joshua and I overheard more than a few dominants hoping to set up a scene with you."

"I'm afraid not. I have other matters requiring my attention tonight."

The orgasm Mark had given her took the edge off, but her core still pulsed with need. As much as she liked the idea of going back for more, it would be beyond unprofessional to play in the dungeon. Aside from that, she wasn't sure how she felt about what she'd done. No good ever came from getting involved with a coworker, and she'd let Mark do...

Hell. She couldn't even say it to herself.

"A pity." He held out a large, callused hand. "It was a pleasure meeting you, Ms. Hall. I can't wait to see what you do with the place."

"You as well." She shook his hand, then added, "I'll be right back."

After running his card, she returned it plus the receipt, then went to find Jake. As she walked into the kitchen, she stopped, her feet frozen when she saw Mark emptying a bus pan into an industrial dishwasher.

The last thing she wanted to do was talk to Mark. He was too tempting—especially now that she knew he wasn't a complete asshole and could make her body sing with pleasure.

"I didn't know you moonlighted as a waitress," he said before she could sneak away.

"I didn't know dishwashing was your side hustle."

He chuckled and rinsed out the bus pan with a sprayer. "It hasn't been since we opened, but we lost some key employees in the last few weeks."

Kendra thanked her lucky stars he decided to talk about business instead of more intimate topics. "I wish someone had brought that to my attention this morning."

His jaw tightened, but he nodded. "We had no idea you'd manage to get rid of the protesters on your first day, or that so many people would learn about it. Housekeeping is fine, but as you can see, the restaurant needs more help if you're going to keep increasing our occupancy."

"Well, I'm sure Jake can manage his own staff. As for why so many people showed up, I used the bulk email service you're paying for and told them about it. The open rate wasn't great, but I guess it was good enough."

"I'm almost glad more people didn't show up," Mark muttered, gazing at the untidy kitchen. "Jake is out of food."

"And Jake is heartily delighted," he said, striding toward them. Without warning, he swung Kendra into a hug and kissed her full on the mouth. "Also, we're keeping Kendra. Quit pissing her off."

To her surprise, a low growl rumbled from Mark's chest, making her shiver. His eyes narrowed and a tic worked in his jaw as he glared at Jake.

Was he...jealous? That didn't make any sense. They barely knew each other, and while they were no longer actively antagonistic, she wasn't dumb enough to consider them friends—much less involved.

"It's fine." Gently, she extricated herself from Jake's embrace. "Mark and I have worked out our differences."

"Mr. McBride, sir?"

A young woman with the most amazing golden-brown complexion peered up through thick eyelashes at Jake. Her shoulders hunched and she didn't seem to want him to see her.

Her skin was so perfect that Kendra couldn't even discern her pores. Pushing down a surge of jealousy, she smiled at the other woman. "Sorry, I'll get out of your way."

"No, it's good. I just...can I start cleaning? I have to be back at the halfway house by one and it's a long walk."

"Excuse me?"

"I'm sorry. I have to—"

"I heard you. You're not walking."

"But—"

"Get to work on the grill. I'll drive you." He pinched the skin between his eyes and shook his head. "Actually, no. You disobeyed me and never took a break. There's leftover lobster mac and cheese, plus some braised lamb shanks in the break room. I'll have someone call and let them know you'll be late getting in."

"Sir, I—"

"Get your ass in the break room now, Olivia. I don't want to see you back here for at least thirty minutes."

The woman scurried away, still wearing her apron and hairnet, but not before Kendra caught the glimmer of tears in her huge brown eyes.

Jake started to follow, but Kendra laid a hand on his shoulder and shook her head. "I have no idea what went on here, but if you're going to terminate her employment, you can do it more professionally."

He scowled, then pressed his lips together. "I'll apologize," he finally said. "It's just that...never mind." He turned toward the grill and walked away without another word, then started scraping the cooking surface like it offended him.

"Olivia kept working when he asked her to take a break earlier," Mark whispered, his breath tickling the hair above her ear. "He's...let's just say he doesn't like to be disobeyed."

"What does that even mean? None of us had time for breaks. We were too busy."

Mark studied her for a moment, then shook his head. "I keep forgetting how innocent you are. Jake demands total submission from his partners."

She knew exactly what Mark was trying not to say. Total power exchange. It was the last thing she'd expected of Jake, but she wasn't truly surprised. Although kind and generous to a fault, she couldn't help but remember how he'd behaved when he brought her lunch.

However, that wasn't going to work with the staff, and if

Jake didn't know better by now, she'd be happy to educate him.

"Olivia is his employee—not his partner. There's an ugly word for people who misuse their authority over their staff."

He winced and turned back to the dishwasher. "I'll talk to him," he promised.

"Good. Thank you. I'll help you finish, then I'm going to bed. It's been a long day and I have early appointments tomorrow morning."

"On a Sunday?"

"I'm house hunting."

"You have a suite here."

"I'm sure you'd rather have that room filled with a paying guest, and I prefer not to live where I work."

He nodded and scooted over, letting her take over the dishwasher while he scrubbed the pots. "We always keep one free just in case, so if you have to stay late or the weather is bad, you won't have to drive home."

"There might be times I take advantage of it. It's a good idea to leave a room or two free anyway. You never know when a toilet might clog, and you have to move someone."

"True. It's never happened, but that doesn't mean it won't."

Carrying a full bus pan, Olivia crept in as they were finishing with the last of the dishes. A tremulous smile crept over her face, then vanished when she caught Jake glaring at her.

"Go back to the break room, Olivia," Jake barked. "It hasn't been thirty minutes."

She scraped a plate into the waste bucket, then loaded it into the dishwasher. "I'm okay, sir. Thank you for supper. It was very good."

Jake's expression softened for a split second before the scowl returned. "I gave you an order, little girl."

"Enough, Jake," Kendra interrupted. "Since you're still being a jerk, I'll take Olivia home."

Olivia's eyes widened and she flushed, the skin over her cheekbones darkening. "But—"

Kendra dropped her apron in the laundry cart, then held up a hand. "Come on. You don't need to listen to Jake's bullshit anymore and I promise he'll be in a better mood tomorrow."

She glared at Jake, leaving the *or else* unspoken. The Horsemen were going to be the death of her.

9

MARK

The women walked out, leaving him and Jake in a mostly clean kitchen. Mark sighed and rubbed his face, then turned to Jake. "Well, I promised Kendra I'd talk to you. This seems as good a time as any to tell you to stop being an ass."

"I don't need you of all people telling me that," Jake retorted. "It's just...there's something up with Olivia and I can't figure it out."

"What do you mean?"

"She said she was experienced, but I had to show her how to make vinaigrette, and she had no idea what roux was when I asked her to make bechamel for the creamed spinach. About the only thing she did well was chopping vegetables."

"You think she falsified her application?"

"I'm not sure." Jake frowned and emptied the dish-washer. "Not that it matters since it looks like I'm stuck with her."

"Where did she say she learned to cook?"

"Prison cafeteria and YouTube."

Mark chuckled and grabbed a broom to sweep up. He needed to get back to the dungeon, but Sean and Ryan were already there to keep an eye on things, meaning he could afford the time to help Jake.

"She probably has a lot of experience opening cans of industrial gruel, but maybe not with Michelin starred food. Do you think you can teach her what she needs to know?"

"Yeah." Jake filled the mop bucket with hot water and cleaner. "Maybe some remedial lessons during the lunch service if she comes back. Kendra was right. I was a dick."

"Seems to be going around." Mark finished sweeping and hung up his broom as Jake mopped behind him. "So far, Ryan is the only one who hasn't caught a case of jackassery."

"Give him time. I'm sure it's contagious."

Mark laughed, then disinfected the steel countertops. "I need to get back to the dungeon. Are you good?"

"Yeah. I can finish up, then I need to put a couple of orders in for more food. The pantry is tapped out." He grinned, then added, "We haven't had a night like this in months. I had almost a thousand dollars' worth of prime rib

I was about to cook and deliver to the homeless shelters in Flagstaff, so it didn't go to waste."

"Let's just hope we get some rooms rented." Mark washed his hands, then gave Jake a wave. "See you later."

With a spring in his step, he strode into the dungeon and smiled. Several couples had scenes going on, and the scents and sounds of arousal and pleasured pain almost drowned out the music emanating from the overhead speakers. It was like he'd stepped back in time to their first year when the place was full, and the novelty brought guests from all over the southwest.

This was what they'd dreamed of back when the old motel was still desert refuse left to die under the Arizona sun. He might not want Kendra around, and he definitely didn't appreciate her coming in and barking orders like she owned the joint, but he couldn't deny the results.

And he certainly wasn't going to deny the chemistry and sparks between them.

It was partially his fault though. Maybe she'd have had a better attitude if he hadn't been so antagonistic. He let out a breath and tried to tell himself to give her a chance. She'd already proven she could do the job Ryan hired her to do, and she hadn't done what he'd been afraid of—namely changing the dungeon. The few things she had asked for were common sense and safety-related, but he couldn't help wondering if they were small things meant to make him relax before she demanded more.

His arms crossed, Sean watched a couple make use of the suspension area. The dom was carefully laying another wrap of colored hemp rope around his sub's outstretched leg, his expression intent.

"Good to see them here," he murmured, standing next to Sean. "It's been a while."

"Yeah. I'm their spotter for tonight. Ryan is watching everyone else."

"Thanks."

"My foot is tingling," the woman called.

Sean hurried to the couple and touched the man's arm, gaining his attention. His hands moved quickly as he signed the sub's words. The dom frowned and repositioned the ropes, then gave her a tender kiss before checking the rest of her extremities.

The couple was the embodiment of safe and sane, and their adoration for each other was something to see. Every scene they did was gorgeous. It had been worth learning ASL just to watch them, and Sean was a lucky bastard to be asked to be their spotter.

Mark spent a few moments watching, only leaving when the dom hoisted his submissive into the air. Her blissed-out expression as she flew made him smile.

Randy and Joshua were sitting on a couch watching a sub being caned by his domme on the bondage horse. Joshua's sleepy eyes met his and he smiled, then cuddled closer to Randy. Judging by the blanket around Joshua's shoulders, it was obvious they'd already had a scene and were simply watching while things wound down for the night.

"Good night," Ryan said, as the domme untied her sub, then knelt to cup his face. "Wish I'd hired Kendra ages ago. I overheard several people talk about getting rooms."

"Nice."

Everything was as it should be, and Mark didn't understand why he still felt like it would all go wrong.

KENDRA

"Thank you for driving me," Olivia murmured as Kendra pulled into the driveway fronting the small group home.

Olivia had barely said a word for the entire drive, and hunched in her seat, her spine curved like she expected something bad to happen.

"You're a few minutes late. I'll come in with you, so you don't get in trouble."

"No, it's okay. I don't want to put you out."

Kendra shook her head and turned the engine off. "You're out past curfew because of work. That makes it my responsibility. I want to talk to them anyway to see if we can get it extended."

"Um... I..." Pressing her lips together, Olivia shook her head. "Never mind."

"Is there a problem?"

"No, I just have to... I'll be okay. You really don't have to come in."

She might not understand what Olivia was going through, or why she'd been incarcerated in the first place, but her reticence and obvious nerves had Kendra's Spidey senses tingling.

"Let's go in," she finally said, keeping her tone soft. "We'll get this taken care of and I promise everything will be fine."

Olivia nodded, but her hands trembled as she unfastened her seatbelt and got out. Kendra followed her up the cracked concrete path, noting the porch light was broken. The only illumination came from a streetlight on the corner.

"Well, look what the cat dragged in," a soft male voice said. "And you brought a friend."

"Go away, Carlos," Olivia said, tightening her hands into fists.

"Oooh, did the little *muñequita* get brave with her fancy new job?"

The man stepped from the shadows and gave Olivia a sneering grin. Shorter than Kendra, he bulged with muscle under a white T-shirt and tight jeans.

Another man flanked him, his eyes narrowed and mean.

"Do you have to stay here as a condition of your parole?" Kendra asked quietly.

"No, but—"

"Get in the car. We're leaving."

A third man appeared behind her, blocking her way. He was shaved bald, and his scalp was decorated with tattoos spilling over his temples. Although slim and wiry, he radiated menace.

"And miss the party? That would be..." He twisted his lips into a smile. "...unfortunate."

His hand shot forward, and he grabbed her throat. Kendra barely had time to set her feet before he squeezed, nearly cutting off her air. Behind her, Olivia screamed, a sound filled with rage and terror.

Instinct kicked in and Kendra slammed the heel of her hand into her assailant's nose. He cursed and let go, but before she could escape, he backhanded her and sent her to the ground. Almost immediately, his booted foot met her ribs, and she cried out, the excruciating pain making black spots cross her vision.

He smirked through the blood trickling from his nose, then grabbed her hair and hauled her to her feet.

"*Puta*." His heated breath washed over her face, smelling of alcohol.

"Let her go!" Olivia shouted, struggling against the two men holding her back.

The man holding Kendra sniffed derisively and slammed

her against her car, then turned away as she slid to the ground. "You'll be making it up to us, right?"

Olivia jerked her head in a nod and looked away. "Yes, just leave her alone."

Oh, hell no.

Kendra staggered to her feet and touched her busted lip. Wetness coated her fingers, and she tasted the copper of fresh blood. Thankfully, the men weren't paying her any heed as they hauled Olivia toward an overgrown stand of bushes.

Crossing her fingers, she opened the back door of her car and felt around the floorboards. When her fingers met canvas, she almost cried with relief. The sound of the zipper seemed loud to her, yet no one turned to see what she was doing. Hands trembling, she eased her grandfather's shotgun from its bag and loaded two cartridges.

Kendra staggered to her feet and fired the first into the dirt. Olivia screamed and the men holding her spun around, expressions of shocked fear on their faces.

"I. Have. Had. Enough." She pumped the shotgun, the ominous metallic thud making them take off running.

"Let's go," Olivia said, grabbing her hand. "We need to get out of here."

"Yeah."

Kendra unloaded the remaining cartridge and laid the shotgun in the back seat. As she drove away, she wondered if they should have called the police, but one look at Olivia's stricken face made her push the idea away. It was more important to get to safety.

She wiped at her lip with a tissue, trying to ignore the aches in her head and ribs. Once she thought she was calm enough to speak without shouting, she asked, "Does that happen often?"

"No, ma'am. I...well, they threatened it if they caught me alone, but I didn't believe them."

"Don't call me ma'am. It makes me feel ancient."

"Sorry, it's a habit." Olivia looked out the window as they approached Club Apocalypse. "And...thanks."

"You're welcome."

Olivia snorted out a giggle, then slapped a hand over her mouth as if surprised by the laughter. "I can't believe you pulled a gun on them. How come you have a shotgun in your car?"

"They had it coming." Kendra slowed and turned into the parking lot, then pulled into a spot near the door. "It was my grandfather's. I've been learning to trap shoot."

"Sounds like fun." Olivia went silent and chewed on her lip, then added, "I wish I didn't have to go back there."

"You don't. We'll find you somewhere else to live and get your stuff tomorrow."

10

MARK

He grinned and waved as the last few stragglers left the dungeon. It had been ages since there'd been good scenes, and he was still riding the adrenaline rush of witnessing everyone having such a great time.

It had nothing to do with giving Kendra an orgasm, or the little humming sounds she made for the few seconds she let him cuddle her. Or by how much he wanted to chase her when she bolted.

"We had a good night," Sean said. He reached up as if to clap Mark on the shoulder, then dropped his hand. "It was nice to see the dungeon get some use for a change."

"I'm almost tempted to say I told you so, but I had no

idea Kendra would work so fast," Ryan replied, getting cleaning supplies from the utility closet. "It's unnatural."

"That's one word for it," Mark murmured, using spray disinfectant and a rag to clean the bondage horse. "Let's do the floor in the morning. I'm exhausted."

"Same." Sean helped Mary Alice, the bartender, load glasses into the dishwasher, then started it.

"We'll put those away tomorrow," Mary Alice said, tossing her apron into a hamper. "I'm headed out. The receipts and used drink tickets are locked in the office already."

"Thanks," Mark replied. "Drive safe."

His phone chimed with a message as he put chairs up on the tables in preparation for morning cleaning. He pulled it out and frowned at the terse message from Sierra.

"Let's go," he said to his friends. "Sierra says there's a problem in the lobby."

Sean wiped his hands and dropped the bar rag in the hamper. "Did she call security?"

"She didn't say." Mark left the cleaning supplies on a table and led the way from the dungeon, Sean and Ryan following his quick pace.

As they passed the restaurant, Jake caught up with them, carrying a large bag of ice and several dishtowels. "Do you know what happened? Sierra asked me to bring ice and towels."

"Maybe someone fell," Ryan replied, breaking into a jog.

"Housekeeping was supposed to be waxing the floor in the lobby overnight, weren't they?"

Sean shook his head. "Not until later. Besides, they—"

"Not here, Sierra! The guests— Ouch! Fuck, that hurts!"

"Quit whining and watch your language, little girl."

Mark stopped, trying to make sense of what he was seeing. Scowling darkly, Sierra had Kendra on the couch and was pressing a bloodstained tissue to her lip. More blood droplets were scattered on the front of Kendra's shirt, and her pants were torn and covered in dirt.

Someone had obviously hit her, and he quelled the immediate urge to find the asshole and rearrange their limbs.

"Pretty sure I have a few years on you," Kendra snapped, jerking out of Sierra's reach.

"Jake is coming with ice. Just let me finish cleaning the blood up before you make a mess on the couch."

"I'm okay. Olivia has some big bruises on her arms. Take care of her first."

"You have an odd definition of *okay*. Olivia isn't actively bleeding on the furniture. Now, stop fussing before I spank your butt."

"Damn it. I'll be right back with my first aid kit," Ryan said before hurrying away.

"I'll check the cameras to see if we can find out who hit you," Sean added, sitting next to Kendra.

"It happened at Olivia's group home," Kendra said.

"There were three men, late twenties. One was named Carlos. I didn't catch anyone else's name."

"What possessed you to go there after dark?" Mark asked softly, fury clouding his vision. "Of all the dumbass things to do—"

Kendra held up a hand, meeting his angry glare with one of her own as Jake held ice to her face. "Stop right there before you say something I'll make you regret. To answer your question, I was driving Olivia home, as you well know."

Before he could reply, or better yet, turn the stubborn woman over his knee, Ryan returned with his kit and knelt in front of her.

Carefully, he pulled the ice away and held a piece of gauze to her lower lip. "Here we go," he said, his tone soft as he helped her replace the ice bag. "I think we've got the bleeding stopped, but let's keep the ice on it."

"I'm fine, but thanks." Turning to Sierra, Kendra asked, "Do we have a room available for Olivia? She's not going back there."

"I can put her next door to Dr. Knox," Sierra replied. "Sean and I can take her to get her stuff tomorrow."

"I was thinking all of the Horsemen, but not you, and definitely not Olivia."

"And deny me the opportunity to explain to them that hitting a woman can be bad for their health? Forget it." Her teeth bared in a vicious smile, Sierra cleaned up the bloody tissues.

"Actually, we need you here," Sean said. "You have to mind the store while we're gone. We'll meet with Olivia's parole officer on Monday."

Sierra rolled her eyes and sighed. "You spoil all my fun, Death."

"I'll make it up to you." He held out an arm for Olivia. "We can scare you up some sweats or something until we get your stuff. Are you okay?"

"Thank you, sir. I'm a little stiff, but I'll be fine." She gave Kendra a shy smile, hero worship shining from her large brown eyes. "Kendra saved me. I've never had anyone stand up for me before."

Kendra shook her head and stood, then grimaced as she rubbed her side over a suspicious dirty spot on her shirt. "Yeah, yeah. Self-rescuing princess thanks to her granddaddy's shotgun." Despite her words, her cheeks flamed with a blush. "Speaking of which, I need to get it out of my car."

"Give me your keys," Sierra ordered, holding out her hand. "I'll have one of the valets bring it to your room."

Ignoring Kendra's squawk of surprise, Mark swept her into his arms, unwilling to let anyone else take care of her. Judging by the way she moved, she was more injured than she'd let on.

"I can walk, you know." She wriggled but stilled when he tightened his arms around her.

Mark grunted, not trusting himself to reply. When he reached her room, he swiped his master keycard through the lock and carried her inside. Reluctantly, he put her down and took a step back. With time and a lot of counseling, he'd forced himself to tolerate casual contact. But this...

The woman had some kind of voodoo. It was the only thing he could think of that might explain his inability to let her go.

"Take off your shirt."

Her warm brown eyes chilled and narrowed. "Excuse me?"

"You don't have anything I haven't seen before. I need to look at the bruises you didn't tell Ryan about."

"How did you...never mind. I forgot your superhero powers of observation." Grumbling irritably, she unbuttoned her shirt and winced when she lifted her arm to pull it from the sleeve.

"Let me help." He eased the shirt away and cursed softly at the reddened contusion on her side. "Which one of them kicked you?"

"We weren't properly introduced."

Without thinking, he gave her butt a firm swat for the snark. Before he could apologize, she jerked away.

"What was that for?" She flushed and rubbed the spot where he'd spanked her.

Forcibly, he kept his hands at his sides to stop himself from helping her rub the sting away. "It was for the smart-ass comment, but I shouldn't have done it when you're already injured. I'm sorry."

_____

KENDRA

An apology was the last thing she expected to hear from Mark, and she couldn't help the surge of pleasure the words gave her.

The spank hadn't hurt at all. It certainly didn't measure up to the ache in her ribs or her swelling face. Yet her bruises seemed to pulse under the weight of his gaze. It was as if he'd stripped her completely bare.

"Thank you," she finally replied. "But as you can see, I'm okay."

"Sierra was right. You have an odd definition of that word." Tsking, he traced the edges of the sore spot over her ribs. "This needs ice."

"I'll be—"

A knock at the door interrupted her. Mark frowned, then grabbed a throw from the couch and wrapped it around her shoulders. "Stay here. I'll get it."

Without waiting for her to answer, he opened the door, blocking it with his muscular body. A moment later, he tugged a room service cart inside, then accepted her shotgun case from the person in the corridor.

"What's that?" she asked as he laid the case on the dresser.

"Looks like more ice packs, a bottle of Prosecco and..." He

lifted a cloche from a plate and smiled. "Jake's limoncello pound cake. He says it cures all ills."

Kendra's mouth watered and she swallowed before she drooled. "There's a fitness center on the property, right?"

Laughing softly, he broke off a piece of cake and held it to her lips. "One small taste to go with the pain medicine Ryan added to the cart. You can have half a glass of wine later."

His dark brown eyes glinted with humor. He was teasing her with that sexy, slumbrous bedroom gaze, but her girly parts woke up and did a happy dance. Two could play at his game though. She opened her mouth and sucked the lemony treat from his fingers, chasing crumbs with the tip of her tongue.

When he hissed out a breath, she smirked inwardly and took a step back. "I'm going to grab a shower."

He straightened and ruddy color decorated his sharp cheekbones. Nodding, he turned to the cart and picked up a glass of water along with a small paper cup containing two white tablets. "Take these first," he ordered.

"Thanks." She swallowed the pills, then chased them with a sip of water, knowing they'd need time to take the edge off her aches and pains. "But I could really use a glass of wine about now."

"I thought you wanted a shower."

The sexy glint returned to his gaze, and she shivered, goosebumps erupting on her arms. Between Mark's off-the-charts sex appeal and Jake's cooking, it was a wonder Kendra had a brain left in her damned head.

"Yeah. I mean... I'll be... Just leave everything. I promise to use the ice."

He hummed in acknowledgement and poured himself some wine. Taking a sip, he peered at her over the rim of the glass. "I think I'll stick around in case you need help."

"But—"

"Shower, baby girl. It's late and you've had a busy day."

Kendra pressed her lips together and strode to the suitcase she hadn't bothered to unpack for a pair of sweats and a clean T-shirt. She had no idea what was up with the people here treating her like she was a child.

That wasn't entirely fair though. Everyone had accepted her plans for Club Apocalypse like they'd been spoken from on high and she could see improvement after only one day. The insulting diminutives only came out when they thought she needed to be cared for.

Gritting her teeth at the pain in her ribs, she folded the blanket and laid it on the bathroom vanity, then swallowed a whine as she wriggled out of her shoes and trousers. Tears popped in her eyes when she had to reach behind herself to unfasten her bra.

"Fuck, that hurts."

She dropped the bra to the floor with the rest of her clothes and stepped into the stall. After adjusting the temperature to something only slightly cooler than the surface of the sun, she positioned herself under the spray and groaned as the hot water went to work on her battered body.

Although Kendra knew Mark was scant feet away on the other side of the door, she felt...safe—as if he was guarding her. Grabbing a sponge and her favorite lavender soap, she washed as best she could, letting the sweet fragrance soothe her jangled nerves.

Closing her eyes, she leaned against the tile and let her mind wander while the massaging spray eased the stiffness in her back. Stupidly, the only place her thoughts wanted to go was back to Mark carrying her down the corridor like a bride on her wedding night.

Some small noise brought her out of her reverie and she opened her eyes, then screamed at the sight of a tall figure standing outside the frosted glass shower enclosure. Kendra grabbed a shampoo bottle. It was a poor weapon, but when the glass opened, she aimed for his head and threw it.

Mark ducked, then grabbed a towel and held it up for her. "Whoa! It's just me! I'm sorry I scared you, but I knocked twice and got worried when you didn't answer."

Abject relief coupled with humiliation made her knees shake and nearly buckle. Trying to stay upright, she grabbed the towel and wrapped it around herself with shaking hands.

She shivered at the sudden absence of heat, and her teeth chattered as she said, "I... I'm okay."

"No, you're not." He grabbed another towel and wrapped her hair into a turban, then carefully patted her dry. "Let's get you into bed."

"I need to get dressed."

"It can wait. You need to lie down and get some ice on those bruises."

"You are so stubborn."

"So I'm told." Careful of her bruised ribs, he wrapped an arm around her waist and helped her to the bed. With one hand, he tossed back the covers and pointed. "Get in. I'll bring the ice and your snack."

She grumbled under her breath but obeyed and slid between the silky bamboo sheets. After a few minutes of painful maneuvering, she managed to position herself on her side and handed him the damp towel from under the covers.

He tossed it over his shoulder and gave her a large ice bag. "That one is for your ribs, and I have a smaller one for your face after you eat."

"Thanks."

Being naked around him should have made her uncomfortable—especially after their...whatever it was. Yet he didn't make it awkward. Instead of staring at her body, he met her eyes easily.

After returning the towel to the bathroom, he said, "Ready for your cake and wine? I can feed you while we ice your bruises."

"Please." She rearranged her pillow to lift her head up, and her vision caught on the dresser. "Why is my shotgun in pieces?"

"I started cleaning it while you were in the shower." He carried a plate and a glass of wine to her and set them on the nightstand.

"Um... Thanks, but just leave it and I'll take care of it tomorrow."

He smiled, the expression wrinkling the skin around his eyes as he fed her a bite of cake. She almost wanted to tell him to stop grinning at her like that because if she had panties on, they'd be soaked, and she'd be throwing them at him.

"You trust me to blindfold you for a scene, but not with your gun?" He sat on the bed next to her and held the wine-glass so she could take a sip.

"Well, when you put it that way..." She winced and looked away. "I didn't mean to be insulting, but it was my grandfather's."

"You mentioned that. It's a gorgeous antique. You obviously already know it's safe to fire, but you might want to consider buying something new, so it doesn't get damaged."

"I wanted to see if I liked it before I invested money in a hobby, but I enjoy shooting clay birds." Kendra didn't tell him she imagined her ex-husband's face on the targets. It was her own personal brand of therapy. "I did think to get it insured though."

He fed her another bite of cake. "I have one you can borrow. We could go out sometime."

"Mr. Luciano, are you asking me on a date?"

He stole the last of her wine but let her finish the cake. "It depends. If you don't say no, then I suppose I am."

They were coworkers. It would be unprofessional and inappropriate for them to see each other socially, yet the excuse rang hollow, considering he'd had his fingers inside her and made her come.

Aside from that, she really wanted to say yes.

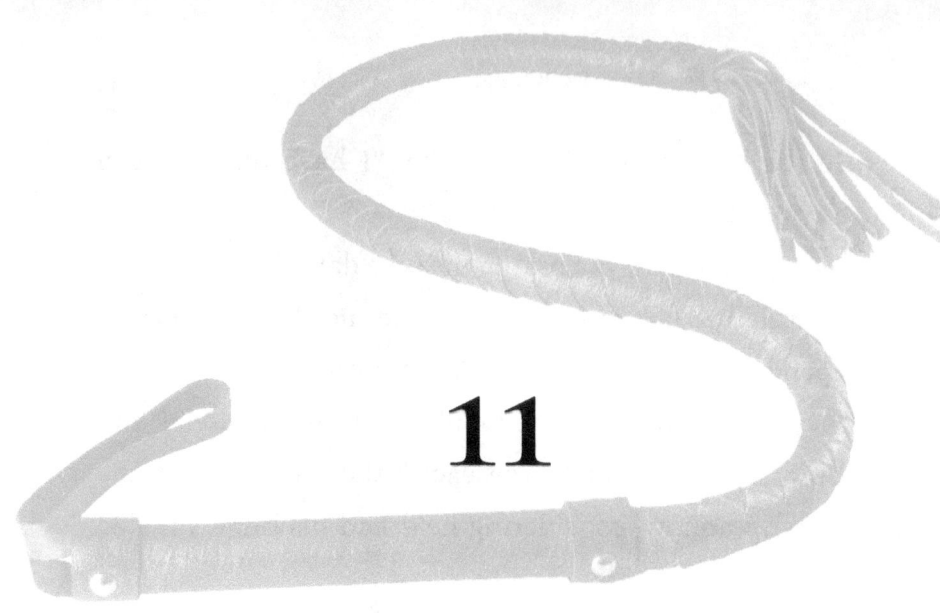

11

MARK

He studied Kendra while she put the ice on her face. Wet hair spread across the pillow, and she looked almost childlike with one hand fisted on the covers.

"Are you feeling better?" he finally asked.

"Yeah. Whatever was in those pills helped, but I'm way too old to be doing any more street fighting."

"Is there ever a good age for that?"

Laughing softly, she closed her eyes. "Definitely not. I'm just glad I had the presence of mind to scare them off. They were going to hurt Olivia."

"She thinks you're a hero."

Her nose wrinkled and she pulled the ice bag from under

the covers. "A hero wouldn't have gotten her ass handed to her. Besides, I was scared shitless."

"You know what they always say about bravery." He took the ice from her, hoping it had helped.

"No idea."

"Bravery is being scared and doing what needs to be done anyway."

"You're quoting a movie. I'm too tired and I can't remember which one."

"Doesn't mean it isn't true." He pushed a piece of hair out of her face, then bent close and kissed her forehead, surprising himself as much as her. "Go to sleep, superhero."

"Asshole."

The insult didn't have any heat, and Mark laughed softly, then kissed her again. "Be careful. Little girls who swear might get their mouths washed out with soap."

She lifted the ice from her face and arched a groomed brow. "I'm sure you have a better imagination than that."

"You have no idea." He gave her shoulder a gentle squeeze, then tucked the covers under her chin. "Get some rest."

Although he wanted to stay, he stood and made his feet move toward the door. Every touch made him want to draw that much closer to her, but what could he offer?

He couldn't make any promises when he wasn't sure if his aversion to physical contact would come back. He'd managed to keep it at bay with other partners—for a while anyway—but it always, always returned. Mark couldn't picture himself telling Kendra, a woman who had stood down a gang of thugs with an heirloom shotgun, that he was afraid of people touching him.

Of course, it was probably already too late now that he'd been a dumbass and asked her out. Maybe a trip to the gun range wasn't exactly a date, but it would be the closest he'd come to one since college.

"Hey, Mark?"

"Hmm?"

"Yes." She pulled the ice from her face and laid it on the nightstand. "Also, will you stay with me until I fall asleep?"

"Yes, to what?"

"To a date at the gun range. We'll have Jake pack us a picnic for after you teach me your witchy firearm ways. No cake though. I have to stop eating his sweets." She snuggled under the covers, her words and ease of movement letting him know the acetaminophen with a small bonus of codeine had done the trick. "Just lay next to me so I can hear you breathe."

He couldn't decide whether to laugh or run so fast he left a contrail. This wasn't him. He didn't touch people, and he certainly didn't go to bed with a woman unless he planned to fuck her to unconsciousness. Always from behind, so he didn't risk inadvertent contact, and he never, ever stayed the night.

Damn it, he wanted to. He wanted to be the one to give

her comfort. Worse, she might call in one of the other Horsemen if he didn't give her what she wanted.

Not in this lifetime.

Before he could think about it too hard, he turned off the lights and removed his boots, then crawled into bed with her and tried to forget she was naked.

Mark left several inches between them, unwilling to risk her touching him if he wasn't ready for it. He'd been known to lash out in his sleep, and hurting Kendra was the last thing he wanted to do.

Well, not like that, anyway. He wouldn't mind exploring sensation play with her again. She might like a Wartenburg wheel, given her reaction to the vampire glove. Maybe drip hot wax in more interesting places...

To his shock, Kendra squirmed and scooted backward until she was firmly nestled against his chest. Letting out a soft sigh, she relaxed, and her breathing slowed.

"Kendra, I—"

"Shh. We're sleeping now. We have a busy day tomorrow."

We?

Almost against his will, his hand moved to cup her hip. It wasn't quite an embrace but brought her closer until he could smell the soap she'd used. It was something sweet and floral he thought he should have recognized, but he couldn't place it. To his surprise, his lids grew heavy as the scent and the sound of her breathing lulled him into a doze.

Maybe it would be okay. He could rest for a few minutes, then leave once she was fast asleep. He inhaled her sweet perfume and closed his eyes.

A faint click and a change in air pressure brought him to full alertness. His instincts, honed to detect a threat, forced him into stillness as he allowed his vision to adjust to the dim light of dawn creeping past the blackout curtains. Slowly, he moved his hand toward Kendra, but found only cold sheets.

Her absence coupled with the knowledge that he'd slept all fucking night in her bed without a single nightmare messed with his head, but Mark would have to think about it later. A faint shadow moved into the room, and he held his breath, waiting for it to come closer.

Mark sprang from the bed and took the figure down, realizing his mistake far too late to do anything about it.

————

KENDRA

"God dammit! Get off me!"

Mark had been sleeping peacefully and hadn't stirred when she left. Even though it was past dawn, Kendra had tried not to wake him, but it was more than obvious she'd failed. Still cursing, she slapped at the hands around her neck, finally making him leap off her.

"I am so sorry. Let me help you."

Still trying to catch her breath from being tackled to the carpet with over two hundred pounds of belligerent male sitting on her chest, she accepted his outstretched hand and staggered to her feet. The ache in her ribs sprang to life once more and she clutched at her side, trying to breathe through the pain.

Given his military history, it was possible he suffered from post-traumatic stress. She was positive his attack hadn't been malicious, and he clearly felt horrible about it. Aside from that, having him on top of her had been strangely arousing. She tried to brush off the sensation of his weight and heat trapping her, but her core pulsed with inconvenient need.

"Remind me to use a fire hose if I have to wake you up again."

"Or just dump ice water on my head." He turned on a lamp, revealing his reddened face and a shamefaced smile. "I'm really sorry. Are you okay?"

It hurt, but she laughed softly. "I'm fine. I apologize for surprising you. I thought I was being quiet enough not to wake you."

Cupping her elbow, he helped her to a chair and made her sit. "Stay right there. I'll get more ice for your ribs. I also have another dose of pain meds from Ryan."

"Don't worry about it. I have breakfast coming, and then I have to go back out."

His thumb traced her still-thundering pulse and he frowned. "Where did you go so early?"

"I went to get Olivia's things. They're in that suitcase by the door. She didn't have much, and—"

"Excuse me? I don't believe I heard you properly." A vein pulsed in his temple and his voice deepened with a warning she chose to ignore.

"The people who attacked us are probably still sleeping off whatever mischief they got up to last night. I figured I could get in and get out with no one the wiser. What do you care anyway? I saved you a trip."

All expression left his face as he straightened. "Do you mean to tell me you went back to the place where you were attacked, by yourself, for a stranger's clothes?"

"So? I certainly wasn't going to let Olivia do it!"

His hands tightened into fists, and he pressed his lips into a thin line. A knock interrupted whatever he'd been about to say, and he stomped to the door and opened it. Still scowling darkly enough to frighten children, he accepted a breakfast tray, then let the door shut behind him.

"Thanks," she said, rising to her feet.

"Sit. Down." China clattered when he set the tray on a table. Folding his arms over his chest, he turned to glare at her.

Kendra frowned at the barked order, then ignored him and poured herself a cup of coffee. "I'm sure you meant to thank me for ordering breakfast."

"No, actually, I'm trying to remind myself that you're not my sub and I probably shouldn't beat your ass for putting yourself at risk like that."

Locking her trembling knees, she took a sip of coffee in an attempt to convince her body not to melt into a puddle. The idea made her twitch with need, yet she was certain he wasn't thinking of a fun spanking.

"You might also remember that I'm your employee." She grabbed a mini quiche from a plate and popped it into her mouth. "And that I'm a grown woman who can make her own choices."

"More's the pity," he muttered. "Are you planning to do anything stupid after breakfast?"

"No. If you'll recall, I told you I have plans to look for a house."

His jaw worked, but he nodded and retrieved a paper cup from the desk. "Take these. I'll drive you."

She shook her head at the sight of the two pills in the cup. "That isn't—"

"Kendra, I can see you're still in pain. Take the damned medicine before I change my mind about spanking you."

"That doesn't make sense. Why would you—"

He jerked her close, making the coffee cup fall to the table and spill. The heat of his body scalded her as his scent of warm male musk filled her lungs. Before she could pull away, he took her mouth in a punishing kiss, brutalizing her lips with the force of it. Yet his hand was achingly gentle as he cupped her nape, tilting her head to deepen the kiss. His tongue swept into her, penetrating her mouth as if he was desperate to taste her—like he was making love to her.

"You make me not make sense," he husked, kissing a scorching path across her jaw. Without warning, he pulled away and touched her swollen lower lip.

The scant brush of his finger over the small cut made her shiver with a mix of need and trepidation. "What was that for?"

"It seemed like the only way to shut you up."

The minute she opened her mouth to yell at him, he pushed the pain relievers between her lips, then poured her a fresh cup of coffee. "Swallow, Kendra."

She considered spitting them at him but chased the pills down with a sip of her drink. "You're such an asshole," she muttered.

The medicine meant she wouldn't be able to drive herself, meaning she'd be stuck with Mark for the next several hours. It wasn't how she planned to spend her day but couldn't deny the warm feeling his care gave her.

To be fair, she'd taken a risk going back to the halfway house, but she couldn't let her fear control her. She'd spent too long doubting herself to allow it to continue.

"I know." Wrapping an arm around her waist, he escorted her back to the chair. "Sit, and I'll bring you the rest of your breakfast. I'll grab a shower and change while you're eating."

"Um—"

Ignoring her, he filled a plate with treats and laid it on her lap, along with a napkin. "And don't move from that spot while I'm gone, little girl."

"I'm hardly little."

He laughed softly and held a piece of cinnamon roll to her lips. "You are when you're being naughty."

Scowling, she ate the roll from his hand, but nipped his finger. "Shoo. If you're going to be so insistent on playing knight in shining armor, you don't have much time."

Still chuckling, he tapped her nose. "I'll be about ten minutes. Behave yourself."

The minute Mark shut the door behind him, Kendra slumped in her chair. Her hand trembled as she lifted her coffee cup. The pain medicine hadn't had time to work on her battered body, and although she'd never admit to it, she hurt. In fact, if she hadn't been so desperate for her own space, she'd have seriously considered canceling her meeting and stayed in bed with a bag of ice.

Of course, spending that much time with her own thoughts would have sent her right back to how his touch made her feel. She touched her tingling lips and pushed the thought firmly out of her head. That way lay madness. Mark was her boss. She didn't have time to date, and most definitely wasn't ready for another relationship.

Maybe Mark had a point about bravery. Going back to that halfway house had been a lot like leaving her ex-husband. Both were terrifying, and both required pulling on big-girl panties and doing it even though there wasn't much difference between bravery and stupidity sometimes.

She grimaced at the plate of pastries. As much as she loved Jake's food, it would be better for her to be in her own place and out of the way of temptation. Then again, she didn't have to listen to Daniel's cutting remarks every time she stepped on a scale. What did it matter if she gained a few pounds? She reached for a treat, then remembered she'd have to buy new clothes if she went too far overboard.

"Screw it."

She took a huge bite of the custard-filled Napoleon and hummed her appreciation. Before she could swallow, the door opened. Freshly showered and changed, Mark stepped into the room and grinned.

"You know, most people make that kind of noise during sex."

12

MARK

A pink flush decorated Kendra's cheeks, but she finished her pastry and wiped a drop of cream from her lower lip.

It was a good thing too. Mark was a few steps away from taking care of it himself. With his tongue. The woman was a hazard, and his only saving grace was that she didn't know how much she affected him.

She seemed overdressed for a Sunday morning in sleek houndstooth trousers and a fitted white Oxford. Instead of heels, she wore black flats with a pointed toe. Not counting the maxi dress she'd worn for her road trip, he suspected this was as casual as she ever got.

"Sorry, not sorry." She gazed at him, humor making her

eyes sparkle as she took another pastry. "Jake is the real reason I can't live at the resort. I'd rather buy real estate than a new wardrobe and his food is better than sex."

Unable to help himself, he leaned over her and wrapped his fingers around her wrist, then ate the pastry in her hand. "Sounds like you haven't been doing it right."

"Maybe I haven't." She parted her lips as if she had something else to say, then ducked under his arm and escaped. "Ready to go?"

Naughty girl.

Mark still couldn't explain why he had such a raging need to touch her—and to let her touch him. Despite their previous personality conflicts, he decided to go with it and see where things went. His friends had been after him for years to find a partner—or at least someone he could tolerate for more than an evening.

He caught up as she slowed to grab her purse. "Where's our first stop?"

"I have a few possibilities in Happy Jack, then Flagstaff if I can't find anything closer."

"Those are both over an hour away."

"I know, but there isn't a lot of available real estate in the area." She walked out, then followed him toward employee parking. "Where are you and the other owners living?"

"We have an apartment on the other side of the dungeon facing the back of the property." He clicked the fob to unlock his truck, then helped her in. "It's more like a college dorm suite, but we're used to being together." He hurried around the hood and got in, then turned onto the main road.

Kendra looked out the window, seeming to forget he was with her. "Sounds convenient," she finally said. "No commute time."

"That was one reason, yes." It might have seemed odd for four grown men to live together, but she didn't sound judgmental about their living arrangements. "And we were broke after finishing the renovations to Club Apocalypse."

She turned to face him and grinned. "So, what's keeping you there?"

"Laziness. And considering we're losing our shirts, it's probably best if we don't take out mortgages."

"Well, I hope to fix that part for you. Don't count out a place of your own quite yet."

He grunted in acknowledgement but didn't answer right away. Despite what she'd done over the weekend, he still wasn't sure whether Kendra could get Club Apocalypse back on track. It seemed almost too good to be true—especially her promise not to mess around with the dungeon.

The reminder of how close they were to going out of business soured his mood. Maybe it would be better to let the property go and sell it to a developer like Kendra suggested instead of watching her turn it into some dumbass theme park. She'd said she wouldn't be doing that, but he still wasn't sure.

An hour later, he slowed to turn into a small subdivision

of log homes. It was farther than he'd be willing to commute, but the houses were attractive and well secluded with ponderosa pines and aspen.

"It's that one," Kendra said, pointing at a home with a steeply pitched roof and a curving driveway.

"Nice. I like the log construction."

"Me too. I always wanted to live in a log cabin, but... anyway, looks like the realtor is already here."

Nodding, he parked next to a white minivan, then got out. After helping her from his truck, they passed an open house sign and went inside.

"Oh, it's so pretty." Kendra spun in place and looked up at the vaulted ceiling. Expansive windows revealed the wooded property and a set of French doors opened to a deck with comfortable seating and a freestanding firepit.

"Hi!" A man dressed in a sport coat and jeans walked toward her, his hand outstretched. "I'm Ted Matthews. Welcome!"

"Thank you." Kendra shook his hand, then moved toward the large open-plan kitchen. "I'm Kendra Hall. We spoke on the phone last week."

"It's good to meet you. How was your trip from Houston?"

"Uneventful, thankfully. Do you mind if we wander?"

"Not at all. I'm sure you and your..." He glanced at Mark, an eyebrow raised in question.

"This is my coworker, Mark Luciano."

"A pleasure, Mr. Luciano." Ted pushed his glasses up his nose and handed her a copy of the printed listing. "You mentioned you were relocating for a new job, but I didn't catch where you'd be working."

She ran her hand over an exposed log doorframe. "I accepted a position as vice-president of operations for Club Apocalypse."

Ted's ingratiating smile faded, and he looked away before clearing his throat. "Well, I... Congratulations."

"Thanks. I'm looking forward to the new opportunity." She wandered into the kitchen and Mark heard her giggle. "This is gorgeous! I love the farmhouse sink."

Hurrying after her, Ted said, "Ms. Hall, would a property in Winslow or Holbrook be a better choice? This would be quite a commute for you."

"I don't mind the commute, and I was looking for a wooded property. There isn't anything of that nature in either of those towns, and you're the one who mentioned Happy Jack." She turned and crossed her arms over her chest. "This house is well within my budget, and I've already been preapproved for double the asking price."

"Well..." He took a handkerchief from his inner pocket and wiped his forehead. "That is to say, Ms. Hall—"

"What is the problem?"

Ted returned his handkerchief to his pocket and sighed. "This is a Christian community. I can't refuse to sell to you, but I'm afraid the other residents wouldn't take kindly to a... Well, I'm not sure how to put this politely, but—"

"Put what politely?" She gazed at him steadily, then arched a brow. "Mr. Matthews?"

Looking down, the realtor didn't meet her eyes. "A...well, an S. E. X. worker."

"I see. When did a vice-president of one of the county's largest employers become a prostitute?"

He flushed, his cheeks turning scarlet. "Well, I'm sure that's... Ms. Hall, there are children living in this neighborhood."

Kendra gave him an expressionless nod. "If you'll excuse us, I'll find another real estate agent who isn't quite such a sanctimonious prick. Have the day you deserve."

Without waiting for an answer, she lifted her chin and strode out.

Mark snorted out a laugh and followed her from the house. "I can't believe he spelled out sex like a child saying a bad word."

"Hmm." She accepted his hand and allowed him to help her into the truck. "That explains the protesters at the resort. Maybe I need to approach this a different way."

Frowning, he drove them north back to Winslow. "You already got rid of them."

"For the moment, anyway. I think we'll need to do more. Maybe community outreach or something along those lines."

"Well, we donate unused food to the Flagstaff food pantries all the time."

"Why not closer?"

Mark spared a glance at her as she typed notes into her phone. "Most of the local charities wouldn't accept it."

"Then start your own."

———

KENDRA

She couldn't decide whether to be furious, humiliated, or a sickening mixture of both. Ted Matthews had called her a whore. To her face.

She truly hated people some days.

"What do you mean, start our own?" Mark asked.

"Just what I said. Take me back to the resort, please. I need to run some numbers."

"What about finding a place to live?"

"I'll just buy land and build something. It's fine."

It wasn't really. New construction would take months. Then again, she wouldn't have a bunch of aggravating neighbors. After living cheek-by-jowl in a Houston subdivision with lots the size of postage stamps, she wanted more space and privacy.

"Kendra, it isn't fine." Mark reached over and squeezed her knee. "I'm sorry that happened."

"Thanks, but it wasn't your fault." She took a deep breath and released it in an attempt to let go of her irritation. "Actually, it might be a good thing. I'm probably better off living where there isn't a homeowner's association."

It was poor consolation, but there was some truth in it too. The HOA in Houston had thrown a fit over the pirate flag she'd once tried to hang on the porch. Daniel had too, calling it childish and unbecoming of his station as a pillar of the community. The man couldn't take a joke—unless it was at her expense.

"I couldn't deal with it either. Anyway, what did you have in mind for outreach?"

"Not sure yet. I'll look at the county demographics and see what's available. I want something to fill a need that isn't already met."

"Maybe something with animals," he mused. "We could do pet adoption events."

She tapped a note into her phone, even though she was too focused on her housing issues to pay it much attention. "That's a good idea. I'll put a few proposals together and present them late next week."

Seeming to know she didn't want to talk any further, Mark held his peace and turned on some music. Thankfully, the pain medicine was soothing the worst of her aches, but by the time they made it back to the resort, Kendra could barely keep her eyes open.

Mark walked her to her room, his hand on the middle of

her back as if he wanted to support her but wasn't quite sure how. When they reached her door, he said, "Have dinner with me."

"Sure you want to be seen with the Navajo County wh—"

He put a hand over her mouth and his expression darkened. She shivered at the sudden anger on his face as his fingers dug into her cheeks. "Do. Not. Ever..." He loosened his grip and seemed to forcibly calm himself. "First off, there's nothing wrong with being a sex worker."

"I know that." She tried to pull away, but he laid his hands on her shoulders to keep her still.

A tiny part of her wondered if she ought to feel threatened. Even without counting the incident at the halfway house, she hadn't had good experiences with men grabbing her. Daniel had never been shy about doing it and often left bruises on her arms.

Yet another reason she should have left him years before she got up the nerve to actually do it.

Despite his obvious anger, Mark didn't frighten her. Instead, insidious warmth curled in her belly. He wasn't mad at her—he was furious on her behalf.

"Second, you're a brilliant, astute businessperson."

"You say that like sex workers can't be."

He quirked his lips into a half grin and slid his hands down her arms, warming her cold fingers with his touch. "Touché. The point is, I'm not going to allow you to denigrate yourself because one small-minded, provincial asshole insulted you."

"Allow? You're not the boss of me." She returned his smile to ease the sting of her words. She couldn't remember the last time anyone had stood up for her. It was strange yet thrilling in a way she couldn't explain.

"Actually, according to the contract you signed, I am." Reaching around her, he slid his keycard through the lock to open the door, then swatted her ass. "Go. Take a nap. We'll meet for supper at five, okay?"

"I—"

"Great. Wear jeans you won't mind getting dirty, boots with a low heel, and bring a jacket. I have a surprise for you. Also, don't take Ryan's meds if he left you another dose. Stick to ibuprofen if you need it."

Shocking the hell out of her, he kissed her forehead, then sauntered away.

"Hey! Wait!"

"Five o'clock, Ms. Hall. Don't be late." He turned and walked backward for a few steps and touched two fingers to his forehead. "I might have to punish you for tardiness this time."

Whuh.

Kendra let the door shut gently, then leaned against it with her hand over her pounding heart. This was such a bad idea on so many levels.

He was her boss.

Well, more a coworker, her subconscious told her.

He'd been unconscionably rude to her.

And took care of you after you got beat up, complimented you after that realtor insulted you, and don't forget the hot wax and vampire glove, and—

"Shut up." That was the last thing Kendra needed to remember, but she couldn't help thinking about the heated streams of wax sliding along skin already sensitized from the glove and the ice. Unbidden, an image of her strapped to one of those pieces of bondage furniture came to mind. She'd be bared to him, helpless, and...

Firmly, she erased the scene from her head and moved deeper into the room. It had been freshly straightened, and there was a towel folded into a swan on the bed. The breakfast tray was gone, but housekeeping had wrapped the leftover pastries and put them in a white bakery box. Along with the food, she found another dose of pain meds, plus a bottle of water in an ice bucket. There was a folded piece of paper in front of the bucket with her name on it.

She unfolded the paper and rolled her eyes at Ryan's terse note, which said, "Rest, take your medicine, and be a good girl or you'll get spanked."

"I'm not your sub, Mr. Wood. Kindly piss off."

With luck, she wouldn't need the meds. A nap wasn't a bad idea, although she didn't have that much time to figure out her living arrangements. An indefinite stay in a guest suite wasn't a good option—especially when business started picking up.

Deciding to research community outreach later, Kendra stripped down to her panties, then crawled into bed and set an alarm on her phone. Like many hotels—especially those in arid climates—housekeeping didn't change the sheets every day unless there was a new guest, and she still smelled Mark's aftershave on the pillow he'd used.

It was ridiculous, but she tugged the pillow close and wrapped her arms around it, then let his scent carry her into sleep.

13

MARK

He rushed through his chores, barely speaking to the staff as they did a weekly deep-clean of the dungeon.

"What's the hurry?" Ryan called from the triage room. "You dropped a pillowcase."

Scowling, Mark juggled the armload of linens and crouched to pick it up. "None of your business."

"Hmm." Ryan examined a package of electrolyte solution for an expiration date and slid it back into the cupboard. "Would it have anything to do with spending all morning driving Kendra around? When did you turn into a chauffeur?"

"Since you gave her meds, and she couldn't drive

herself."

Cocking his head, Ryan grabbed a laundry basket and helped him with the armload of linens. "And where was she going? I'm assuming you didn't try to run her off again."

"She was looking for a house to buy."

"Any luck?"

"No." He'd considered not telling Ryan what had happened, but if Kendra was right and the protesters came back, he would want to know. "The realtor all but called Kendra a prostitute to her face when she told him where she works."

"Is he still walking under his own power? We don't have much of a bail fund, but for Kendra—"

Mark barked out a laugh and shook his head. "No, she called him a sanctimonious prick and walked out like a queen. It was epic."

"Good for her." Ryan sobered and shook his head. "Can't say I'm surprised, but I'm also kind of glad. I'd rather have her stay on the property for security."

"She wants her own place and thinks we'll start doing enough business to need the suite."

"Hmm." Ryan crossed his hands behind his back as if he was at parade rest. "We still have that five-hundred-acre parcel north of the resort property. We could sell her part of it and let her build."

"Yeah, I guess."

Homes of their own had been their plan all along, and

the reason they'd never let go of the additional acreage. It seemed a pipe dream now, and it was probably for the best that none of them had started building.

"I mean, how much room does she need to build a house for one person? We'll offer her that weird little ten-acre corner on the southwest."

"Ten acres where?" Jake asked, pushing in a cart loaded with water and packaged snacks for the aftercare rooms.

"We're selling the southwest ten acres to Kendra so she can build a house," Ryan replied.

"Just give it to her as an additional signing bonus. God knows, she's earning it." Jake put a few bottles of water into the glass-fronted refrigerator. "We've all picked out our spots, and I've already bought the plans for the house I want."

As usual, Jake was disgustingly optimistic. He truly thought everything would work out and they wouldn't end up selling the resort before they went out of business. Mark wasn't so sure but didn't have the heart to contradict him.

Hell, maybe Dr. Knox would buy it. She had the money and would probably do it just to piss off Sean. The idea made him smile wryly. Jolene Stratton, their landscape architect, had always dreamed of turning the property into a nature preserve as a memorial for her first husband, who had died of cancer. They could make it a non-profit, giving Jolene her wish and Dr. Knox a nice tax deduction.

"I'm good with that," Ryan said, dragging Mark's attention back to the conversation. "We'll check with Sean and make the offer tomorrow if he's okay with it."

Best of all, it fit in with his plans for his date with Kendra. He'd intended to take her out there to shoot anyway, and it would give him the opportunity to present the idea to her.

"Hey, Jake, is there enough food in the kitchen to make a picnic supper for Kendra and me? I was planning to take her out there for a little target practice anyway, so I might as well tell her our news."

"No, let's make it a surprise," Ryan said. "You could get an idea of whether she'd appreciate it though. There's no point in offering if she doesn't want to live there."

"Good idea." Jake finished stocking the aftercare rooms. "If she wants it, we can present it to her at tomorrow's staff meeting. What time do you want your picnic?"

"Four-thirty, I guess. I told her to be ready at five."

"On it. Any requests for the menu?"

"Surprise us. You know what Kendra likes, and I'll eat anything. Speaking of which, do either of you mind if I borrow the shotguns? Kendra's is an heirloom and I want to let her try a few of ours to see what she likes."

Ryan and Jake looked at each other and shrugged. "I don't care," Ryan said.

"Me either, and Sean won't mind." Jake pushed his cart from the room, then added, "Stop by the kitchen on your way out. I'll have your picnic ready by four-thirty."

"Thanks." He lifted the basket, propping it on a hip. "I'll take care of the linens and finish the floor. The benches and fixtures are already done."

"Great." Ryan finished his inventory and washed his hands. "I'm going to do payroll, then see if Dr. Knox needs anything."

"She's gone," Jake replied. "Well, her car is gone, so I'm assuming she's with it."

The men were silent for several seconds, then Ryan let out a soft curse. "Someone, please tell me Sean wasn't an asshole again."

"Doubt it. He's not here either," Jake replied. "He might have gone to get Olivia's stuff."

"Crap. I forgot to say something." Mark cursed himself, then added, "Kendra got everything early this morning."

His friends gave him matching scowls. "And you let her?" Ryan asked.

"She's a grown-ass woman. Aside from that, I was asleep, and she didn't ask my permission. I'll text Sean and let him know not to bother."

"I'm adding a paddle to your picnic," Jake said. "That woman needs her butt spanked."

"You'll get no argument from me," Mark muttered.

Leaving his friends, he dumped the laundry in one of the industrial washers, then grabbed fresh linens. After making the aftercare beds, he went back to the small apartment he shared with his friends and collected several shotguns and other supplies from the communal gun locker in the living room.

It might not be a traditional first date, but it was the one he'd mentioned to Kendra. Knowing that didn't explain why he was so nervous though. Mark felt nothing about making play partners come until they cried, but the thought of a vanilla date with a picnic made his palms sweat.

———

KENDRA

She woke long before her alarm went off, feeling refreshed and in much less pain. Sitting up in bed, she browsed her phone for rental companies. Maybe buying a house wasn't going to work out, but there were a few charming houses south of Winslow. She called the property manager of her favorite and left a message, not expecting a return call on a Sunday.

After answering a few emails, she got up and dug through her suitcase for something like Mark had requested. Most of her clothes and personal belongings had been shipped to a nearby storage facility so she didn't have much, but eventually found a pair of jeans and a T-shirt, plus hiking boots.

As Kendra finished dressing, her phone rang. Glancing at the number in surprise, she answered.

"Hello, this is Kendra Hall."

"Hi Kendra. This is Rachel Garret from Navajo Property Management returning your call about the Lakeside house you found on our website. Would tomorrow be a better time to talk?"

"Thank you for returning my call. I didn't expect to hear from you today, but I'm happy to talk about it."

"I was in the office getting some paperwork done anyway. The house is still available, so if you're interested, fill out the online application. I should be able to get the background check finished up in a few days, then you can come by the office to sign the lease and pay your deposit."

"Wonderful. Is it still available for a six-month lease?"

"Yes, but the owner might consider extending it."

"That won't be necessary. I plan to build, so six months is perfect."

"Great! I'll keep an eye out for your application. It was a pleasure speaking with you."

"Thanks. You too."

Smiling, Kendra ended the call and felt tension leave her shoulders as she completed the online application. It was probably dishonest, but Kendra put the name of the Horsemen's corporation as her employer, not the club itself. There was no sense ruining her chances for another house with the information—especially since it was one of the few that was furnished. To be fair, she wasn't truly lying. The corporation was her employer.

Glancing at the time, she hurriedly tied her boots, then grabbed a bottle of sunscreen and applied it liberally to her arms and face. Given what Mark had asked her to wear, she was fairly certain whatever he planned would take place outside.

The sudden knock at her door made her jump with surprise, but she opened it to reveal Mark. He wore jeans and a blue polo with the resort logo stitched on the breast. Boots covered his large feet, and he had a leather jacket tossed over one arm.

Given his attire, she felt better about her choices.

"Hi. I just need to grab a jacket, then I'm ready to go."

"You're right on time," he murmured, giving her an appreciative gaze. "And you look perfect."

"Thanks. I'm lucky I had something. Most of my clothes are in storage."

"Do you need a jacket? I have one you can borrow."

"Nope. I'm good." She reached into the closet and retrieved a baseball cap and a windbreaker lined with polar fleece she knew would keep her warm after sundown, then got a pair of sunglasses from her purse. "So, what are we doing?"

"It's a surprise." Offering her his arm, he escorted her down the corridor, but didn't go out the main entrance. Instead, he led her past the restaurant to a service exit near the dungeon.

A large ATV with a trailer was parked a few yards from

the door, loaded with a cooler, a portable propane grill, a folded table, and two canvas chairs. There was also a duffel bag, plus a target thrower.

Smiling happily, she pointed at the thrower. "You should have said something. Do you mind waiting while I grab my shotgun?"

"You don't need it. I have several I thought you might want to try, including a couple of actual trap guns. You can figure out what you like without spending for rental fees. Jake put us together a picnic too."

"Wow, thank you. That was very thoughtful."

It was more than thoughtful. It was exactly what she'd wanted to do. Tears burned in her eyes, and she blinked them back before he saw her crying. She wasn't a crier and didn't understand why she wanted to do it now.

"No problem." He grabbed a helmet and handed it to her. "Ready to go?"

"Sure. How far is it?" She put her jacket and cap into the trailer, then slid the helmet over her head.

"About ten minutes." He swung a long leg over the seat, then held out a hand to help her on. "Watch your step."

"Thanks." She settled behind him, her pulse quickening at the feel of his hard body between her thighs and swallowed a gasp as he shifted his weight to start the ATV. If she hadn't known better, she'd have sworn he did it on purpose.

"Hold on tight," he murmured, taking her hands to wrap them around his waist.

His muscles twitched and rippled under her palms, and she resisted the urge to pet him. Thankfully, the engine noise prevented conversation. The vibrations, combined with the occasional bump on the trail, made her think of how Mark had touched her. How he...

She tried not to think about it, but by the time he parked the ATV in the shade of a gnarled tree, Kendra was about an inch away from tearing off her clothes and jumping Mark's bones. Warm wetness trickled from her core to dampen her panties and she closed her lips on a whimper as she climbed off the vehicle. Even the touch of his hand on her elbow sent a surge of electric desire into her belly.

"Do you want to eat first or start playing?" he asked, unloading the trailer.

"Let's shoot first. We've got a couple of hours until sunset." Using a firearm would keep her mind off her damp panties. Hopefully anyway.

"Okay." He set up the target thrower several yards from the ATV and pointed it toward the desert.

"Who does this property belong to? Do we have permission to shoot here?"

"It's ours. This is the southwest corner of a five-hundred-acre parcel we got along with the resort property."

"It's gorgeous." Although it wasn't the wooded property she'd wanted, its austerity made it strangely compelling. The late afternoon sunlight bathed a distant ridge in red, making it appear to glow, and she imagined the landscape would be filled with desert wildflowers after a rain. She could almost picture a Spanish-style hacienda facing the ridge. The living room would look out over...

She had to forcibly push away the idea of asking him to sell it to her. Five hundred acres was more than she needed, and she wouldn't have time to care for it like it deserved. Deciding to make herself useful, she followed him, carrying a box of clay pigeons, and set it down. "Here you go. Do you want me to load the thrower?"

"Sure. I'll grab the shotguns and be right back."

Two hours later, her shoulder ached and the detritus of a whole box of targets littered the desert. Laughing happily, she snapped a quick photo of her favorite of the shotguns he'd brought her to try, meaning to order her own later.

She still loved the one her grandfather had left her, but the elegant trap gun felt like it had been made for her and was a dream to shoot. "How much should I budget for this?" she asked, returning it to him.

He zipped a padded gun case closed around it, then stowed it in the duffel bag. "A couple of thousand, probably. It's a good choice for you, but there's no rush. You can use this one whenever you want. You can also store yours in the gun locker in our apartment if you prefer."

"Thanks. I'd feel better if it was secured. And thank you for setting this up. I think this is the best date I've ever had."

Returning her grin, he collected the target thrower. "And I haven't even fed you supper yet."

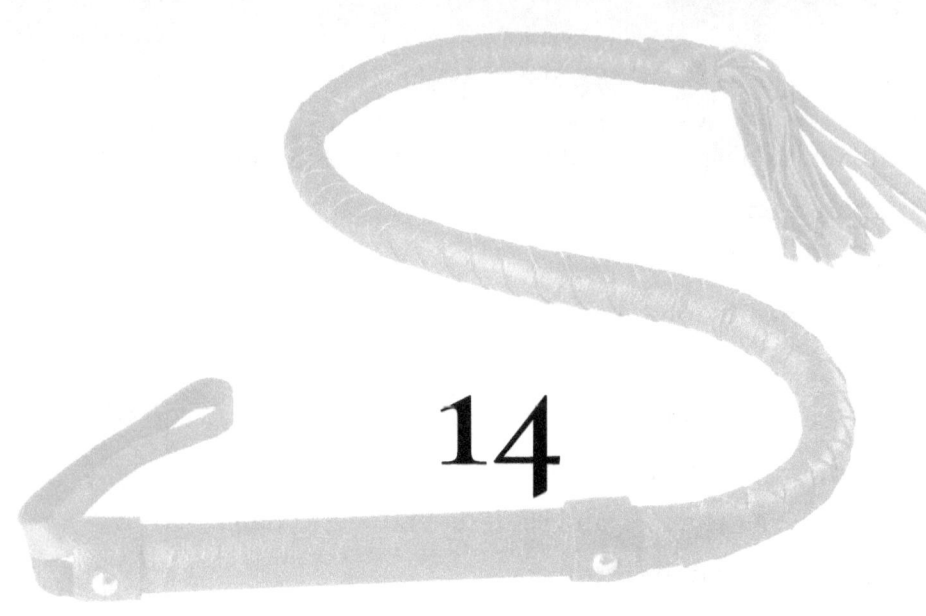

14

MARK

Although he was impressed with himself for keeping his hands off Kendra for a whole two hours, Mark knew it wouldn't last. Every time he caught a whiff of her floral perfume as he corrected her form or moved past her to reload the target thrower made it that much more difficult to keep his distance.

In an effort to get his mind off her deliciously curved backside which still needed to be spanked, he grabbed the folding chairs and table from the ATV trailer.

"Let me help."

"Sure." While she took care of the table and chairs, he set up the grill and used the attached sparker to light it.

"I'm dying to see what Jake packed for us, but I hope he included instructions. I'm not much of a cook." She glanced over his head at the setting sun and smiled. "The scenery is gorgeous too."

"I wouldn't say I'm on Jake's level, but I don't do too badly with a grill."

Squeezing next to him, she peered into the cooler and retrieved a bottle of wine, plus a pair of stemless glasses. "This is my idea of cooking. I'm great with a corkscrew."

Laughing, he glanced at the sheet of instructions taped to the inside of the cooler lid. "Looks like Jake gave us leftovers. We're having grilled lamb kebabs with fingerling potatoes and Brussels sprouts."

"That sounds delicious." She poured the wine and handed him a glass. "Here's to the best leftovers I've ever eaten."

"I'm not a fan of Brussels sprouts."

"Me neither, but I didn't like artichoke dip until I tried his." She tipped her glass toward him and drank. "Besides, if we both hate them, we'll just scatter them for the critters and eat everything else. I also have a plateful of pastries left over from breakfast."

Chuckling, he put the foil-wrapped vegetables on the grill, then checked the time. "He has flourless chocolate cake for dessert, so I doubt we'll need to dig into your stash."

"I'd like to say I have enough self-control to skip dessert, but…" She shrugged, then took another sip of wine. "I really don't."

"He's trying to impress you. I promise, we don't usually eat like this. Well, not for breakfast and lunch anyway. We get kitchen leftovers for supper, and it never includes dessert."

"Jake had me with his prime rib. He doesn't need to work that hard." She set her glass on the table and leaned forward on her elbows. "Truthfully, you've all impressed me with the way you've given new life to an old motel."

"You want a lot of changes for someone who's impressed."

Her smile faded and he wanted to kick himself for bringing business into what was supposed to have been a pleasant evening. "Are there any you truly object to?"

"I'm sorry," he finally said. "That was out of line."

Reaching over the table, she touched his hand, sending tingles up his arm. "Club Apocalypse is your baby, Mark. You, Ryan, Sean, and Jake have poured your souls into it, and you're understandably protective. I'm not asking you to change what makes it special. I'm asking you to let me help you keep it alive."

"I know." He went silent for a moment as he tried to put his thoughts into words. "I guess it's just…hell, I can't explain it and make it sound at all logical or professional, much less adult. I know we need help, but—"

"Let me ask you something. Is it me personally you object to?"

"No." He drained his wineglass but held a hand over it when she offered a refill. "But in some ways, yes, even though I know you're the best at what you do."

"I think I'm flattered?" She gave him a wry smile, then added, "I don't want to watch Club Apocalypse go under, so tell me what I can do to alleviate your concerns."

He studied her for a moment, wondering if he dared tell her what he was thinking. Unfortunately, he didn't have another answer she might accept. "Intellectually, I know you're trying to help, but since you aren't into D/s, I'm not sure you understand what having a safe, secure place to play means to our members."

"Who says I'm not into it?"

Mark opened his mouth, then closed it again and shook his head. "You never said one way or the other, did you?" he murmured. "You also took off like someone set fire to your tail when I tried to give you aftercare."

"You never asked, and at best, it's only tangentially related to my job. To answer your question, I'm curious but you've seen the extent of my experience." She finished the last of her wine and corked the bottle. "As far as your after-care, I..."

She let her words trail off and shivered, then thanked him when he got her jacket and helped her put it on.

"What about aftercare?" he prodded gently.

"It seemed too intimate, and we're coworkers. I felt like if I let it happen, I...we would be crossing a line."

Instead of answering, he rose and tended the grill as he considered her words. "You're right," he finally said, not looking at her.

He couldn't let her see the disappointment on his face. It occurred to him to demand her resignation so he could introduce her to his world, but Sean, Jake, and Ryan would throw a fit if he did something that stupid. It drove him nuts to know the one woman he actually enjoyed touching was off-limits—especially after her admission of interest in D/s.

She laid her hand on his back, making him hide a flinch of surprise. He'd been so lost in his thoughts that he hadn't heard her approach. Gently, she pushed his shoulder to turn him.

"I rarely say this, but there are times I hate being right." Despite her words, she stepped closer into his space, bathing him with the warmth of her body. "I think I don't care."

The gentle brush of her lips over his turned his blood to flame, the conflagration burning him from the inside as he cupped the back of her head and deepened their kiss. She tasted like wine and passion, and he swept his tongue into her mouth, desperate for more of her heady essence.

Mark had never been one for kissing. At best, he could usually manage a perfunctory cheek kiss for a partner after a scene, but with Kendra...

He never wanted to stop.

———————

KENDRA

An explosion sounded overhead, storybook fireworks from true love's first kiss. If she hadn't been afraid of falling over, she'd have lifted her foot.

Breathing hard, Mark pulled away and swore as he looked up. "We have to go now."

"But—"

"Now, Kendra!" Grabbing her hand, he dragged her to the ATV.

Without warning, the sky opened up, drenching them both as lightning forked across the sky. The temperature dropped, going from pleasantly cool to freezing in mere seconds.

"What about the—"

"Forget it." Quickly, he unhooked the trailer and mounted the ATV, then pulled her behind him. "I'll come back for everything later."

Pressure rose in her ears, and it seemed as if she'd gone momentarily deaf as the ATV rocketed toward the resort. She caught a faint scent of ozone a split second before a scrub oak barely ten feet away exploded in a flash of lightning and flame.

She closed her mouth, stifling the whimper of fear bubbling in her throat. It was just a desert thunderstorm, but her mind gave her images of flash floods sweeping them away in a deluge.

They hadn't even taken the time to put on their helmets, but Mark sped toward the resort as if they weren't in danger of crashing. Yet the thought of wrecking didn't scare her as much as the storm raging overhead.

"Almost there," he said, his voice barely discernible over the roaring ATV. He took one hand off the controls and squeezed her wrist. "We'll be fine."

"I know." She tightened her arms around his waist, then closed her eyes and laid her cheek on his muscular back. Her words were absolute truth. Kendra barely knew Mark, but she had no doubt he'd get them to safety.

The rain beat down on her like a hammer, the drops stinging until she thought they might draw blood. Yet the storm stopped just as suddenly as it started, and she lifted her head to look up into a brilliantly clear early evening sky. The resort was a scant hundred yards in front of them.

She choked out a laugh that might have been a sob of relief as they slowed to a stop by the service entrance. "Looks like Mother Nature is done with her tantrum. We can go back out if you want."

"No." He slid off the ATV and lifted her into his arms, then used his keycard to unlock the door. "It's freezing and we're soaked."

He carried her inside but didn't go to the dungeon or her suite. Instead, he strode down a short hallway to a door marked employees only and entered a code into a keypad. The door opened into a comfortable living room with a couch and four recliners. There was a massive television mounted on the far wall with a gaming system on a media stand underneath it.

The room widened into a spotless open-plan kitchen with a breakfast bar and four stools. It was modern and efficient, but simply designed with inexpensive appliances and fixtures. Judging by the four doors closed against her perusal, this was the apartment shared by the Horsemen. Aside from the television, it was more than obvious they'd spent the bulk of their savings on the public areas of the property.

"This is nice."

"Thankfully, it's clean," he muttered.

"Oh! Speaking of clean, we need to go back for the trailer."

"Don't worry about it." He carried her into the room on the far right and straight into a large bathroom. "Get undressed and in the shower. I'll find you a robe and be right back."

Without waiting for her to answer, he left, shutting the door behind him.

"I was going to help," she muttered. Unfortunately, he was probably right about her need to get warm. Her teeth were chattering, and she shivered so hard it was almost impossible to untie her boots.

By the time she managed to wriggle out of her sodden clothes, she was exhausted, but stepped into the large shower enclosure and turned on the water, gritting her teeth as the heated spray struck her chilled skin.

As she contemplated using Mark's soap and shampoo, he knocked, then stepped into the bathroom and stripped, revealing cut muscles and a dark treasure trail leading to his flaccid cock. Goosebumps pebbled his skin, and his lips were tinged blue.

"Damn it, Mark!" She opened the glass door and yanked him into the shower, then pushed him under the spray. "You're frozen! Get in here."

"Bossy." He spoke the word between clenched teeth but tried to smile. "My fault you got wet."

"Hush." She grabbed his soap, then washed his shoulders and back until he stopped shivering and relaxed. As his skin warmed, her touch became less clinical and more... sensual. Languid, yet purposeful.

Despite her touch and the warmth of the water, Mark seemed to stiffen into rigidity, unmoving as he stared at the shower wall. In another attempt to bring his body temperature back up, she turned him to face the shower spray.

Without warning, he jerked out of reach and took a step back. Instead of meeting her eyes, he kept his gaze fixed over her head. "If you're warm enough, I'll finish up while you get dressed. Do you need someone to walk you back to your room?"

"No, thank you." Anger, humiliation, and hurt turned in her stomach, but she stepped from the shower. After drying off, she dressed in the robe, then grabbed her clothes and strode from the apartment without saying goodbye. Considering he didn't even offer to walk her back himself; he didn't deserve the courtesy.

How could she have gotten it so wrong? She would have sworn her interest was mutual, and now she looked like a needy... No. She wasn't going to call herself that—even if that was what she appeared to be.

Daniel would have certainly called her a whore if she dared ask for sex. According to him, women didn't have needs.

Worse, she now had to do a walk of shame back to her room when she hadn't done a single damned thing to earn it. Then again, Club Apocalypse was an adult resort. It was highly unlikely she was the first person to creep back to a room wearing a bathrobe. Or nothing at all. Straightening her shoulders, she pasted a smile on her face as she crossed the lobby.

"Are you okay?" Sierra asked from her position behind the front desk. "I heard you and Mark got caught in the storm."

"I'm fine, thanks. No harm done."

"Good. Have a great evening."

"You too."

Praying no one else stopped her, she kept her footsteps measured and unhurried, unwilling to let anyone know how fucking furious she was. Thank goodness she was moving soon, and that she'd never gone beyond a few kisses with Mark. That would have killed her.

15

MARK

He wondered how many times he could bang his head against the tile before he lost consciousness. Not that unconsciousness would help. He'd still be the dumbass who froze when a beautiful woman touched him.

The afternoon had been perfect. He and Kendra had found a shared hobby they both enjoyed. The conversation was easy and interesting. Kissing her was...

Sublime. Arousing.

Incredible.

Even the storm hadn't been so bad. He'd long since gotten used to the random thunderstorms popping up without warning. They disappeared as fast as they arrived and left blooming wildflowers behind.

He would have loved to show them to her, but he had to go and be a whacked-out idiot. Worse, he'd completely forgotten about feeding her, and had left a mess behind.

"Fuck." He turned off the water, then grabbed a towel and dried off.

Maybe it was for the best. She had a point about them working together, and it was going to be awkward enough to face her in the morning without adding sex to the mix.

Mark had to tell her something though. Judging by the lack of expression on her face, she was angry and hurt and he didn't blame her. His logical inner self said she would understand if he told her about his issues, but he couldn't picture himself getting the words out.

Hey, you're gorgeous and brilliant, and I really love touching you, but you can never touch me back.

He didn't have to imagine how well that would fly, but he had to try. She deserved an apology and an explanation.

After dressing in fresh clothes, he took the ATV back out to collect everything they'd left behind, then stored it in the utility shed. Once that chore was taken care of, he crossed the property to the eastern wing housing the guest suites, unwilling to risk encountering anyone.

Letting himself in through the side entrance, he walked to her door and forced himself to knock. He'd stalled long enough, and it was time to face the music.

He heard nothing from the other side of the door and wondered if she'd already gone to bed. As he was considering whether to knock again, the door opened a few inches, allowing him to see only part of her face.

"Can I help you with something?" she asked, giving him an impassive stare.

"I..." He rubbed his face and shifted his weight in an attempt to get a better look at her. "Can we talk? Please?"

Kendra studied him for a moment, then nodded and opened the door to allow him in. She crossed the room and sat at the workstation but didn't glance at the open laptop.

As he entered, he saw the robe in a pile with a few dirty towels. She'd changed into yoga pants and a loose gray T-shirt. Her silky hair was clipped in a messy bun, and his fingers itched to release it.

"What can I do for you, Mr. Luciano?"

He sat across from her, suddenly unsure of himself. In the dungeon, he was Master Mark, yet that persona wouldn't help him explain what he needed to tell her. After several seconds of silence, in which her impatience obviously grew, judging by the way she drummed her fingers on the table, he finally spoke.

"I have an aversion to touch. I thought I had it under control and that we could..." He let out a sigh and stood. "Anyway, I'm sorry."

She gazed at him, then cracked the tiniest of smiles. "You

do realize, of course, that you could have said a safe word instead of chewing your arm off to escape."

"I—"

"In fact," She rose from her chair and stepped closer, but didn't invade his space. "I seem to remember someone taking great pains to impress upon me how well they work, but his name escapes me."

"I can't imagine who that might have been," he murmured. "Sounds like a veritable genius."

"Yes, I thought so too." Kendra moved around him and went to the minibar. "There's a decent bottle of wine here, and I still have leftover pastries. Want to try again for that supper date?"

"Well, considering this was about when I thought you'd be throwing me out, why not?" He joined her at the minibar and opened the wine while she carried the pastries to the table. "I thought you'd still be angry."

"I am." She unwrapped the pastries, then grabbed a few washcloths to serve as napkins. "I'm mad that you didn't tell me—not that you're touch averse."

He nodded and poured their wine, then sat across from her. "You have every right to be."

"So, why didn't you?"

He took a bite of his pastry, more to give himself time to think than out of hunger. "I thought I had it under control," he finally said. "We slept in the same bed. I touched you all night, and it was perfectly fine."

"I see."

"No, it was better than fine. I haven't slept that well in years." He stood and turned away, then pushed his hands through his hair in frustration. "I just don't get it."

"Mark, will you do me a favor?"

"Yes, of course." He turned to face her, wondering what she needed. The conversation wasn't going as he'd planned, and he had no idea where things would end up.

"Repeat what you said, please."

"I was better than fine—"

"No, just before that."

He frowned at her abrupt tone, then said, "Something about I touched you all night."

She stood and put her arms behind her back in a classic submissive pose that made him want to bend her over the nearest object and either spank her ass or fuck her. "Touch me."

"No. That isn't a good idea, Kendra."

"Humor me." She stood calmly, as if waiting to see what he'd do.

Letting out a soft curse, he approached her and put a hand on her shoulder. Her floral perfume wafted around him, the scent warm and calming as he stroked her upper arm, then trailed his fingers over the outer curve of her breast. She inhaled, then let out a soft murmur of appreciation.

Still petting her, he waited for the inevitable panic. He'd

start to sweat, then freeze, and if he got very lucky, he wouldn't throw up.

Yet it never came, and the tension in his shoulders eased as he breathed her in. He didn't know if it was because of that enticing fragrance, or because it was Kendra—the one woman he'd actually wanted to touch.

"I... Can I kiss you?"

"Go for it." Lifting her chin, she closed her eyes, letting him take his time.

He brushed a gentle kiss over the corner of her mouth, and it felt as perfect as he remembered. His cock thickened with the reminder of holding her in his arms.

Before he could deepen their kiss, she took a step back and dropped her arms, then smiled. "You don't like being touched. You're perfectly fine if you're doing the touching."

Mark froze, considering the idea. It had been distasteful, but he'd been able to touch Shelby Baldwin without having a panic attack. He'd also handled dozens of demos and had even managed intimacy on a few rare occasions if his partners were restrained.

Maybe Kendra was right. He'd never really thought about it, but it made sense. His worst meltdowns always came when people touched him without warning, or he was forced by circumstance or proximity to tolerate lingering contact.

Would it be different with Kendra?

He didn't know, but he wanted to find out.

KENDRA

She returned to her seat and tipped her wineglass toward him. "Fascinating discovery, isn't it?"

Instead of answering, he gazed over her head as if he was lost in thought. She waited patiently, giving him time to digest the information.

Although Kendra was still annoyed, she didn't want to take it out on Mark. It wasn't his fault he was touch averse. It was just...a thing—and it wasn't much different from her constant notetaking. She hadn't lied about why she was angry either but decided to let it go since he'd already apologized. That didn't mean she'd let him get away with bullshitting her again.

"It sounds stupid," he finally said, giving her a wry smile. "It's like a kid thinking if they can't see you, you can't see them."

"No, it really doesn't. Brains are weird."

He sat across from her and took her hand, watching himself stroke her knuckles as if the gesture surprised him. "Your brain isn't."

"Actually, my therapist told me they were, so..." She shrugged, letting the rest go unsaid.

"Why would you need therapy? Unlike me, you've got your shit together."

"No, I just make crazy look good." Kendra smiled briefly, then let out a sigh. "My ex-husband is a narcissist and spent ten years destroying my self-confidence. He gaslit me so badly, I became convinced I was suffering from early-onset Alzheimer's, so I went to a doctor. The doc got suspicious and sent me to a counselor specializing in spousal abuse."

Expressions flashed across Mark's face so quickly she almost couldn't follow them. Shock, horror, surprise, then anger. His fingers tightened almost painfully on her hand, and he rumbled out an ugly curse. "I had no idea. I'm sorry. You were incredibly strong to get yourself out."

"Thanks." She tried to ignore the warm glow of his approval. "Anyway, the counselor gave me some coping tips, and recommended I start taking notes about every conversation."

"What happened?"

"We had a prenuptial agreement separating our finances. I filed for divorce when he tried to have me declared mentally incompetent so he could seize my assets. All those notes, recorded conversations, and medical exams were used as evidence." She snorted out an ugly laugh. "He was so convinced he had me on the ropes he agreed to let me record him in front of a room full of witnesses."

The memory of the incident crawled through her mind, making her stomach churn. Daniel had publicly humiliated her at a charity ball, telling everyone she was too mentally impaired to follow a conversation without recording it.

"I have a burning desire to drive to Houston and beat him up." He didn't stop petting her hand, and asked, "Is that why you're always writing things down?"

Her face heated and she nodded. "Yeah. Logically, I know I don't need to do it anymore, but—"

Mark nodded and softened his touch on her hand. "It's a comfort mechanism, and I took it away from you the first time we met. I'm sorry."

"It's okay. You had no idea. Besides, I should have thought about using a notepad instead of my phone without being told." Unwilling to push her luck, she eased her hand away and took a sip of wine. "Maybe you could find your own that isn't quite so obviously bizarre. It's like a crutch for me, you know? I still need proof that I'm not losing my mind. Hell, I question myself every time I misplace my keys."

"We're all mad here," he murmured, his lips quirking into a sexy half-grin.

She barked out a surprised laugh, remembering him call her Alice the first time he took her into the dungeon. "But I don't want to go among mad people."

"Too late. You're already here, and we're keeping you." He stood and held out a hand. "Want to help me with a little research?"

She stood and took his hand. Although he shivered, he squeezed her fingers instead of letting her go. "What kind of research?"

"Bring your legal pad. I want to see how good your notes are when I'm touching you in the dungeon."

Even knowing intimacy with Mark was a bad idea, Kendra wanted it. There was just something about him... He was the sexiest man she'd ever met, but it was more than that. Maybe it was that touch of vulnerability underneath the surly bluster, or the way he'd dropped everything to keep her safe from the storm.

It might have been realizing he was a little bit broken just like she was, and she wanted to believe their jagged edges would fit together.

He grinned with excitement, then sobered when she didn't immediately reply. "Well, if you agree anyway. You don't have to say yes. I just thought—"

"Let me get some shoes." She went to her closet and slid her feet into a pair of flip-flops. "And this time, I won't run if you want to give me aftercare."

16

MARK

He held Kendra's hand as they walked down the corridor and had absolutely no desire to let her go. In fact, he almost wished there were people around so he could show off.

Not only had Kendra agreed to let him touch her, she was willing to be seen in public with him. Well, sort of public. The dungeon was closed on Sunday, and their only guests were hikers planning to take advantage of Apocalypse's proximity to Homolovi, plus a few retirees who had stopped to visit the iconic corner of Second and Kinsley in Winslow with its statue of a guitar player.

Sierra was busy on the phone as they passed the front desk, but she gave their clasped hands a pointed glance and smirked at him. His face heating, Mark surreptitiously flipped her off behind his back.

As he swiped his master keycard through the lock, he said, "Remember, you can bail at any time. You don't even need to use a safe word. Just ask me to stop."

Laughing softly, she squeezed past him and pushed the curtain aside. "I should be telling you that."

He followed but couldn't decide whether he should spank her cute butt for the snark. He wasn't used to people teasing him—especially not a woman he desperately wanted to make love to.

Mark's footsteps stalled as the words rang through his mind. He fucked. He didn't make love. Not ever. It implied connection and intimacy, and he didn't know if he could do it.

But he wasn't going to give up without trying first.

After taking a moment to pull himself together, Mark let out a cleansing breath and dimmed the house lights until the dungeon was lit with a warm, muted glow. Standing in the middle of the room close to the center stage, Kendra looked like she'd been washed in amber, the light turning her into a gilded angel. She turned in place, watching the play of illumination across the wall of erotic art.

When he reached her, he held up his hand. "I do solemnly swear to use a safe word instead of chewing off a limb to escape."

"And I promise to let you give me as much aftercare as

you're able to do." She flipped to a clean sheet of paper and scrawled her name on the page. "Should we both sign on it?"

Nodding, he took the pad from her and wrote his name, then handed it back.

She smiled at the page and gazed at him, her warm brown eyes sparkling with humor. "Master Mark?"

"In here, at least, but never when we're working." He moved behind her and removed the clip from her hair, allowing her blonde curls to spill past her shoulders. "Whatever we do will be between the two of us unless we both decide we're okay with other people knowing."

"Um…" She licked her lips, then swallowed. "Yes, that would be for the best. We're doing something kind of unprofessional, and I don't want things to get awkward."

Wasn't that the truth? Crossing his fingers, he prayed he wasn't making a mistake.

"Shh. This is just for us. We're both too old and sensible to make this a thing. Tomorrow morning, we go back to being Mr. Luciano and Ms. Hall. I'll go out of my way to irritate you and be slightly jealous you like Jake's food better than you like me. You'll spend part of your day arguing with me while you chase Sean away from Dr. Knox."

She laughed, then glanced over her shoulder. "Yes, Master Mark, but to be fair, Jake's food is pretty amazing." Sobering, she added, "For what it's worth, I don't want to argue with you."

He didn't want to argue with her either—especially when she seemed to be right more than she was wrong.

So far, at least.

He lifted her silky hair in his hands, resisting the urge to bury his nose in it. Slowly, he braided it, then secured the end with a hair tie from his pocket.

"You're being a very good girl," he murmured close to her ear. "Do you like being called a good girl?"

"I..." She let her head fall back, allowing him access to the smooth skin of her throat. "Yes, Master Mark."

Mark wrapped his arms around her and steadied the notepad. "Write what you're feeling when I tell you what a good girl you are."

With the notepad and pen in her hands, Kendra wouldn't be able to touch him back. The feeling of her in his arms was like nothing he'd ever experienced and hadn't realized he'd been missing.

The warmth of another person against his body. The silk of her hair against his cheek. He gazed over her shoulder as she wrote.

Happy. Turned on.

"Is that all?" He brushed a kiss over the smooth skin under her ear, relishing the sensation. It was like sparks tingling against his lips.

She shivered and wrote down another word, her penmanship as ragged and shaky as her breathing.

Wet.

"What else?" He nipped her earlobe then kissed the sting away.

Her fingers tightened around the pen as if she was afraid she'd drop it. "Scared," she whispered.

Kicking himself, he took a single step backward, then another. He outweighed her by at least fifty pounds, and she was by herself with a man she barely knew. Yet that didn't seem quite right. Kendra didn't strike him as a woman to panic over something like that, but he knew better than anyone that fear wasn't always logical.

"I'm sorry. I didn't mean to—"

She turned and blinked with surprise, then reached for him before pulling her hand back. "I'm not afraid of you. I'm afraid of me."

———

KENDRA

Mark nodded, then took her hand. "Let's sit down and talk about it."

She forced herself to keep her touch impersonal instead of holding him tight like she wanted. It would kill her to drive him away again. Yet when he sat, he pulled her into his lap, destroying her determination to keep her distance.

"What—"

"Shh. It's okay." He nuzzled her shoulder. "Tell me why you're afraid."

"I..." She huffed out a breath and tried to extricate herself from his lap without touching him. "I can't talk to you while I'm sitting here."

"Sure you can." He tightened his arms to keep her still.

"This isn't helping. Let me up."

He petted her thigh with long, languorous strokes as if he was gentling a wild animal. Kendra bit back a moan as his callused hand brushed her hip. Maybe this was better though. In his lap, she didn't have to look at him, and he couldn't see the desperate need she was sure was on her face.

"I can do this all night, baby girl." He feathered his fingers up her rib cage to brush the underside of her breast. "Or you can tell me what I want to hear. Why are you afraid of yourself?"

Every touch brought her that much closer to the edge of something she'd sworn not to do. It was as if his hands had a direct line to her clit, and she had to remind herself he was touch averse. She tightened her fists in an effort to keep her hands to herself, but she was growing desperate to feel his bare skin.

Swallowing hard, she closed her eyes. "You're a sadist."

"Very good guess." His breath tickled the back of her neck. "I'm particularly fond of mind fucks."

"I've had my mind fucked quite enough, thanks."

"No, not like your asshole ex did." The scruff of his beard rasped against the skin under her ear and she nearly whimpered. "I want to tease you. I want to surprise you, confuse you, make you wonder when the next orgasm will come. Will it be now?"

He drew his hand up her stomach, then over her breast, sending a shockwave of pleasure through her body as he brushed her nipple.

"Or will it be later?" His hand settled on her thigh. "But I promise I won't hurt you beyond your ability to take, and I will never, ever abuse your trust."

"I'm afraid you're going to make me break your hard limit and touch you!" she burst out. "I'm afraid you're going to do all those things, and I won't be able to help myself. And then you'll freeze or run, or—"

He chuckled softly, then helped her up as he stood. "That's the last thing you need to worry about."

"What are you talking about? Of course, I'm worried! I don't want to abuse your trust either."

He hummed a response, then laid a hand on her lower back to escort her to a leather-covered spanking bench with brushed steel eyebolts set where her wrists and ankles would be. Kendra swallowed past the dryness in her throat, imagining herself shackled in place, unable to move while he did dirty, filthy things to her body.

"What's your color, Kendra?" Mark asked, surprising her from her aroused fugue.

"Chartreuse?"

"Not quite yellow, not quite green." He turned her to face him, his hands gentle on her shoulders. "Tell me what would move you to green."

"Don't..." She hauled in a breath, hoping Mark didn't take offense. "Don't restrain me. I know it's a lot to ask, but if something happens, you'll have to touch me to let me go."

"I see."

His face lost every hint of expression and she cringed inwardly. It hadn't been her intent to hurt his feelings or make more of his aversion to touch than there was, but it was a valid concern. She could just picture herself secured to the bondage bench, waiting for someone to let her free. Mark would be embarrassed and struggling, and she'd be in no position to help.

She didn't want that for him or for herself.

"I just don't want to make things worse, you know?"

He brushed his lips over her mouth in a painfully sweet kiss, then rested his forehead against hers. The gesture was incredibly intimate and made her heart stall, then leap in her chest.

"Sweetheart, that would be impossible because you only make things better."

Before she could call him a liar, he straightened and let her go, then went to the bar and fiddled with the sound system. A song she recognized but couldn't name emanated from recessed speakers. It wasn't too loud, yet the thumping beat seemed to penetrate her body.

Carrying a small duffel bag, Mark returned and circled her slowly, grazing her shoulders with his fingertips. "There's just something about you," he murmured, not giving her a chance to speak. "I almost want you to touch me."

Although the sentiment was nice, there wasn't anything special about her, and Kendra shook her head. "I don't think that's how an aversion works."

Gently, he took the notepad and pen from her and set them aside, then positioned her wrists behind her back with her elbows bent. "Do you know what honor bondage is?"

"No, not really."

"It means I'm trusting you to leave your hands where I put them."

Soft breath smelling of wine and chocolate warmed the back of her neck, sending a delicious shiver down her spine. Kendra tightened her fingers on her elbows as she remembered the haunted expression on his face when she touched him in the shower. Mark was good at hiding his feelings, but he wasn't that good and the last thing she wanted was to make him look like that again.

"I...okay. I'm ready."

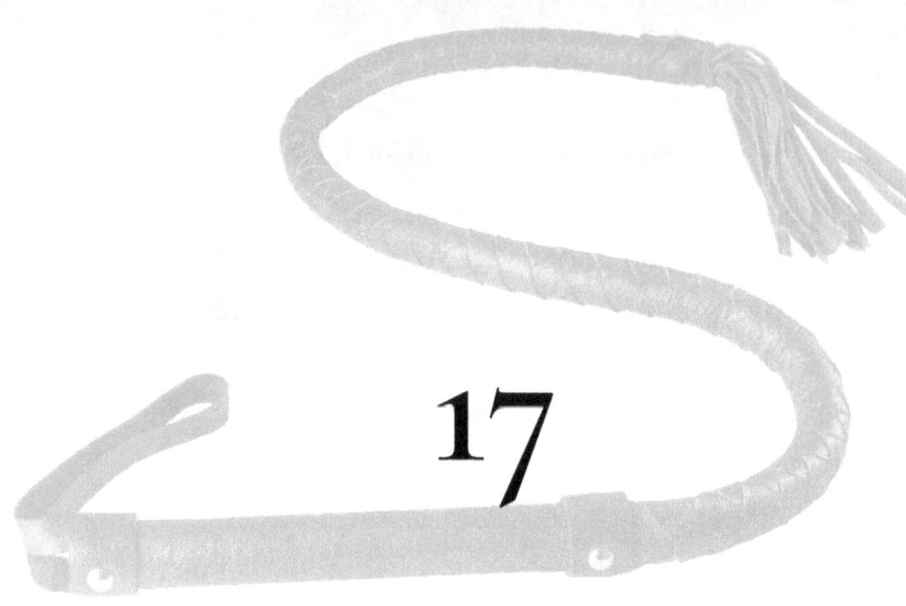

17

MARK

Goosebumps blossomed on Kendra's arms, following his fingertips as he touched her. Although she shivered, she didn't drop her arms. The position altered her posture, forcing her to move her shoulders and arch her back.

She might not have been bound, but she looked every inch the perfect submissive. Her beautiful breasts rose and fell with her breathing, making his mouth water for a taste.

"Are you comfortable undressing for me?" The question was rote, and one any good dominant would ask. Just because a woman agreed to play once didn't mean it would happen again.

"It's just us, right?" Without moving her hands, she

turned to face him. "I'm not sure I'm ready for a crowd to see all my old lady flab."

Mark shook his head and laughed softly. "First, you're not old, nor are you flabby. Even if you were, Club Apocalypse was founded on body positivity and acceptance. That means you never have to show more skin than you're comfortable with."

Her cheeks turned pink, and she lowered her head. "And what's the second thing?"

"The dungeon is closed on Sundays. Nobody will bother us."

"Okay. I...okay." She stepped away from him and dropped her hands, then closed her eyes. "Can't believe I'm doing this."

She shimmied out of her leggings, making him wish he could see her ass wiggle, then yanked her T-shirt over her head like she was angry at it. Pressing her lips together, she dropped it and folded her arms behind her back once more.

The diamond piercing her navel winked at him like a target, just waiting for him to play with it. Neatly trimmed blonde curls a shade darker than her hair guarded her sex. Her lush hips curved into a trim waist, drawing his eye up to the fullness of her breasts.

Maybe it was a dumb cliché, but they were a perfect handful, well-proportioned to her frame and tipped with the prettiest brown nipples he'd ever seen.

"Do I pass muster?" she asked, forcing him to meet her gaze.

"More than." He shook his head and gave her a smile, knowing he was acting like an adolescent. "Sorry. You're just really pretty. I almost wish Natalie Mercer was here to paint you."

Blushing, she returned his smile and her shoulders dropped almost imperceptibly. "That's um...a little out of my green zone, cowboy."

He moved behind her and rubbed her shoulders, further easing the tension. "I won't do anything that takes you out of that zone, Kendra."

"I know." Her rigid posture eased. "I'm ready to start whenever you are."

"Baby, we already have."

"Huh? I don't understand." She tried to turn, but he kept her in place, still kneading her shoulders. "This isn't what I expected."

"I know. Remember how I told you I like mind fucks?"

"Oh." Her muscles tightened again, and she shifted her weight as if she was about to escape.

"But I won't be cruel, and it will never be anything like what your ex-husband did." He turned her to face him with a careful touch on her arm. "That wasn't a mind fuck. It was abuse, and someone really needs to kick his ass for it."

"Couldn't agree more," she muttered.

Mark tilted her chin up to make her meet his eyes. "If

what we do isn't fun for you, it's definitely not going to be fun for me."

She let out a breath and lifted a hand to touch her forehead. "I know it up here. The rest of me is nervous."

"Oh, good." He swatted her butt gently after she'd folded her arm behind her back. "As long as you aren't scared, I like you being nervous."

Kendra's eyes sparkled with amusement. "No, I'm not scared."

"Hmm. Do you like roller coasters?"

She blinked at the off-topic question, then curved her plump lips into a fond smile. "I'm an addict for them, even the rickety wooden ones at state fairs that are a few loose bolts away from killing people."

Why was he not surprised?

"Interesting. Seems like you like being scared." Lowering his head, he nipped the tendon on the side of her neck. "Maybe I like you a little scared too. Ready to buckle up and enjoy the ride?"

KENDRA

She locked her knees before she keeled over. Mercy, the man was pushing all her buttons. She wouldn't have thought his mix of gentle understanding and sensual threat would have done it for her, but it really did.

Who would have thought she'd be willing to stand naked in public with a man she barely knew, where someone could walk in at any time? The dungeon was closed, but there were plenty of staff members wandering around, including the other three owners.

The idea of getting caught—of having an audience—made her even more aroused.

"Would you like to close your eyes, or would you prefer a blindfold?"

"I thought you made the decisions. You're the master, right?"

"Within reason." He stroked a hand down her spine, then palmed her ass. "You decide where we're going, but I decide how we get there."

"I'm not sure I understand."

"Good girl for telling me that." He patted her butt and gave it a gentle squeeze. "I don't want you to see what I'm doing, so I want you to either close your eyes and keep them closed or let me blindfold you. You get to pick which one."

"Didn't you want me to write things down?"

"You can take notes later, but I want to read them if you do." Giving her a half-smile, he added, "Now, the blindfold or keeping your eyes closed?"

"The blindfold."

"Okay." He pulled a length of black cloth from his bag,

then moved to stand behind her and tied it over her eyes without catching her hair in the knot. "Not too tight?"

She blinked, then let her eyes close. It seemed almost like cheating to try to peek. "No. It's comfortable."

"Good." He laid a hand on her elbow and walked her forward. "Just a few more steps to the bench, then I'll help you up."

Every word Mark spoke pulled her deeper under his spell. His voice was both soothing and tempting, yet she couldn't help remembering the *hold still* game they'd played and prayed he didn't make her do it again.

He was going to though. She shouldn't have bothered praying for that, but it didn't matter. He was trusting her to keep her hands to herself, and she wasn't about to abuse his faith in her.

"Careful, sweetheart, you're—"

Her knee hit something, and he caught her when she stumbled. "Ouch. Sorry."

"No, my fault. I didn't warn you in time. Are you okay?"

The concern in his voice warmed her and she nodded. "No harm done. I'm fine." She couldn't help a nervous giggle, and added, "Some sadist you are, worried over a little knee bump."

His hand landed on her ass in a hard spank that made her yelp. "That snarky mouth is going to get you in trouble, little girl."

The spank stung, but quickly turned into heat that

moved into her core like lava. Pressing her lips together, she tried to hold back another giggle. Judging by the tone of his voice, Mark was trying to stifle laughter too.

How had she missed this all these years? Sure, she'd read about it, but had believed the characters to be made up. Men who laughed during sex didn't exist.

But maybe she'd been wrong. Maybe she just hadn't found the right partner. There was one thing she did know. She wanted to hear him laugh again.

She felt him move and then the touch of his finger on her chin. Pressing gently, he made her lift her head and kissed her, tracing the seam of her lips with the tip of his tongue. It felt like she was balanced on the knife edge of need—desperate to deepen their kiss but unwilling to drive him away.

"Being a sadist doesn't always mean hurting people, Kendra," he murmured, brushing his lips over her ear. "It can, and I'm not going to say I won't hurt you, but I promise you're going to love it."

"And I say yellow if I don't, right?"

"Exactly. Or red if you need to, but I hope you'll use yellow first."

"I don't want to use either one."

He breathed out a soft curse and cupped her face in warm palms. "Kendra, this is very important. I have to trust that you will use a safe word if you need to."

"But—"

Mark kissed her again, probably to silence her. "It would be a dream come true to have a perfect scene where your only color is green, but you're a novice and we never did take time to go through limits."

"No body waste, no blood, no permanent marks." She wanted to kiss him again but didn't dare unless he initiated it. Aside from that, she had no idea if he was close enough. "I trust you, and I promise to use a safe word if I need it."

18

MARK

Talk about pressure.

His hands shaking, he helped Kendra mount the spanking bench. Her knees rested on the bolster, and she bent over the body of the bench to grab the eyebolts set in the frame, revealing the smooth expanse of her bare back.

He had no idea why he was so worried. He'd done hundreds of scenes with novice submissives, and not a one had ever called red. Logically, he recognized Kendra as an alpha sub. She submitted only at her own will and would probably flay the skin from his body with that acidic wit before she said a safe word.

Her treatment of anyone who crossed Gabby and Olivia

was more than enough evidence of that. Luckily, her shotgun was locked away in her suite. For someone just starting the hobby, she was an excellent shot.

This scene had to be perfect. He wanted to give her everything—all the pain and pleasure he could muster. It was more than wanting to make up for being a jerk to her, although that was in there too.

It had to be perfect because she was the first partner who knew his secret and didn't care. More than that, she was the first person who actively tried to make things work. She wasn't a masochist who wanted nothing but pain, or a brat who thought she could change him.

Or three best friends who thought he was broken.

Acceptance was a heady thing, and he couldn't stand the idea of fucking it up.

Letting out a breath, he stroked her back, feeling her muscles move under his hand as she relaxed into his caress.

"I love touching you," he finally said. "Your skin is like silk."

"I like it when you touch me." She arched against him like a spoiled cat but didn't protest when he moved his hand away.

Fuck, she was perfect.

Mark reached into his play bag and retrieved a soft doeskin flogger. It was gentle enough for a warmup but could deliver a decent sting if used correctly. Shaking the falls out, he limbered up his wrist, then let it fly to the lower curve of her bottom. Although she flinched and let out a soft squeak, she didn't move from her position.

"What's your color, Kendra?"

"Green. That was... Can you do it again?"

"Ask and you shall receive." Moving in a figure-eight pattern, he painted her gorgeous ass with the flogger until her skin blushed a faint pink, then slowly worked his way up, avoiding the area over her kidneys.

Moaning softly, she shifted her weight and stretched, relaxing under the gentle flogging. He wanted to do so much, yet the list of things he wanted to try would take days. Carefully, he slowed the warmup, then delivered a stinging blow to her ass.

"Ahh!" Her head rose and she stiffened as ruddy lines blossomed on her bottom. "Jesus, fuck!"

"Give me a color, honey."

"More green." She blew out an audible breath, then added, "Is it weird that I want you to do that again?"

He coughed out a laugh, then tossed the flogger aside and readjusted himself in his jeans. His dick wanted nothing more than to be buried in her slick heat. "No, but I have other things in store for you."

"Can't wait."

"Oh, really? Let's try something else." He tugged his master keycard from his pocket, unable to help a wicked grin. What he planned might make her call yellow, but he couldn't resist a small mind fuck.

He turned the card in his hand and used the edge to trace a line across her upper back. "What do you think about knives, little girl?"

She went still and even stopped breathing for a split second before relaxing again. "You're not going to cut me," she replied, surprising him. "But it is a little scary."

"Good." He pressed harder with the edge of the keycard, then drew a deeper line into the outer curve of her breast. "I love that you trust me, but I like scaring you too."

"Before you ask, I'm still green."

"Guess I better up my game." He pulled one of his favorite tricks from his bag of treats and unwrapped it. The pungent aroma of ginger surrounded them, spicy, yet sweet.

With a more experienced submissive, he'd insert the whole root into their anal opening, but Kendra was a novice. Instead, he brushed the root over her clit, making her flinch, then buck her hips, obviously seeking more of the glancing contact.

"Ginger? Are we doing aromatherapy?" she asked, her voice halting and breathless.

"Something like that." He opened the plastic bag, meaning to put the ginger away, but a wholly evil idea crept into his brain. "I think you deserve a reward for being such a good girl."

Using the tip of the root, he circled her clit, making sure to rub the juice over as much of her tender sex as he could.

"Mmmm." She pressed against him, shifting her position

to encourage him to push the root into her channel. "Feels good."

"I'm glad. Still green, I assume?"

"As grass, Master Mark."

"Perfect." He put the root away, ignoring her disgruntled muttering, then picked up the flogger.

"Not much of a reward," she said under her breath. "I—"

He delivered a stinging blow to her upper thighs, and she screeched, the sound like music. Again and again, he let the flogger strike her thighs, until she parted her knees to reveal her swollen pussy.

His mouth watered for a taste, and he cursed himself, remembering the ginger. This wasn't about him—it was all for Kendra, but sooner or later he'd tie her ass down and feast. Adjusting his aim, he sent one more delicate lash to her pulsing center.

"Fuck!" She bucked and tightened her hands on the eyebolts, but her knees almost slid off the bolster.

Mark caught her before she fell and settled her back on the bench but couldn't resist scattering a few kisses on her shoulders. "Give me a color, sweetheart. Are you okay?"

She caught her breath and shuddered, then slumped. "Green, and I have no idea."

———

KENDRA

She didn't know how the hell she was going to tell Mark she'd had a mini orgasm when he whipped her pussy.

Who did that?

He had her tied up and turned into knots, yet there was nothing binding her but his desire and her will. It was everything she'd ever imagined but didn't believe possible. Pain and pleasure melded together into a perfect storm of sensation, and she never wanted it to end.

She was desperate to touch him. Feel those hard muscles like velvet over steel. Yet doing so would break their fragile trust and he'd already given her so much.

Passion beyond imagining. Care. Attention. If she never got to have her hands on him, it would be enough. She refused to entertain the possibility of a *someday*. Even if she was his partner, she had no business expecting him to change for her.

Been there, done that. Had the mental scars to prove it.

"You have no idea, huh?" He palmed her ass and swirled a finger around her clit.

The immediate shock of burning arousal pulled her back into the moment and she let out an unintelligible whine. Chuckling, he removed his hand, yet the heat didn't fade. Instead, it felt as if he held a candle to her pussy.

She shifted her hips, desperate for something to alleviate

the tingling burn. Her core throbbed in time with her heart-beat. "I...no, but I feel like I'm on fire."

"You don't say. I wonder how that happened." He eased a finger into her channel, then rubbed her clit.

"Ahhh! Mark, please!" She'd thought physical contact would help, but it made things both better and worse. The fiery sensation crested until she thought she might go mad, yet every touch sent liquid passion seeping from her core.

"Does that help?"

"No! Yes! Fuck!"

He laughed and delivered an open-handed slap to her exposed pussy. The pulse of another mini-orgasm stole her breath, yet it teased instead of relieving her need. She let out a scream of frustration as tears pricked her eyes behind the blindfold.

"Poor baby. Let's see if I can make you feel better."

He moved behind her, making her wish she could see. She'd thought the blindfold would make him more comfort-able with her. If she couldn't see him, she couldn't touch him. Yet she had to be honest with herself.

Kendra liked not knowing what was going to happen. It was exactly like a roller coaster, and the laughter in his voice told her she was in for the ride of her life.

She felt a brush of air on her core, then...

"Fucking hell!"

Ice, freezing and wet, surrounded her core, but it did

nothing to alleviate the growing burn. Instead, it spread, burrowing deep as if the ice pushed it into her body.

"Language," he chided, pushing the ice into her channel.

"Oh, God! Dammit, Mark, fuck me please!"

"Well, if you insist, I'm sure I can oblige."

The words were smooth and innocuous, but a twinge of warning penetrated her need-fogged brain when she heard a click behind her. Something hard and cool touched her, then eased its way into her spasming channel. She felt a split second of relief, then heard another click.

Without warning, the object came to life and buzzed merrily against her g-spot. The sudden climax pulled her down like an undertow, stealing her breath until she didn't have enough air left to scream.

"Aww, baby, you came without permission," Mark purred. "Do you think that deserves a punishment?"

"Ungh." Warm hands massaged her shoulders, helping her remember to breathe. Even if she hadn't been blindfolded, she probably wouldn't have been able to see.

She almost wished she knew what kind of vibrator he used. It had rocked her world, but maybe it was more Mark than the toy.

He let out a murmur of approval, then pressed a kiss to her forehead over the blindfold. "What's your color, Kendra? Are you okay to continue, or do you need to stop?"

"I said, ungh."

"That's not an answer, but it was funny."

"So glad you're amused." She let out another breath and tried to get her brain back online. "Green. I'm green, but..." The words trailed off as he massaged her shoulders and back. "Will you make love to me?"

His hand on her back stilled and he didn't answer, making her realize what she'd asked. Making love meant touching and intimacy—something she knew he didn't want. Jerking away, she threw herself from the bench and staggered when her knees nearly gave out.

"Kendra, I—"

"Sorry! I'm sorry." Her hands shook as she pulled the blindfold away. He gazed at her, frowning in conflicted confusion. "I'll just...never mind. I'm sorry."

Crouching, she grabbed her pants and shirt, then tried to make her shaking legs carry her to the door.

"Stop, little girl."

She ignored the growled warning and forced herself to move faster. Just a few more steps and she'd be free of the mess she'd made.

A heavy weight slammed into her back as she reached the exit, pressing her against the wall. She gasped as Mark's hand circled her throat and squeezed.

"Big mistake, sweetheart. You should know better than to run from me."

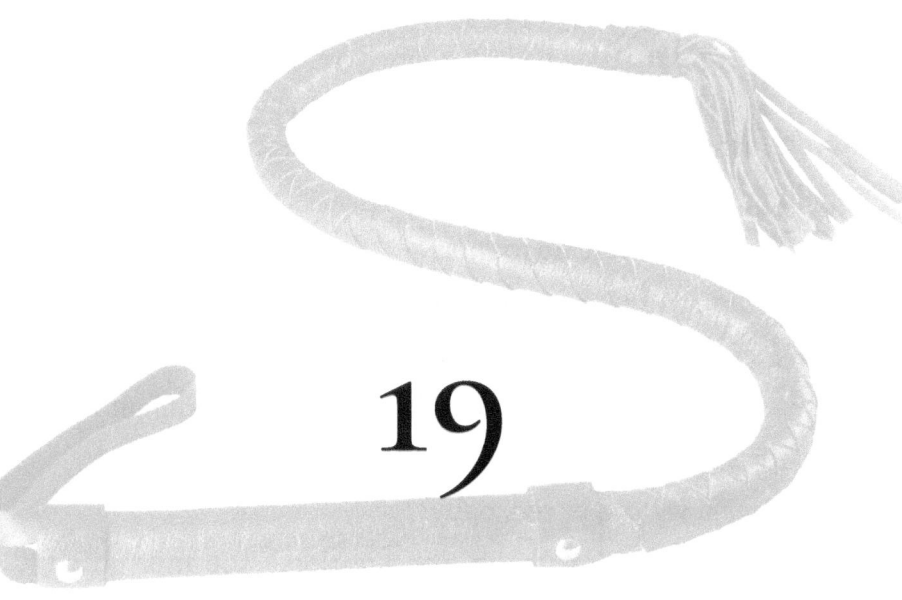

19

MARK

What was wrong with him?

He kept asking himself that question as he tossed Kendra over his shoulder, then strode to the aftercare rooms.

Her suite would be more comfortable, but he wasn't willing to wait, because fuck yes, he wanted to make love to her more than he'd ever wanted anything in his life. More than that, he needed it enough to risk the inevitable loss of control.

Hell, he'd already lost it. All he could focus on was reaching a bed and condoms as quickly as possible.

"Mark! Stop!" She clutched at his shirt, tugging the fabric almost enough to tear. "Listen to me!"

"Hush." He swatted her butt hard enough to sting, making her let out a surprised squawk, then carried her into the first of the aftercare rooms.

Without a word, he tossed her to the bed. She bounced once, then was off like a shot. He caught her before she could take more than a few steps and laid her down again, pinning her arms over her head.

"Green, yellow, or red, baby?"

"That was going to be my question," she murmured, gazing at him with those expressive brown eyes. Instead of shooting sparks of anger, they were warm and inviting, yet curious.

He softened his hold and touched his forehead to hers. "You're the first person who's ever asked me that."

"And what's the answer?"

"Grass, baby. Green as grass." Instead of letting her reply, he cupped the back of her head and kissed her, stroking her silken body with his free hand.

Her hands moved, making him stiffen, but instead of touching him, she grabbed his shirt. "As much as I want to admire the eye candy, leave this on so I have something to hang on to when you fuck me until I speak in tongues."

The words were a whispered breath against his lips and his cock surged against the zipper of his jeans, making him desperate to strip away the constricting fabric.

"You're fucking brilliant."

"How good of you to finally recognize that." She flexed her hips and bent her knee, opening herself for him.

The sweetly perfumed skin of her throat beckoned, and he trailed kisses to her shoulder, then nipped her. "Smart ass."

"Uh huh. Are you going to let me save a horse and ride a cowboy?"

Her eyes sparkled with humor, and he wanted to gaze into them for the rest of his life. "Condom, but I'm clean. I can give you my test results."

She let go of his shirt and stretched to grab one from the bowl on the nightstand. "Same and same."

Mark took the condom from her but hesitated when she stretched her arms over her head and laced her fingers together. His tongue felt thick, and he wanted to say something, but the words wouldn't come. He'd have to show her instead.

Scooting down the bed, he wedged his shoulders between her thighs and did what he'd wanted to do all along. Her pussy was so slick and warm, and she smelled like salt and feminine musk mixed with a faint hint of ginger. He slid his tongue between her folds, relishing her spicy sweetness, then lashed her clit with his tongue.

"Ah! God!"

She shuddered and lifted her hips, allowing him better access. More than anything, he wanted to devour her pussy until she came on his face. His cock ached and throbbed painfully, but he didn't dare take off his pants. It had been too long, and he wasn't about to go off like a teenager.

Tightening one hand on her hip, he pushed a finger into her channel, then added a second as he sucked her clit into his mouth. Crying out, she thrashed and bucked under him.

He lifted his head, then said, "Come for me, Kendra."

She shook her head and her back bowed as she gripped the sheets and tore them free. "I—"

Her voice broke on a scream when he increased the suction on her clit and curled his fingers, stabbing them hard into her g-spot. She exploded with a rush of liquid pleasure.

Smirking, Mark eased his touch. She'd be sensitive, and he wasn't quite done. Her eyes soft and slumberous, she gazed at him as he stripped off his boots and jeans, then tore the condom wrapper open and sheathed himself.

"You can leave your shirt on," she sang, slightly off key. "C'mere, cowboy."

He thought she'd reach for him, but she left her hands tangled in the sheets as if she'd bound herself. "You're very demanding," he murmured.

The twinkle in her eye made him bite back a laugh. "Cock inside me, now."

"I thought I was the dom." He knelt on the bed and crawled up to position himself between her thighs. She tilted her hips, actively seeking his cock and he felt the wet heat of her pussy through the thin latex.

"You already know I'm not above begging. Let's save some—"

She let out a choked scream as he reached between their bodies and positioned himself at her entrance, then thrust into her.

"Love to hear you scream," he gritted out, sliding a hand under her ass to deepen his penetration. He fucked her hard, barely noticing the bed slamming against the wall as she cried out under him.

"More, please!" Her begs were a repetitive catechism, spurring him on.

He was so lost in her, he barely noticed when she grabbed his shirt, fisting the fabric until the shoulder seams popped. Yet she never touched him. Not even when her eyes fluttered closed and she let out a breathless scream as her channel tightened and pulsed, drawing him down with her into the storm of passion.

———

KENDRA

Mark rolled away too quickly, and she tried not to let it hurt. She'd pushed too hard, too fast. Been too demanding. Too something. Instead of reaching out, she turned to her side, facing away from him.

"Hey, Mark?"

"Hmm?" She felt the bed move as he sat up, probably dealing with the condom.

"What's your color?"

Tears pricked her eyes when he didn't immediately answer, and she tightened her muscles to get up. With luck, she could dress before the awkward apology. Before she could move, he slid into bed behind her and pulled her against his chest, his long arms banding around her as tightly as rope.

"I'm the best shade of green there is. Bright green as plastic grass put in a kid's Easter basket. Maybe interstate sign green. Green as a primary color green. Green like—"

A tear escaped to trickle down her cheek, but she laughed. "Okay, I get it. I feel like I should give you aftercare though."

He rumbled out a pleasured sigh and buried his face in her hair. "Baby, you already are. Just decompress for a few minutes and I'll get you a snack and some water."

"Sure. You got it." She felt him relax against her, and within moments, he snored softly into her hair, his body softening with sleep. Carefully, she turned in his arms to face him.

In slumber, he looked younger. More innocent somehow, although that would never be a word she'd use to describe Mark Luciano.

As much as she wanted to stay, she wasn't interested in the inevitable morning-after. Kendra eased out of his arms, careful not to wake him. There would be questions, halting explanations, and discomfort, but she was going to meet it on her own terms—not naked with the evidence of their passion dripping down her thighs.

Her time with Mark might be one of his future regrets, but it wouldn't be hers. Kendra doubted she'd ever forget how he'd touched her.

After grabbing her clothes, she crept from the room and slid the pocket door shut behind her before dressing. She had no idea what had happened to her flip-flops but didn't have time to look for them. Thankfully, she had her keycard in the pocket of her leggings, which would give her access to the external doors.

She slipped from the dungeon and out the service exit, then ran past the pool to the west wing like all the hounds of hell were chasing her. Thankfully, she made it back to her suite without encountering anyone. Once she had the security deadbolt engaged, she stumbled into the shower.

The scent of ginger chased her, seeming to rise with the steam. A small laugh escaped as she belatedly realized he'd used it on her sex for the burn. Thankfully, it faded under her lavender body wash.

"Dumbass," she muttered to herself as she turned off the water and dried off. "Seriously, aromatherapy is all you came up with?" Still appalled at her own stupidity, she put on panties and a clean T-shirt, then crawled into bed. With luck, everything would be fine in the morning.

To her surprise, Mark didn't say a word the next morning. Or the next. In fact, he became so good at avoiding her,
two weeks went by without a single conversation between
them that wasn't related to business. The few times she
managed to catch him, he was actively dismissive and
seemed almost angry.

She tried to tell herself she was fine with it. Workplace
romances were a bad idea all around, and they shouldn't
have done it in the first place. Maybe it was for the best, but
it still stung.

*And maybe she shouldn't have been a coward and escaped
like a thief in the night.*

The only place Mark seemed like himself was in the
dungeon, yet it was his domain. She didn't go in there
without a very good reason, but the few times she'd braved
meeting the lion in his den, it had been filled with happy
people enjoying themselves.

Despite Mark's perplexing distance, the resort flourished. Memberships were up by over twenty percent, and
weekend room occupancy was back to capacity. There had
been no protesters camped out on the road, and the cyber
incursions had stopped, thanks to Gabby's new computer
system.

The atrium was coming together nicely. There was a
traveler's store carrying tasteful branded merchandise and
the first of their new vendors had set up shop. She'd even

managed to outline ideas for the day spa that had been in the original business plan.

Best of all, she had a Horseman-free rental a reasonable commute from the resort. They'd offered her ten acres surrounding the place Mark had taken her to shoot, yet she'd declined the generous offer. The longer she suffered Mark's animosity, the more she wondered if Club Apocalypse would be a good long-term fit for her. It didn't seem wise to build if she wasn't sure she'd stay.

After finishing the last task of the day, she detoured to the kitchen for her customary takeout salad before heading home.

As she left the kitchen, Sierra hurried to intercept her. "We have a problem in the lobby."

"What happened?"

"The sheriff is here." Sierra took a deep breath and a muscle in her jaw twitched. "We're apparently being raided for running a brothel."

"You're joking, right?"

"Do I fucking look like I'm joking?" She pressed her fists into her eyes and her shoulders visibly slumped. "I'm sorry, that was rude. They're asking for a manager, but I can't find any of the Horsemen."

"Okay." She handed her boxed salad to a passing server and strode to the lobby, forcing Sierra to keep up. "Do they have a warrant?"

"I...shit, I didn't even ask."

"No problem. They would have shown it first thing if they had one. I'll take care of it."

As she walked, she threw her shoulders back and lengthened her stride, knowing the sound of her heels on the ceramic tile floor in the lobby would help make her entrance.

Two deputies stood in front of the front desk, but one was trying to peek over at the papers on the workspace. "Do you have any personal information where they could see it?" she asked Sierra, keeping her voice to a soft murmur.

"No, I was working on the schedule for housekeeping."

"Okay. Follow me in, then take your place behind the desk." Without waiting for an answer, she pasted a smile on her face and strode into the lobby.

"Good evening, gentlemen. Welcome to Club Apocalypse. I'm Kendra Hall, the vice-president of operations."

Both officers were fairly young, certainly no older than thirty if Kendra had to guess. Both had dark hair and brown eyes, and neither would meet her gaze. Glancing at their badges, she committed their names to memory.

Deputy Steubens took off his hat and lifted his chin. "Ms. Hall, we—"

"Kendra, please. If you'll follow me to the lounge, we'll have a seat and discuss your concerns."

After leading the deputies to a comfortable conversation pit adjacent to the lobby, she seated herself across from them and gave them both an easy smile. "Now, my night manager tells me you're investigating us for running an illegal brothel, is that correct?"

"Yes, ma'am. We've had a report of illicit activities from this location," Deputy Zimmerman said, glancing at his partner.

"I see." She leaned back, giving the very picture of calm equanimity. "I won't ask for you to breach your informant's confidentiality, of course, but may I ask what evidence they presented? Secondly, how can I help to alleviate your concerns?"

"She said you're running some sort of sex club here, and the employees are required to perform sex acts with customers."

"Ah. What did she say she was required to do?" She leaned forward and picked up her notepad. "And who required her to do it?"

"She said it was Mark Luciano, and that he fired her when she wouldn't have sex with him."

Kendra blinked and cocked her head to the side, trying to decide how she felt. Hearing about something like that after sharing intimacy with him was a gut punch, but it didn't sound like Mark at all.

"That's a very serious accusation," she murmured. "Do you have physical evidence?"

Deputy Zimmerman cleared his throat, then scowled. "We have witness testimony that Mr. Luciano forced a woman to kneel on dry rice as punishment, causing her mental distress."

That did sound like something Mark would do. It was probably harmless, but she could imagine it being very painful, much like stepping on a LEGO block.

"I—"

"The woman you're talking about is named Shelby Baldwin. She's a former employee," Mark said, striding toward them with a thunderous scowl on his face.

"I beg your pardon?" Deputy Steubens asked.

"I'm Mark Luciano, one of the owners. The scene you described happened over two weeks ago. Shelby chose to quit when I asked her to do her job instead of standing around all night. If you'll follow me, I'll take you to our security center so you can view the video footage."

"Mark," Kendra said softly. "I can take care of this. Please don't say anything else." She lifted a hand to touch his arm, but he jerked away and gave her a glare as if he wished her anywhere else but near him.

Leaning down, he whispered, "You've done quite enough, Ms. Hall, and I think it's more than obvious your little media campaign had exactly the wrong results. Go home...if you think you can make it."

He walked away, gesturing to the deputies to follow.

"What the actual fuck?"

"He doesn't like the changes," Sierra said softly, coming to stand next to her. "I'm not sure if you know this, but he's touch averse, and it's hard for him to get enough space when the dungeon is crowded."

"Shit." Kendra rubbed her forehead to ease a burgeoning headache. "I knew, but if the dungeon isn't full, this resort will fail."

Things weren't going to work out with Mark romantically, and it wasn't as if they'd ever be friends, but she felt terrible. Worse, she couldn't think of a single way to make it better.

"I know." Sierra squeezed her shoulder. "Good news is, he does have video of Shelby Baldwin hitting on him, then getting a right proper mind fuck when she wouldn't give it up."

"Then maybe she does have a case—at least for harassment."

"You're kidding, right?" Sierra snorted and shook her head. "You're the only person he's willingly touched in the entire five years I've known him. He didn't lay a hand on that woman, and she got exactly what she asked for."

Kendra wasn't sure why, but the information made her feel somehow better, even though she was still pissed at Mark for being a jerk. Again.

"I'll call the lawyer tomorrow and make sure Shelby knows better than to spout off lies. I'm sure we still have her signed NDA on file."

"Good idea, but that leads me to something else. I was on my way to find you when the police showed up but..." She shook her head and pointed to the front entry. "Well, maybe you better look for yourself."

Frowning, Kendra walked outside, then pushed her way between two security guards as a pair of large tour buses parked on the road and disgorged dozens of people to join with the crowd already in place. Shouted bible verses echoed across the desert as they organized themselves into rows blocking the entrance to the parking lot.

"Son of a bitch!"

20

MARK

"Thank you for coming out, gentlemen. I'm happy we could address your concerns in a satisfactory manner."

Deputy Steubens held out his hand, and Mark forced himself to smile and return the handshake. As much as he hated it, he had to channel his inner Kendra before he kicked a law enforcement officer off his property.

Mark almost wished he'd let her deal with the issue, but she'd done more than enough to make his life miserable, and he didn't want to see what she'd come up with next.

He should have known her plans wouldn't work. The dungeon was so full, he couldn't stand to be there. What was once his safe place was filled with people, all uncaring about keeping their distance.

That was just one of the things that made him furious at Kendra. It wasn't enough that she'd turned his dungeon into a carnival, she'd disappeared after a scene—again—and pretended like it never happened.

Of course, Club Apocalypse was operating in the black again, which made everyone else happy. He supposed he should be thankful for that, at least.

"Thank you for being so helpful. It was much appreciated," Steubens replied as his partner nodded.

"My pleasure. If possible, may we have the report Ms. Baldwin filed? We have her signed nondisclosure agreement on file, and I'd like to pursue legal proceedings against her in addition to whatever penalty she'll face for filing a false report."

They glanced at each other and nodded. "I think that would be okay," Zimmerman said. "It's not like you didn't remind her of it when she quit."

"That's very true." Mark forced another smile as he walked them to the exit. "Thank you again for coming."

"No problem. We'll drop the report by tomorrow," Steubens replied. "Have a good evening."

"You too." He turned and trudged back to his office behind the dungeon, praying for just a little peace, when he heard the familiar, but welcome voice of Edie, one of his favorite guests.

"You have a pest problem outside, Luciano. Do you have any idea how hard it is to get religious zealot off a paint job? And poor Kendra must be furious."

Mark couldn't help a smile, but he wondered if Kendra had managed to make it past the protesters. The stubborn woman refused to listen to reason and insisted on off-site housing. Then again, they didn't have a suite to spare these days.

Just as she'd promised.

"Behave yourself, little one." Wrapping an arm around her waist, Edie's husband said, "We didn't hit anyone, but it was a near thing."

Still spry and active despite their years, the couple were deeply in love. Edie was as luminously beautiful as she'd been in her wedding photo taken decades before. His hair a thick shock of silver instead of brown, Fred carried himself like a proud member of the Jolly Green from his days in Vietnam.

"Thanks for coming," Mark replied, meaning it. Married fifty years, Edie and Fred were two of his favorite people. "Actually, I'm glad to see you. We have—"

"I imagine Kendra's about to shoot steam out her ears," Edie interrupted, grinning impishly. "Fred and I got a suite for the weekend so we can see the fireworks."

"Mostly, we're here to see the suspension demo," Fred said before kissing Edie's cheek.

"That too." Edie smiled wistfully, then sighed. "Sure do miss the ropes, but too much arthritis in these old joints."

"I was about to tell you we have a master artist in from Chicago." Mark cupped her elbow to escort her to the dungeon. "He's a surprise addition and specializes in adaptive suspension for people with health issues."

"Seriously?"

The glimmer of hope in Edie's green eyes made his chest feel tight. Mark had already arranged for a demo partner for the rope master, but it was easy enough to fix. "Serious as a heart attack. In fact, he might be looking for a demo dolly."

Edie jerked away and broke into a limping trot toward the dungeon, leaving him and Fred behind.

"Guess I better catch up before she gets herself into trouble," Fred said, leaving Mark to follow his wife.

Mark couldn't help but smile. He might be pissed as fuck at Kendra, but he couldn't deny her results. As much as he hated the crowds in his space, he loved seeing people like Edie and Fred enjoy themselves.

Stupidly, despite everything she'd done to ruin his life, he...missed her. He couldn't keep pretending she didn't exist and forgetting everything they'd shared wasn't possible—not when he dreamed of her every fucking night.

He winced, remembering the hurt on her face when he spouted off. It wasn't fair to blame her for doing her job. She'd been right about how close they were to going out of business, and it was something he'd have to learn to manage.

It was past time to make things right.

"I'll walk with you," Mark said. "I'm headed that way anyway."

After escorting Fred to the dungeon and arranging for Edie to be the rope master's demo partner, he detoured to the offices, fully expecting Kendra to be gone. To his surprise, she was still there, and paced her office as she spoke into a wireless headset.

She paused, her back to him, then laughed at something the other person said. "I know how much you like tormenting religious nutjobs, but you really are doing me a huge favor and I appreciate it... Yes, bring everyone who's willing to come. If those inbred fuckers want a fight, we'll give them one."

———

KENDRA

Something tickled her spine, as if the air pressure in her office had changed. Barely hearing her best friend Linda's words, she turned and caught her breath at the sight of Mark in her doorway.

He hadn't purposely come anywhere near her in days, and she tried to control her irritation, knowing he was bringing some new level of hell when she'd already worked a fourteen-hour day.

"I... Sorry, I have to go." Her hand shaking, she fumbled for the button to end the call.

"Don't you dare hang up, young lady."

She choked out a helpless laugh and made an attempt to sit behind her desk without collapsing in her chair. "I'm still here. Was there something you needed?"

"Take off that damned headset I know you're wearing and put me on speaker."

"Bully." Kendra laid the headset on her desk and tapped her phone to let the call play through the speaker.

"You know it. Relax your shoulders and do the breathing exercises we practiced."

Silently, Mark walked in and sat across from her, pinning her with enigmatic brown eyes.

"How did you know I was stressed?"

"My mystical powers were installed when they gave me a priest's collar. Stop talking, heifer."

"Bossy bully," Kendra muttered, scowling at Mark's amused smile.

"Listen, peace is a state of mind. You cannot control outside influences, but you can separate yourself from them."

"I know."

"You're talking, but not breathing. Breathe, sweetie. Just...breathe. Nothing can touch you if you don't let it."

She met Mark's eyes as Linda spoke. His hands relaxed and he inhaled, then let the breath out on a soft whisper of sound.

"There you go," Linda said softly. "I could almost hear the ugly shit floating away."

Talking to Linda always made her feel better, but this was different. Tension she hadn't been aware of left her body as she matched her breathing with Mark's, leaving her feeling almost weightless, but so, so tired.

It was almost like sharing Linda's self-care advice made it more powerful. "Thanks. Can't wait to see you," she finally said, trying to force the words past the lump in her throat.

"Me too. And get a massage. There's some kind of fuckery with your chakras."

"Bully."

"Heifer."

"Love you."

"Right back atcha. I'll see you soon. And tell the person in your office they need to breathe too."

The call dropped and Kendra resisted the urge to put her head down for a nap. Unfortunately, Mark was still sitting across from her, meaning there was yet another fire to put out.

To her surprise, he cleared his throat and gave her a fleeting smile. "Your friend is...interesting."

"I'm almost afraid to see what she's planning. Linda is a

force of nature, but..." She shook her head and tried to organize her notes. "Anyway, what can I help you with?"

"At the moment, nothing. What were you going to say about Linda?"

"I wish I hadn't asked her to come here." Kendra slid the papers across the desk. "I took a few photos and tracked down who rented the tour buses. The Shepherds of the Coming Peace are camped on our doorstep, and they're bad news."

He scanned the printouts revealing the cult's suspected activities. "I didn't realize they ever left their compound."

"Why am I not surprised they have a compound?" She sighed and pinched the skin between her brows. "Okay. I'll take care of it soon."

"Seems you didn't listen to your friend," Mark countered. "You cannot control outside influences, but you can separate yourself from them."

"Sounds like Linda has another fan."

"I'm wondering if there's some fuckery with my chakras too." He leaned back in his chair and studied her. "Why did you leave?"

Kendra swallowed hard and rose from her chair, then faced the small window looking out over the desert. It wouldn't do any good to pretend she didn't know what he was talking about. "I was afraid."

"Of what?"

"Of me, mostly. Of making you uncomfortable because I

pushed too hard. Of accidentally touching you while we were asleep. Of the awkward morning-after, of—"

"A very smart woman once related a story to me about a man who told her that words have power." He moved to stand behind her, but she didn't dare look at him when he laid a warm hand on her shoulder. "Safe words, in particular."

Kendra couldn't decide whether to step out of his reach or melt against him. She settled for holding herself as still as possible, but he closed the distance between them and rested his chin on her head.

"I'm thinking we'll run out of arms if we keep chewing them off to avoid what's going on between us." Moving slowly and ever so gently, he turned her to face him, then took her hands. "And I really want there to be something between us."

To her shock, he lifted her hands and laid them on his cheeks. It was innocent...a sweet gesture, yet profoundly intimate and all the more surprising given his aversion to touch. The warmth of his skin sent a shockwave of need into her core.

"I'm sorry," she blurted out. "I shouldn't have—"

"Me too, and same. I've been a dick to you for two weeks, and you didn't deserve it." He shivered under her touch but smiled.

"Yeah, I really did deserve it. I mean, I left you, then

changed everything in your dungeon like I promised I wouldn't do."

"You didn't change a thing except the number of people enjoying it," he countered. "We both fucked up when you ran, and I let you go. I should have chased you down the minute I woke up instead of letting it get to me." He kissed her forehead, then added, "And I definitely shouldn't have told you that your work wasn't anything short of amazing."

"Thank you, but I shouldn't have run in the first place."

"I should have chased you. So, I want us to start over, from the beginning." He let go of her, then crooked an elbow, offering her his arm. "How do you feel about forgetting the protesters for an evening so I can escort you to the dungeon?"

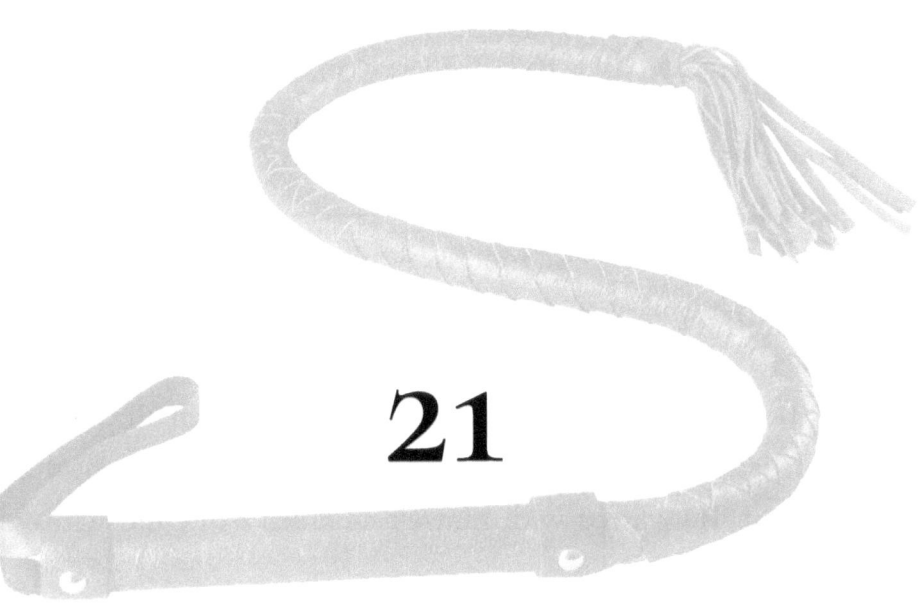

21

MARK

You cannot control outside influences, but you can separate yourself from them.

Just...breathe. Nothing can touch you if you don't let it.

The woman's words burrowed deep, her hypnotic voice still echoing in his mind as if she'd been talking directly to him. She'd made it sound so simple, but he knew better. Such a massive shift in his perception... Inwardly, he shook his head. Going through BUD/S again would be easier than training himself not to throw up when someone put their hands on him.

Well, everyone except Kendra, anyway.

Her hand around his arm felt like coming home. Mark

would probably never know what it was about her that made her touch okay when he couldn't stand it from anyone else—even his closest friends. Maybe it was because the stubborn woman refused to lay a hand on him unless he put it there.

He wondered if the nickname he'd been given all those years ago during training was more apropos than he'd thought. He warred with himself as much as he did with Kendra.

"Sierra told me you were having problems in the dungeon," she said, pulling him from his thoughts.

"It's crowded now, which is great, but..." He shrugged and let the words trail off, knowing she'd understand.

"I'm sorry for that too. I don't know how to make it right." She went silent for several seconds as they approached the dungeon. "You can ask for my resignation. I won't fight it, but I'd like to wait until after we get rid of the Shepherds."

Oh, hell no.

He spun and pushed her against the wall, caging her with his body. "You are not resigning. Do you hear me?"

"But—"

Lowering his head, he kissed her brutally, taking her mouth like he needed it to live. She was a heady treat he couldn't get enough of, and when she fisted her hand in the fabric of his shirt, he pressed closer.

"Touch me, Kendra. Not my shirt."

"I...no!" She tried to wriggle free, but he wasn't about to let her go.

"Do it!"

Her palm met his ribs just above his waist and he groaned, then eased a scant few inches away. Kendra jerked her hand back like she'd been burned and looked up at him, chewing on her swollen lower lip. The need to hide her away before everyone saw her inherent submission surprised him.

"I—"

"Shh." He touched her lip with a fingertip, gently easing it free of her teeth. "This is a me problem, not yours. And I'll be God damned if I let it drive you away."

"I think it's our problem, Mark," she countered. Despite her words, her lips twitched into a smile. "Maybe...will you let me help?"

"Would you stop if I said no?"

A giggle burst free, and she blinked as if it surprised her. "You could always save your arms and use a safe word."

"Smart ass."

Sobering, she lifted a hand as if she wanted to touch him again, then let it fall. "I promise I'll figure something out to help you in the dungeon. Hopefully, I'll have some ideas later tonight."

"No. You're going to spend at least a few hours enjoying what you've done. You haven't been in there in days, so you have no idea what it looks like when it's full of people."

"I've peeked in a few times."

"Going no further than the vestibule. I've talked to the greeters."

"Sneaky dom."

"Stubborn wench."

She snorted out a giggle, then let her hand hover over his arm, forcing him to put it where it belonged before he opened the door leading into the dungeon. He wished she didn't feel like she had to be so careful with him yet wasn't stupid enough to think his issues with touch would be solved overnight. Hadn't the shrink from the VA told him that?

Yeah, before you stopped going four years ago.

He escorted her into the vestibule, then past the curtain into the dungeon. The pressure of too many people hit him almost immediately, yet he wasn't nervous. In fact, nobody was paying a damned bit of attention to him. Everyone's focus was on the suspension area where Edie was being wrapped in lengths of colored hemp rope. Fred sat in a chair close by, smiling as he watched.

This was what Club Apocalypse was for. It wasn't about him or Kendra. It was about all the people who came seeking acceptance and a place where they could be themselves.

And he'd almost lost it.

"Hey, Mark?" Grayson, one of his dungeon masters said as he approached, "we're out of—"

Smiling, Kendra stepped between them and pulled out

her ever-present legal pad, making Grayson stop in his tracks. "I'll be happy to take care of it."

She was...protecting him? Fuck.

Grayson, not being an idiot, knew better than to deny Kendra when she wore what Mark had come to think of as her power shoes. The four-inch stilettos made her almost six feet tall, and combined with the tailored pantsuits she favored, she exuded presence.

Once Grayson was dealt with, she spent the next fifteen minutes using her body to buffer him from anyone who approached, then finally maneuvered him into a secluded corner where they could see the suspension area.

She leaned against the wall and let out a sigh of contentment. "Whew. That was okay, right? Is everything good?"

He crowded her and wrapped his hand around the back of her neck, then brushed his lips against her ear. "No."

———

KENDRA

She hadn't realized how much she'd missed having Mark's warm body against hers. She wanted to run her hands up and down the muscular planes of his back, pet his gorgeous hard flesh, massage the tension from his shoulders...

Forcibly, she pressed her hands against the wall. "What do you mean, no? I didn't let anyone touch you. It's the perfect solution. I just come to the dungeon every night and—"

"What time did you get here this morning?" he interrupted.

"Um...seven?" It was actually closer to six, but she didn't think he'd approve.

"So, what you're telling me is, you're going to work a twelve-hour shift, six days a week, then come babysit me until the dungeon closes?"

"You say that like it isn't doable." It was very doable, but it was going to be exhausting. Still, if it made things right with Mark, she'd deal until he either learned to tolerate the crowds or they came up with another idea.

Leaning away from her, he traced a finger down her jaw. "I didn't say it wasn't doable. I'm saying you aren't going to be doing it."

"But—"

He pulled her into his chest and banded an arm around her torso to keep her still. "Hush and watch the demo. We'll talk about it later."

"Mark, I'm working!" Kendra couldn't bring herself to protest too much though. If he was willing to play the *I can touch you, but you can't touch me* game, she was delighted to go along with it.

It was almost as if he held her in a perpetual state of... honor bondage.

A drip of liquid heat tickled, and she nearly moaned. The

ridge of his cock pressed against her backside, adding to the heady sensation of being trapped. Kendra stopped the line of thought before it got started. Getting turned on by Mark's aversion to touch was more than disrespectful, and he deserved better.

"No, you're off the clock, little girl. Behave yourself, or I might decide to show everyone how beautiful you look on the central spanking bench."

"You say that like it's a bad thing."

"Naughty." He splayed his fingers across her belly, then nipped her earlobe. The slight sting nearly buckled her knees.

In an effort to get her mind on business, Kendra pointed at the older woman on the stage dressed in a tank top and yoga pants, whose expression of bliss made her want to try the rope work herself. "She looks like she's having the time of her life."

"That's Edie, and she is. She loves suspension bondage, but she has arthritis and had to give it up. The rigger is demonstrating adaptive techniques."

With soft words of encouragement, the rigger, an older man with a gray ponytail caught in a tie at the base of his neck, encouraged her to lean back into the embrace of a multitude of colored ropes looped through a large ring hanging from a ceiling beam.

Edie let out a soft murmur of pleasure as the rope caught her weight. Still whispering encouragement, the rigger tugged on one of the ropes and hoisted her into the air, then gestured to a man sitting in a chair off to the side.

Grinning happily, the man approached and gave Edie a lingering kiss that made Kendra's heart skip a beat. "Who is that?"

"Fred, Edie's husband. Watch."

Fred took a step back and laid a hand on Edie's hip, then pushed. Edie spun slowly, the ropes suspending her making her look like a butterfly.

Soft whispers from the crowd softened then stopped as Edie flew, as if no one wanted to interrupt the scene playing out. Eventually, Edie's motion ceased, and Fred caught her and held her in a loose embrace while the rigger untied her.

Tears streamed from Edie's eyes, but she smiled as Fred held her up. Kendra blinked back tears of her own as a dungeon monitor helped Fred escort her into the aftercare area, applause following them.

"That was...intense," she finally said, swallowing a lump in her throat.

"Yes." Mark cleared his throat and pulled her tighter against his chest. "Kendra, I..."

The words broke off and Kendra turned to face him, tucking her hands behind her back so she didn't inadvertently touch him. "What is it?"

"I want to thank you. If you hadn't worked so hard to get Apocalypse back up and running, the rigger wouldn't have come to give a demo, meaning Edie wouldn't have...anyway, thank you."

"You don't have to—"

"If you say you were just doing your job, I will spank your bare ass right here," he warned, a crooked smile easing the threat. "Putting up with my bullshit is not in your job description."

She licked her lips, then kissed the taut line of his jaw. "What if I want it to be?"

His smile faded and he plucked her hands from behind her back and laid them on his hips. The warmth of his body scalded her through his shirt. "Maybe I'd—"

"I have time for one more demo," the rigger called, holding up a section of red rope. "Do we have a newbie in the audience?"

"Right here!" Mark called, holding up her hand. "I volunteer Kendra, our fabulous vice-president of operations, as tribute!"

The audience roared its approval, a few people whistling loudly.

"Wait! I—"

"Front and center, Ms. Hall," Randy shouted, grinning as he wrapped an arm around Josh's shoulders. "I knew she was a sub. Didn't I tell you she's a sub?"

"Yes, sir. You did," Josh replied, grinning at her.

She laughed helplessly, then let Mark drag her to the suspension area. Here, in this place, she was accepted.

Welcomed, even. Her presence, her work, her contribution meant something. It was more than chasing rats out of a Paris cellar or cleaning up a kitchen that should have been in a museum.

Club Apocalypse wasn't just a resort—it was a haven. And she'd helped keep it alive.

Mark let her go and she kicked off her shoes, then dropped her jacket into his arms. "I'm ready."

EPILOGUE

Beauty again tames the beast.

Ryan Wood smirked as Mark gave Kendra the sappiest heart eyes he'd ever seen. Unfortunately, he couldn't decide which of them was beauty and which was beast.

Kendra Hall was a ballbuster. All the Horsemen had learned not to cross her, but she always, *always* got results. She was the last person he thought his best friend Mark Luciano would hook up with.

That wasn't to say Kendra wasn't gorgeous, but she was... well, Kendra. Ryan wouldn't admit it in public, but she scared him a little. He couldn't have hired a better person to get Club Apocalypse back on track and making money.

Still, she looked good in rope. Eyes closed, with an easy

smile, she seemed peaceful—like her brain had turned off and she was allowing herself to relax and enjoy the moment.

Knowing Mark and Kendra were in good hands, Ryan left the dungeon as the rigger brought her down from the suspension. He didn't need to see their aftercare, and the staff would take care of everything else.

Jake was in the kitchen, still scowling at poor Olivia. Lord help her, the woman was trying, but she couldn't seem to do enough to please Jake. Ryan made a note to talk to Jake before Kendra blasted him to hell and back for his behavior toward a staff member.

Dr. Knox was in her office sucking on a lollipop as she worked. She wore a pink plush onesie with cat ears and sat cross-legged in her bean bag chair, looking up at dual monitors on the desk. One of them showed cartoon characters, while the other revealed lines of code he had no hope of understanding. The code was as inexplicable as why she refused to use the perfectly good desk chair they'd given her and sat on the floor.

"It's past your bedtime, sweetheart," he murmured after tapping the doorframe to announce his presence.

"Deadlines." She typed for several seconds and the background on the image changed to a brighter shade of watercolor purple. "I've got you lot managed, so I'm trying to get some real work done while Sean isn't around to bother me."

"That's not insulting at all." He laughed, knowing the

security issues with Club Apocalypse were her idea of a vacation. "One more hour, baby girl. Then bedtime."

She waved him away without replying, her focus returning to the code she was building. It was always good to see a kid from the projects succeed, and he'd miss her when she left to return to her day job in Massachusetts. Not that she was a kid now, but she'd grown up in poverty just like he had.

He passed through the atrium on his way to the lobby to finish his evening rounds. They had two more open spots for vendors, but the preliminary numbers looked good for the first month's revenue.

Hell, aside from several floor pillows in the conversation pit positioned for kneeling submissives, some tropical plants shadowing the corners, and a few paintings on consignment from Natalie Mercer in Minnesota, they hadn't changed a damned thing aside from the vendors. Still, the resort felt more... something. Ryan couldn't quite put his finger on the right words to describe it. The art and accessories made everything more intense. Warmer, but not more comfortable.

It had a seductive edge now, and he understood what Kendra had wanted. The public areas were a challenging tease. They held the promise of pleasure and pain that would only be fulfilled if a guest took that one additional step into the dungeon. She'd told them to create an immersive experience, and it had paid off.

He paused and adjusted a floor pillow, correcting its position. As he straightened, he caught a faint shadow of motion from behind one of the lush potted palms, then heard a soft whimper.

Frowning, he moved slowly to the plant. It almost sounded like a stray animal had gotten inside, and he didn't want to risk scaring the critter before he could catch it. Carefully, he pushed the foliage aside and swore under his breath.

A woman was balled up on the floor, her face hidden under a scarf. She wore a brown burlap dress that covered her from ankle to chin, and shapeless boots with a thick coat of dust. Her arms were wrapped around her calves and her head was touching her knees, giving him no idea of her age or why she was hiding behind one of his plants.

"Hey," he crooned softly, "what's your name?"

"Carrie, sir. Carrie Yost."

He knelt, close enough to speak softly without invading her space. "Hi, Carrie. I'm Ryan. Can you tell me why you're hiding?"

"I'm running away."

Ryan sat back on his heels and frowned, wondering if she was the daughter of one of the protesters. If she was, he had every sympathy, but given her slight stature and soft, somewhat squeaky voice, he suspected she wasn't anywhere close to old enough to be in Club Apocalypse. It didn't sit well with him to return her, given everything

Kendra had learned about the Shepherds of the Coming Peace, but...

"Where are your parents, honey? I bet they're missing you."

"That's probably true."

"Okay. Well, unfortunately, this is an adults-only place. Can I call someone—"

"I'm twenty-two. I ran away because they're trying to force me to marry my uncle."

Ryan didn't bother to hide his distaste. She wasn't looking at him anyway. "And you snuck away from the folks outside when nobody was paying attention, right?"

"Yes, sir."

"Okay, then. We'll give you a safe place to stay for as long as you need it." He quickly tapped out a text asking Sierra to find her a bed for the night. Judging by the somewhat unpleasant odor wafting from her, Carrie would need clean clothes and a hot shower too.

She rubbed her face against her forearm and sniffed but didn't look up. "I can cook, clean, and sew, sir. I'm not useless."

The last words came out louder than she probably intended, as if she was trying to convince herself more than him.

"No, of course you aren't." He stood and held out a hand to help her up.

Carrie scrambled to her feet without assistance yet

wrapped an arm around her ribs as if they pained her. "I can sleep out in the barn. I don't mind. Just need a pile of hay and a blanket if you have one to spare."

Ryan opened his mouth to tell her they didn't have a barn but bit the words back. He had no idea what her life had been like and didn't want to risk insulting her, but barns weren't really a thing at the resort. "Let's get you something to eat. I bet you're hungry."

"No, sir. I'm okay." Her shoulders hunched and she pulled her scarf further over her face, then tried to sidle around him.

"Look at me, Carrie."

She lifted her head and straightened but kept her gaze on his feet. Purple and black contusions covered her face, and one eye was swollen shut. A steady trickle of blood leaked from her nose and dripped down her chin.

"Oh, Carrie." Ryan handed her a handkerchief from his pocket, then pressed his lips together before he said anything else. He wanted to kill whoever hit her. He wasn't a sniper, but the protesters were less than five hundred yards out. He could tag a good number of them before someone called the cops. Ryan shook the thought away. Revenge could wait until he had Carrie physically stable—and wouldn't get him thrown into jail where he couldn't protect her.

Despite the bruises and swelling, she was the most beautiful woman he'd ever seen. Disheveled red curls framed her heart-shaped face. The mix of trust and hope in her startling green eyes made something squeeze inside his chest, and he almost lifted his hand to touch the silvery scar under her trembling lower lip.

Firmly, he kept his hands at his sides and focused on what he needed to do instead of the sudden urge to pull her into his arms and show her the wonders of Club Apocalypse.

The idea was laughable. He had no right to haul an innocent twenty-two-year-old cult survivor through a bondage dungeon. Hell, he couldn't even risk using the triage room to take care of her injuries.

"Let's get you settled in. We'll get some ice for your bruises too," he finally said, before leading her to the front desk. Carrie wouldn't be staying long. She'd be gone the minute he could get her into a safe location out of the Shepherd's reach.

And out of his too.

PESTILENCE'S CURE
SNEAK PEEK

RYAN

He adjusted his cuffs and gave the visiting police officers a practiced smile. "I'm sorry, gentlemen, but we haven't seen the girl you described."

"Are you sure, Mr. Wood?" Officer Walt Thompson, a man Ryan had known since the day Club Apocalypse opened, held out a picture of an unsmiling young redhead with a scarf covering her head. "Carrie Yost vanished from the Shepherds' protest group last night and her father is frantic."

"It's terrible to have a child go missing," Ryan murmured.

"Her father says she's twenty-two, but he's busting my..." Walt glanced at Kendra and flushed. "Sorry."

Kendra Hall, their vice-president of operations, said, "We'll do everything in our power to help you find Miss Yost. Please assure him we're allowing you full access to the resort property, with the exception of thirty-four occupied suites unless you have the guests' permission to enter. The owners and staff of Club Apocalypse are happy to answer your questions. In fact, I can call in the staff members who were here last night."

Walt sighed and shook his head. "No, that won't be necessary. Knowing your security systems, you wouldn't have missed a redhead in a burlap dress coming in here." Replacing his hat, he shook Ryan's hand. "Cross your fingers she's actually managed to get out of town, and away from... anyway, call me if you see her."

"Of course," Ryan replied smoothly. "Do you need to see the security footage? You might find something we missed."

"No, but thanks for the offer."

"Will you let us know if..." Kendra brushed a finger under one eye and tried to smile. "When she's found?"

Walt's gaze softened and he handed Kendra a tissue from a small packet. "Yes, ma'am. We're sorry to have bothered you."

She sniffed and dabbed at her eyes. "You're never a bother. We hope she's reunited with her family soon."

"Thank you. It's always a pleasure doing business with the Horsemen."

"With you as well," Ryan said. "Let us know when you find her. Despite our issues with them, I'm sure her family is worried sick."

He shut his mouth and tried not to roll his eyes. The Shepherds of the Coming Peace had been waging a protest on the resort's property line for months, demanding they close down. They believed Club Apocalypse was a brothel, and nothing anyone said would change their minds.

"Will do."

Walt and his partner walked out, but Ryan waited until they drove away before he spoke. "Tears, Kendra? How did you manage that?"

She lifted her chin and tossed the tissue into a wastebasket. "Please. When have I ever not acted in the best interest of Club Apocalypse and its guests and staff? If that means tears, I'll turn on the waterworks."

He chuckled and followed her through the lobby to the offices in the west wing. Kendra Hall was a woman who got things done, but he hadn't realized she was such a good actress.

"Where did you stash her?" he asked.

"Mark's office." She glanced at her watch and quickened her pace, the heels of her expensive stilettos echoing on the tile. "He, Jake, and Sean are with her. I assume Sean already altered the security footage of Carrie coming in?"

"Yes, he took care of it last night." Ryan chose not to argue about putting such an innocent young woman in the dungeon. He didn't like the idea, but it was one of the few places inaccessible to guests until it opened for the evening.

"Good. Thank you. I'm putting her in Mark's room in your apartment to keep her out of sight. He'll be moving in with me, so—"

"No."

Kendra stopped, her heels clicking as she turned. "Excuse me?"

"She can't stay with us. It would be inappropriate."

Gazing at him, she lowered her ever-present legal pad. "As inappropriate as someone spotting her in one of the common areas or outside? Can you imagine how much worse the Shepherds are going to be if they know we're hiding Carrie from them?"

Ryan grunted and started walking again. As much as he wanted to keep Carrie as far from the Shepherds as he could get her, he couldn't let her stay so close. She was too sweet and innocent, and those big green eyes just did something to him.

Made him want to protect her and keep her hidden away where no one could find her. Have her waiting at home with a hot meal. She'd have no other worries aside from keeping his house and raising their family and would never have to work. He'd walk in the front door, and she'd kiss his cheek, then...

No. As beautiful as imagining her as his dutiful, stay-at-home wife was, she needed freedom to find her own way. To create a future for herself and discover who and what she was truly meant to be.

"We should let Dr. Knox take her back to Massachusetts. That would get her well out of the Shepherds' reach."

"Dr. Knox has her own business," she reminded him, "and we have no idea if Carrie can take care of herself without support. For better or worse, she's our responsibility until we can find somewhere safe for her to go."

He sighed irritably but nodded. "You're right. Sorry."

"I'm always right." She strode past the restaurant, acknowledging several guests as they enjoyed the expansive buffet breakfast Jake, their chef and one of his best friends set out, then went into the dungeon where Mark's office was tucked out of view behind the bar. It was the safest place for them to meet to discuss what to do with Carrie.

Jake grinned at Kendra as she walked in, then held up a bite-sized quiche. "Ah, caught you before you escaped without breakfast, naughty girl."

She opened her mouth to speak, but Jake shoved the treat between her lips. She glowered at him but chewed and swallowed. "Stop that. I already ate."

"Coffee doesn't count." He held up another. "One more and you can go."

Mark grinned and kissed her cheek. "I told on you."

"I'm going to abjure you one of these days and make it

stick." Despite her words and the dirty look she shot at Mark, she ate the second and dabbed her lips with a napkin. "Spinach, my favorite."

"These are actually low carb with egg whites. You like?"

She took two more. "I like everything you make, but this is something I won't feel guilty for eating. Thanks."

"My pleasure."

Although Carrie's face was still bruised and swollen, she'd gotten a shower and fresh clothing. The housekeeping uniform of khakis and a black polo made her look wan and pale, but it was a significant improvement over the shapeless brown dress she'd been wearing when she arrived.

Giving her a bright smile, Kendra sat behind Mark's desk. "Hi Carrie. I'm Kendra Hall, and we're going to help you, okay?"

"Yes, ma'am." Her shoulders went up around her ears and she stole peeks at the people surrounding her as if they were a threat.

Ryan wanted to take her from the room and hide her away but shook off the ridiculous idea. This was necessary, and they'd both just have to deal with it.

Jake set a plate overflowing with scrambled eggs, bacon, and toast in front of her. "You can eat before we talk, okay?"

"Sir?" She glanced at the food, then back up at him. "I don't understand."

"It's your breakfast, honey."

"But—"

Jake's eyes glittered, transforming him from a slightly goofy chef into a stern dominant. It was a look that would cow even Kendra into good behavior, all the more astonishing because he almost never went that far. "Eat your breakfast, Carrie."

Surprisingly, her shoulders relaxed, and she picked up her fork.

"Good girl," Jake crooned. "Would you like juice, milk, or coffee?"

"Milk, please," Carrie said after swallowing. "This is very good."

"Thanks." Jake put a glass of milk next to her plate, then sat next to Sean and folded his hands over his stomach, watching to make sure Carrie ate everything.

Wearing a pleased smile, Kendra waited until she finished. "Okay, Carrie. You already know everyone, so we'll get started with our meeting. We're going to help you write a statement saying you're here of your own free will, and you don't want to return to the Shepherds. Is that what you want to say?"

"Yes, ma'am."

"Call me Kendra, please." She handed Carrie her notepad. "Now, by your father's own words to the police, you're over eighteen, which means you can go wherever you want. That also means he can't force you to marry against your will."

After laying her fork next to her plate, Carrie dabbed her

lips with her napkin. "This is the second time I've escaped," she finally said. "The first time, I managed to stay away for almost a year before my father dragged me home."

"How old were you?"

"Eighteen. I was working at a diner in Flagstaff when he caught me, and then he... Anyway, I came here to ask if you can help me get far enough away that he can't find me again."

Ryan breathed out through his nose and forced his hands to unclench. He was almost afraid to ask her what she didn't say. Surreptitiously, he sent a text to their on-call counselor, knowing Carrie would need help if what he suspected was true.

Unfortunately, Sean didn't have any qualms about asking her that difficult question. His golden complexion darkened with fury. "Did your father touch you inappropriately?"

"No. Never." She thanked Jake for the glass of water he gave her, then took a sip. "He beat me, then starved me until I agreed to marry the man he chose for me. I did, but—"

"Wait. I thought you ran to escape marrying your uncle." Ryan said, desperately trying to keep his cool. He didn't know if her future husband or her father had abused her, but he didn't care. It was all he could do to stop himself from hunting the bastards down.

"My husband had a bad heart and died two weeks ago. My father wants me to marry his stepbrother."

"I'm very sorry for your loss," Kendra murmured. Like all of them, she was probably wondering how old Carrie's husband had been. Thankfully, Carrie didn't see her pallor or the expression of sick horror on her face.

"Thank you. Benjamin was kind to me, but Josiah won't be."

She twisted her hands in her lap and lowered her chin. Judging by the clenched set of her shoulders, she was scared as hell, and Ryan couldn't blame her.

"Will you help me? I think if I can get to Phoenix, he won't go that far, but he has my birth certificate and ID locked in his office." She laughed mirthlessly, then added, "He keeps all the women's documents locked up now so we can't escape as easily."

Carrie had run and managed to stay away until she was caught, but without ID, it would be much harder for her to find a job and a place to live.

"Is there someone you do want to marry?" Jake asked softly. "You'd need your late husband's death certificate and your documents, but if there was someone else, he couldn't force you."

Shuddering, Carrie shook her head violently. "No. Not ever again."

————

CARRIE

She hadn't quite believed it, but judging by the sexually explicit art, and the massive bar she'd seen in the restaurant, Club Apocalypse was indeed a brothel. She'd even recognized a few pieces of what she thought was bondage furniture in the large room she'd passed through on her way to Mark's office.

It didn't bother her too much though. Valentina, her roommate and best friend in Flagstaff, had been an escort, and Carrie had never met a kinder, more generous person.

Despite her busy schedule with school and work, Valentina had taught her to read using her collection of naughty books, helped her pass her high school equivalency testing, and then helped her find a job. She'd even gotten a driving permit and started learning to drive Valentina's old Toyota.

In fact, Valentina was the reason she was in her current predicament. When her father threatened to hurt her, Carrie had followed him home, meek as a kitten. He hadn't even given her a chance to say goodbye.

Carrie swallowed back a sob, knowing she couldn't go back to Flagstaff. That would be the first place her father would look.

"Okay, no wedding your future," Ryan said, smiling at her. "I think we can help you with your documents though."

"Thank you." She let out a breath, then lifted her head to

meet his eyes. "May I borrow your phone? I want to call my friend in Flagstaff. That will be the first place my father goes to find me."

All four men held out phones, making her blink in surprise. She chose Ryan's and chewed on her lip as she tried to remember Valentina's number. Finally, it came to her, and she tapped the screen to connect the call. Her thumb slipped and she accidentally put the call on speaker but wasn't sure she could turn it off without disconnecting the call.

After a few rings, Valentina picked up, sounding very sleepy. "This is Valentina from cardmember services. If you're dumb enough to give me your credit card number, I'll use it to buy sex toys and a Ferrari."

"Hi, Valentina, it's um... Carrie."

Something crashed to the floor, and she heard a screech before Valentina said, "Chica, I've been worried sick! You don't call, you don't write. It's been three years! Where have you been?"

"I... my father came."

"Oh." The single word held all of Valentina's animosity. "Let me guess. You didn't leave a typed note on our kitchen table telling me you found a job and were moving away. I knew I should have looked for you."

"No, I'm glad you didn't. He said he would hurt you, and... I'm sorry."

"What an asshole." Valentina let out a sigh, and in a

softer voice, said, "I'm just glad you're okay. Dare I hope you've gotten away from the old fuckwit again?"

"I did." She'd almost forgotten what Valentina used to call him. She'd always been taught to honor her father and it had horrified her at first, but the longer she was out of his reach, the more it seemed to fit.

Ryan reached over to squeeze her knee in encouragement, and his lips curved into a smile that made her catch her breath. Lord, that smile. If he'd been the man her father picked, maybe she wouldn't have protested so much.

He wore a dark suit and white shirt without a tie and had onyx cufflinks at his wrists. Gray eyes the color of desert storm clouds were filled with kindness. He even smelled good, like bay rum and soap, and she wanted to inhale the clean, masculine fragrance deep into her lungs.

"Good for you! Where are you? I'll come pick you up."

"I'm actually calling to warn you. Our apartment is the first place he'll look."

"I'm not at all sorry to say he'll be disappointed. I moved to a gated community in Pine Canyon. Now, tell me where you are, and I'll come get you."

How the heck had Valentina managed to afford a house in that neighborhood? Maybe she'd decided to escort full-time after college instead of finding a job. It wasn't for her but if Valentina was happy, Carrie wouldn't judge. At least Valentina wasn't living in their apartment anymore, but that didn't mean her father wouldn't find her.

"I'm at a place called Club Apocalypse."

There was another crash, and it sounded like Valentina had dropped the phone. "Valentina? Are you okay?"

"Did you say Club Apocalypse?"

"Yes. The Shepherds are protesting, and—"

Valentina squealed, making Jake snicker behind his hand. "Oh em gee! Are you like...inside?"

"Yes, I'm in—"

"You utter cow. I've been on their waiting list for months! Oh, my God!" Valentina squeaked again, then said, "Okay, fangirl time over. I'll be there in about two hours to get you, but will you please ask if I can have a tour?"

Ryan held a finger to his lips, then gave her a warm smile. "Valentina, this is Ryan Wood. I'd like to personally invite you for a complimentary stay at Club Apocalypse. We'll discuss your membership when you get here."

"Mr. Wood... Pestilence. Can I call you Pest? Shit, I'm sorry. I promise I'm not usually such a spazz. Actually, I am, but I need to thank you for helping my friend. I don't even care about the membership as long as she's okay."

"Carrie is fine." He grinned at his friends who were all holding back laughter. "And you can call me Ryan. We'd also like to ask a favor of you."

"Anything! I'm on it," Valentina replied.

"Stop somewhere and buy Carrie some clothes. Enough for a couple of weeks, I think. We'll call it your first month's dues. How does that sound?"

"I'll provide for my bestie. She deserves it. I'll be there soon."

The call dropped and Carrie closed her eyes, trying to hold back tears. After so long, Valentina still called her bestie. As much as she'd missed Valentina, it had been worth leaving to keep her safe. Carrie wouldn't have been able to live with herself if something happened to her.

"Thank you," she said, once she thought she could speak without crying. "You don't know what that means to me."

"If your father managed to find you in Flagstaff, he can find your friend," Kendra said. "I'd like all my lost waifs in one place where I can keep an eye on them."

"He'll try, and I can't—" The tears fell, and she choked on a sob. "Valentina is...she taught me to read and... I'm sorry."

"Don't worry." Ryan stroked her hand, sending an electric surge of pleasure into her tummy. "We'll keep you both safe."

———

If anyone can protect Carrie, it's Ryan. Pestilence's Cure is available wherever ebooks are sold.

For sneak peeks and teasers, sign up for my newsletter. You'll also get a free book delivered right to your inbox!

ACKNOWLEDGMENTS

As always, my undying gratitude and love go to Engineer Hubby. Without your support and faith, I wouldn't be writing at all. Love you to the moon and back, baby.

———

Want to see what I'm up to next? Join my Renegades on Facebook. You can also sign up for my newsletter to receive a free short story delivered right to your inbox!

ABOUT RAISA GREYWOOD

USA Today bestselling author of filthy smut, empty nester, and cat snuggler.

Raisa has worked as a teacher, an actuary (her husband called her a bookie—which isn't too far from the truth), mother, and scout leader. She's happily married to her husband of twenty-eight years, and is now enjoying semi-retirement writing the books she always wanted to read with kick-ass heroines and sexy, sexy men.
www.raisagreywood.com

If paranormal romance is your jam, keep reading for a sneak peek of Wicked Truth by her alter-ego Minette Moreau, available FREE at your favorite retailer.
www.minettemoreau.com

facebook.com/AuthorRaisaGreywood

instagram.com/raisagreywood

bookbub.com/authors/raisa-greywood

goodreads.com/raisa_greywood

tiktok.com/@raisagreywood

ALSO BY RAISA GREYWOOD

Club Apocalypse

Grim's Little Reaper: A Club Apocalypse Novella

War's Peace

Pestilence's Cure

Famine's Feast

Death's Desire

Charon's Chaos

Holiday Daddy Doms

Jennifer's Christmas Daddy

A Valentine for Chelsea

Treats for Lucia

Zinnia's Solstice Daddy

Black Light

Black Light: Roulette Rematch

Black Light: Saved

Dad Bod Doms

Henry

Leave Me Breathless

Breaking Donatella

Bridgewater Brides

Their Wanted Bride

Cocky Hero Club

Sexy Scoundrel

Standalone Titles & Anthologies

Ladder 54: Five Firefighter Romances

Masters of the Castle: Witness Protection Program

Happily Never After (written with Sinistre Ange)

Demon Lust

Blood Lust

WICKED TRUTH
WICKED MAGIC BOOK ONE

MINETTE MOREAU

As a child I believed in magic. As a woman, I believe only in the power within me.

The Duke of Denforth has made me his bride, and from him I've received so much more than the title of Duchess. It seems the world is full of wonders beyond any fantasy, and instead of one husband I now have three: the Duke and my guardians, Moses and Liam.

The scandalous passion I share with these men is white hot and undeniable, each of them seeking to explore my every secret. But when a sinister force who would use my power for evil takes me from them, it will be up to me and me alone to embrace who I am, and harness my gifts once and for all.

I am Lily Archer: Duchess, wife, lover, dragon charmer, undefeatable warrior. And nothing I've ever feared will keep me from returning home to the men I love.

BONUS EXCERPT

There was a problem with barricading one's door. When her maid knocked, Lily had to get up and remove the obstacle before the woman could enter without causing a commotion.

"A moment, please, Margaret! I'll be right there!"

"Yes, ma'am. A gentleman has come to call. He says his name is Duke Denforth."

Lily tied the sash of her dressing gown and removed the barricade from the door before opening it. "Did he say what he wanted?"

Whilst Lily rarely asked for her services as a lady's maid, Margaret went straight to Lily's wardrobe, choosing the best of her day dresses. "No, ma'am. He asked to speak with your mother as well. I will try to make her presentable after I dress you."

Lily allowed Margaret to take her dressing gown and assist her into her corset and pink frock. "I don't know him. And the Denforth estate is quite a distance away, if I recall." She bit her lip, wincing when her teeth caught the edge of the scabbed cut Caine had given her. "I don't understand why a duke would call on me."

"I'm sure I don't know, ma'am. Let me do something with your hair before I tend to Mrs. Archer."

"Of course." Lily sat while Margaret brushed her hair, the blonde tresses falling to her waist in a wavy curtain. With deft movements, Margaret soon had the mass pinned into an elegant chignon. Lily's belly growled, and she laid a hand over her abdomen, knowing there would be no time for breakfast while a bloody duke sat in their parlor.

She'd forgotten her stockings, but had no time to bother with them. One didn't keep a duke waiting. Hoping he wouldn't notice, Lily settled for slippers, donning them as Margaret hurried away. Taking a deep breath, she wiped her sweaty palms on her dress and went downstairs.

As she entered the parlor, Jason Martin stood and drew her into his arms. Kissing her cheek, he said, "It's good to see you again. You look beautiful, Lily."

She grinned and hugged him tightly, so glad to see her oldest friend, aside from Elizabeth. "What are you doing here? I thought you were apprenticed to—"

"I came back to see to my brothers and met these gentlemen. They wish to make your acquaintance." Laying a hand on her arm, he kissed her once more and backed away.

A man in a somber gray suit turned away from the window to face her, and she realized he must be Duke Denforth. He looked vaguely familiar, but she couldn't place where she'd seen him. His brown hair was untidy, as if he'd been outside in a gale. His nose was straight and perfect over full lips, and his jaw had just a hint of reddish stubble. He smiled at her, flashing straight, white teeth. He wasn't particularly tall, but his carriage and bulk under the fine wool of his coat lent him quite an imposing appearance.

Two men stood with him; one dark as a midnight sky, and the other fair, with the pale complexion and red hair of an Irishman. Men with dark skin were uncommon in the countryside, and she tried to hide her avid perusal of him. The dark man's bald head and a livid scar across one cheek kept him from being conventionally handsome, but he was the most striking man she'd ever seen. Truly, both Duke Denforth's servants were arresting. The redhead appeared very young until one looked into his blue eyes. They were ancient, hard, and very cool as he caught her peeking.

Both were dressed well in bespoke suits and white shirts. They were most likely Duke Denforth's servants, and she wondered why he'd brought them to meet her.

Yet it was Denforth's eyes that caught most of her attention. She'd never seen such a startling hue before. Pale almost to translucence, the green was otherworldly. She saw dew freshened leaves in his gaze, or perhaps new spring grass. Those eyes held such wisdom, and a bit of mischief.

She dropped into a curtsy, nearly forgetting her manners. "I am very sorry to keep you waiting, Your Grace. Will you all sit? Our maid will be in with tea and scones shortly."

"Don't apologize, please. It is very early, and we have arrived unannounced. It is I who should be giving you an apology."

"Dukes don't apologize." She slapped a hand over her mouth as the redhead snorted out a laugh and her face grew hot. "I do beg your pardon. I have no idea what came over me to say such an impolite thing." Despite her embarrassment, Denforth's laughter charmed her and she smiled as he bowed, then helped her to the low chaise longue. "Will you introduce me to your companions?" she asked.

"Of course, Miss Archer." Pointing first at the mahogany-skinned man, he said, "The bald one is Moses, and the redhead who looks like he's sucked on a lemon is Liam."

They each bowed in turn, making her wonder if they were indeed servants. Both men greeted her with the clipped, modulated speech of educated gentlemen. Moses had an unfamiliar, yet charming accent. Truly, it seemed they had more appropriate manners than their master. She had better sense than to chide Duke Denforth for his poor introduction.

He settled his large body rather too close to her. She relaxed, knowing no impropriety could occur with the parlor door open and Jason in attendance. The situation was so disconcerting. Lily had no idea why he would visit her, nor did she remember ever meeting him. Why, such a man shouldn't have known of her existence, much less visited at such an unseemly hour.

Knowing she had a very short time before her mother appeared, she gathered her nerve and asked, "Why have you come to call on me, Your Grace?"

He smiled softly, his eyes considering and thoughtful. "I will discuss it when your mother arrives. I am led to believe you don't have a male relative, so it is her to whom I will direct my inquiry."

"Yes, Your Grace. My father passed away some time ago." Lily could think of only one reason a man might make such a statement, but couldn't fathom why a duke would ask for the hand of a ruined girl with no title and a miniscule dowry, not to mention the fact that the banns had already been read for her marriage to Caine. As her friend Elizabeth had once said, marriage often involved men of middle age with bad breath and worse habits. All of those things were true of Caine Martin.

Settling back against the cushions, she hid a sigh. Duke Denforth's visit must have something to do with her late father's work. Papa had been a gifted scholar of plants and natural remedies for illness. Many of his experiments still grew in the kitchen garden and in the tiny greenhouse abutting the garden wall. Duke Denforth surely meant to purchase plants, or perhaps one of her father's books.

Truly, she was disappointed that she'd found a reasonable explanation for Denforth's presence. She'd quite liked the idea of a young and attractive duke rescuing her from the distressing fate awaiting her. She looked down at her work-worn hands and short nails. Those fanciful tales never came true except in stories, although Elizabeth seemed happy enough with her handsome earl.

When her mother tottered into the room, leaning heavily on Margaret's arm, Duke Denforth stood and helped her into the overstuffed chair in front of the fire.

Dropping a short curtsy, Margaret said, "I'll return with tea in a moment."

When the door shut behind her, Duke Denforth turned to Lily's mother, and said, "Thank you for accepting my call so early in the morning. I'm sorry to disturb you, but there is a matter I wish to discuss."

"I can't imagine what interest we would hold for you, Your Grace. My late husband had very few debts, and I'm sure they've been paid off." Grimacing, she adjusted the black scarf covering her gray hair. "Did Mr. Archer owe money to you? He did nothing aside from putter in that abysmal garden of his. He kept us fed with his tinctures, I suppose."

"No, he didn't. May I also add my condolences for your

loss." He knelt in front of her chair. "I wish to contract a marriage with your daughter, Lily Archer."

Her mother barked out a laugh, sounding much like a hyena Lily had once seen at the zoo in London. "She's already engaged to the innkeeper. Besides, she's ruined for a decent marriage. As much as I love my daughter, I'm afraid that's the best she's likely to get."

"You would sentence her to a loveless marriage with a man who hits her?"

"She would have better choices had she not..." Lily's mother sighed and dabbed at her eyes with a handkerchief. "I'm afraid the matter is already done, Your Grace. She will be married to Caine Martin next week. It will be a fitting fate for a girl with loose morals."

Lily squeezed her eyes shut to stifle her tears at her mother's words, humiliated beyond anything she'd ever experienced. She'd thought her mother loved her, but Abigail Archer planned to force the marriage to punish Lily for something she hadn't done. She supposed she'd known it, but the proof of her mother's feelings toward her made her heart ache. Was she so unworthy of love and respect that even her own mother believed her to be either losing her wits or a whore? And to say such things in front of guests sent a wave of sick shame through her stomach.

Once again, she wished she'd stood up for herself all those months ago, but looking at her mother's judgmental face, she didn't think it would have helped. To her surprise, Moses and Liam moved to stand behind her, each resting a hand on her shoulders. The gesture was more comforting than she'd expected, and she wondered at their sudden attentiveness.

Duke Denforth got up and shook his head. "I'm afraid you're wrong about that, Mrs. Archer."

"I beg your pardon?"

"I am the man who was in Lily's bedchamber that night. I can also tell you that Lily is as chaste and pure as the day she was born." Turning to Lily, he added, "Even if she's been indiscreet with someone else, which I highly doubt, I don't care. Furthermore, I have enough money and power to prevent that farce of a wedding you have planned."

Her mother's face turned purple with rage and she sputtered. "You have no right to say such things to me! I am Lily's mother, and—"

Duke Denforth held up his hand, cutting off her words. "Someone should have said them to you. Do you not see the bruises on your daughter? What happened to a mother being a safe haven for her child?"

He tossed a piece of parchment into Lily's mother's lap. "The contract with Caine Martin is dissolved, and I have a special license signed by the bishop. Miss Archer will not suffer from abuse, or your vile innuendo any longer. You may keep her damned dowry, and I'll throw in another twenty thousand to cheer your wicked soul."

Lily stood, unsure of what she intended to do. She'd

always wished to see the man who had violated her so thoroughly without ever touching her, and she considered the words she'd wanted to give him.

"Excuse me."

Duke Denforth continued to trade barbs with her mother, but Lily was done listening. She got between them, facing him. "I said, shut your bloody mouths!"

She ought to be ashamed of her appalling language. It had come out almost without her control. Her angry screech brought dead, blessed silence, and she took a deep breath before addressing the rake in front of her. Margaret stood at the door to the parlor, her mouth open in shock as she wisely made herself scarce. Jason sat in his corner, a large grin on his face as he waved an encouraging hand in her direction.

"Did you just say you were the man in my room?" Lily asked.

"Yes, my dear, I will—"

"And you admit in front of witnesses that you didn't touch me?"

Taking her hand, he rubbed her knuckles. "I never laid a hand on you! Please, let me apologize—"

She pulled her hand away. "You let me suffer ruin. You let me get engaged to that foul innkeeper, and you let me debase myself entertaining Caine's filthy customers. Why do you come forth now?"

"I will explain everything after we are—"

Something energized her, a glancing touch of power that

coursed through her veins. She tried to grasp it, but the energy escaped her, and she was too furious to chase it. With a scream of rage, she balled up her fist and planted a facer right to Denforth's nose.

Blood spurted and she backed away before facing her mother. "If he's still here when I return, I will accept Duke Denforth's proposal. We will be married as soon as he cleans up his face, and I will make his life a living hell for the next three hundred and thirty-two days." She stomped her foot and shook out her sore hand. "That is the precise amount of time I have suffered from his carelessness."

Both of Denforth's companions looked as if they were about to burst into laughter, and it made her even more furious, if that was possible. She pushed past them and called for Margaret to fetch Father Reynolds, then went to the kitchen to eat one of Margaret's delicious scones and swallow down a cup of tea.

She shouldn't have punched Duke Denforth. She'd been sorry for it the moment the blood gushed from his nose. And she truly didn't mean to be a shrew. He'd tried to apologize, but she'd been so angry, it was as if something had taken over her voice, making her say all those ugly words without her permission.

Guilt plagued her for her thoughts, but Lily no longer cared about her mother's opinions. It hurt that her mother thought so badly of her when she'd never done a single thing to invite her judgment. It was most likely true she would have gotten no better offer, but that didn't excuse her mother's behavior. What mother purposely pushed her only child into an abusive marriage? Even if she had done what the townspeople accused her of, there was no excuse for such treachery. Why, her mother had even said she should share Caine's bed before their wedding!

As if she would ever do such a thing. She took a deep breath to calm herself and said a prayer of thanks that her father wasn't alive to witness her mother's behavior. He'd been such a kind and gentle soul, and would be horrified by the situation. The thoughts brought a pang of sorrow. Her father would have believed her. He would have protected her.

To her surprise, Jason followed her into the kitchen and poured their tea while she fussed with the plate of scones. Setting jam and cream on the table, she asked, "Did you come to see my humiliation so you could tell your father?"

A flash of hurt darkened his brown eyes. "I followed to make sure you were all right. My father will never trouble you again," Jason replied. "I think between me and your husband-to-be, we've convinced him of the error of his ways."

She felt horrible for her unkind words. Jason wouldn't do such a thing. Laying her hand atop his, she said, "I'm sorry I said that. It was an awful thing to say. But what makes you think I should marry Denforth? By his own admission, he—"

"Came back when you needed him most, Lily." Ignoring

the scones and tea, he squeezed her hand. "He's bought a special license, and left my father in a bleeding heap for you."

"I rather think you did that."

"No, I started it. Duke Denforth finished." Shuddering, he added, "I don't know that I'd have gone that far, but perhaps my father has learned his lesson."

Lily split a scone and spread jam on it. Her appetite had fled, despite her earlier hunger. "I've already said I'll marry him. I suppose we'll just have to wait and see if he stays for the wedding."

"He'll be there when you're ready," Jason said.

Why was Jason so sure of that? She couldn't join him in his faith. But perhaps being known as a termagant would be better than being known as a whore. At least this time, she'd have done what people accused her of.

———

Myrddin wiped the blood from his face. He ignored the shrieking woman in the chair, and grinned. What a magnificent creature his Lily was! Untaught, she'd pulled a thread of his magic away, keeping it for her own to give her enough strength to punch him. And she'd done a bloody fine job of it, to boot.

He held his handkerchief to his face and surreptitiously pushed his broken nose back into place, using a touch of magic to heal the break as Moses and Liam tried to hold back their laughter. Fates, it had been centuries since he'd seen such a powerful familiar. It was no wonder Angeline had wanted her.

"...and I cannot believe my daughter struck you! I swear to you, we brought her up better than that!"

"Do be quiet, Mrs. Archer. I deserve Lily's wrath, but she's given me a bit of a headache."

The older woman scowled, but held her peace. He thanked the heavens for small blessings as he, Moses, and Liam walked outside to wait for his bride to return.

When the door shut behind them, Liam let his laughter burst forth. "I shouldn't laugh, old friend, but the look on your face when that tiny girl punched you..." He sputtered and snorted, his giggles increasing until he had to lean against the side of the house.

"It was a surprise, to be sure," he murmured.

"You're not upset?" Moses asked, looking at him speculatively.

"No, I quite deserved her abuse." He sniffed and rubbed at his sore nose. "Although it is my hope she will keep her fists to herself after we marry."

Nodding, Moses said, "She seems a dutiful and obedient girl under normal circumstances." Wrinkling his nose, he added, "I didn't expect her to have such a sweet disposition, given her mother's appalling behavior."

When he got his laughter under control, Liam said, "I

like her. She has pretty manners, and it was a delight to see her give you your comeuppance."

Myrddin sighed and shook his head. Truly, he'd been shocked at Lily's obviously uncharacteristic fit of temper. Rather than making him leery of marrying her, it only made him more intent upon having her as his wife. Despite her softness, he saw an iron will under the façade of a pale English rose. "We have something to attend to while we wait for my bride to get ready," he said.

"Oh?" Moses asked. "We'll stand with you, and you've got a ring for her. What else do we need?"

"We need to investigate her garden," Myrddin said, gesturing for them to follow as he led the way toward the blackberry bushes. "I found a nasty bit of magic in there last night that seems to siphon its health, and Lily's, too, I believe."

"Whose is it?" Liam asked, his eyes intent upon Myrddin's.

"I think it might be a stray from Angeline. She scattered magic everywhere without considering the consequences, but I didn't have time to investigate it when I was here last. Regardless," he said, walking toward the garden, "I need to make sure it's neutralized so it can't hurt anyone."

"If it was Angeline's, it will fade in good time," Moses said.

"But what if it isn't?" Liam asked.

"Once we have Lily safely in our home, I'll come back

and take care of it." Yet when they reached the wall where the sick plants were, the spell had moved to another section of the garden. The plants had been pruned of blighted leaves, and when he tasted the fruit of the blackberry vine, he found it sweet. Lily's small footprints went back and forth through the beds, and he could see divots where she'd knelt to care for the injured foliage.

"The spell was here before, but now it's moved." As he pointed to the burgeoning blight on a climbing rosebush, he heard conversation from the lane and stood, cutting off his investigation when Lily's maid approached with the reverend.

He had suspicions about the nature of the foul enchantment that sickened this garden, but it didn't make sense that one of the dark Sidhe would set a spell in a place inhabited by a young woman, especially one with a small trace of light Sidhe blood. Why would the dark Sidhe bother with Lily Archer, especially when it would likely raise the ire of King Omer? King Teran of the dark Sidhe wouldn't stand for any risk to the fragile peace existing between them.

"You should ask that dragon you're carrying about," Liam whispered as the reverend walked toward the house. "He might know something."

Once Lily's maid had escorted the reverend inside, Myrddin turned to Liam. "Drako sleeps, as he has for almost a thousand years. He has no interest in conversation," Myrddin replied, unwilling to admit that he'd entertained the idea himself. However, it was always the wisest course of action to let sleeping dragons lie, even if the dragon's massive bulk rested across his shoulders.

A quietly shut door and footsteps on the gravel heralded Jason coming to join them. His lips twitched into a smile as he approached, his large hands tucked behind his back. By the time he got to the small group, he'd erased the expression from his face. But then Liam snorted, his face turning pink as he tried to hold the laughter inside.

Myrddin looked on in disgust mixed with amusement as the younger men collapsed to a marble bench next to a blooming rose bush. Leaning against each other, they laughed helplessly.

"Did you see his face?" Liam asked. "She popped his nose like a tomato!"

"We shouldn't be laughing at a duke, you know," Jason whispered.

"You're laughing, too."

"I can't help it," Jason replied, wiping his eyes with a handkerchief. "Lily is so tiny. I never realized she had it in her!" Sobering, he stood and held his hand out to Myrddin. "I believe that Lily made her displeasure quite clear, Your Grace."

"Indeed," Myrddin replied. He'd left the swelling around his nose to avoid raising suspicion. It would fade in a few hours, and he had no interest in explaining why a bloody nose had suddenly repaired itself. "She has a bit of a temper, doesn't she?"

Jason smiled fondly as he looked toward the house. "Yes," he replied. "It's astonishing because it's so rare, but when she finally explodes, it's best to get out of the way."

"I see."

Turning back to face Myrddin, his expression went flat and sober. "Her fury is nothing compared to what mine will be if I ever learn you've hurt her. I will make what we did to my father look like a Sunday stroll, and I don't give a damn if you're a duke or the Crown Prince himself."

"I have no intention of ever hurting her, Mr. Martin." Leaning closer, Myrddin asked in a soft whisper, "Did you love her that much?"

Jason shook his head. "Yes, but not as a husband should love his wife. Lily has been one of my dearest friends since childhood." He rubbed his chin and added, "Elizabeth Stratton as well, I suppose. Lily gave us both a place to hide when our parents became unmanageable."

Myrddin had no fear of the young man, of course. Despite his size, he was no match for a mage. Yet it cost him nothing to reassure Jason, and perhaps it would please his soon-to-be wife. It also gave him some insight into her character, and he wasn't unhappy with what he found. "She has a very good friend in you. I think she would be happy if you write to her, and it would be my honor to have you visit us after we're settled."

"We'll see, Your Grace." He smiled and shook his head. "I'm just a simple cooper, and I doubt I'd fit in a duke's household. But if it will please Lily, I'll visit." Glancing back at the house, his eyes lit up when he saw Lily's maid waving at them. "It looks like it's time for me to give away the bride."

Myrddin and his companions followed him back to the house. It was surprising how quickly a confirmed bachelor would jump into the parson's mousetrap for the right woman. He wondered if the young Countess Shepton would be amused by his choice. More likely, she'd be furious.

Without another word, they walked into the parlor. He stopped, his hand on the doorframe as he stared at his wife-to-be. Her honey blonde hair hung to her waist in loose curls, and was held back with ivory combs. Her blue dress was a perfect match for her spitefully glittering eyes. The capped sleeves and heart shaped bodice revealed several bruises on her pale skin, and he wanted to slit Caine Martin's throat.

Ignoring the stares and sour expressions from everyone in attendance, save himself, Liam, and Moses, he walked toward her and bowed over her hand. "I've never seen a more beautiful bride. I am honored beyond measure to call you my wife."

Will Lily forgive her handsome duke? Find out in Wicked Truth available FREE wherever ebooks are sold.

For sneak peeks and teasers, sign up for Minette's newsletter. You'll also get a free book delivered right to your inbox!